THE WAY
WE DANCED

By the same author

The Friday Tree

THE WAY
WE DANCED

SOPHIA HILLAN

WARD
RIVER
PRESS

Praise for *The Friday Tree*

"Your writing is an absolute beauty" *David Marcus*

"A vivid and intimate portrayal of childhood's confused stumbling into the complex tragedies of the adult world" *David Park*

"Exquisite ... Because the reader is at all times aware of the horrors that lie ahead, the narrative charm of this delightful novel has an added depth" *Eugene McCabe*

"An engrossing story, elegantly told ... a lovely prose style, crisp and flowing, and imbued with warmth and real humanity" *Donal Ryan*.

"A singular debut novel ... This novel reads already like a classic" *Anthony Glavin*

Published 2016
by Poolbeg Press Ltd
123 Grange Hill, Baldoyle
Dublin 13, Ireland
www.wardriverpress.com

© Sophia Hillan 2016

Copyright for editing, typesetting, layout, design, ebook
© Poolbeg Press Ltd

1

A catalogue record for this book is available from the British Library.

ISBN 978-178199-948-6

Printed and bound by CPI Group (UK) Ltd, Croydon, CR0 4YY

www.poolbeg.com

ABOUT THE AUTHOR

Sophia Hillan began her writing career with a nomination for the Hennessy Award (1980), when she was published in David Marcus's *New Irish Writing* and, as a prizewinner, in Sam Hanna Bell's *Literary Miscellany*. In a parallel life as a university academic, she wrote and published her PhD on the work of Michael McLaverty, who made her one of his literary executors, and she has published widely on Irish literature of the nineteenth and twentieth centuries. Returning with great delight to fiction, she was named a finalist in the Royal Society of Literature's first V.S.Pritchett Memorial Prize (1999) after which her short stories were broadcast by BBC Radio 4, and published in *The Faber Book of Best New Irish Short Stories* (2005). In 2011 she received high praise for *May, Lou and Cass*, the untold true story of Jane Austen's nieces in Ireland, and in 2014 her début novel, *The Friday Tree*, was the first to be published by the newly launched Ward River Press. Previously living in a hollow at the bottom of a hill, she now looks out, like *The Friday Tree*'s Brigid, at Belfast's Black Mountain. Her house is filled with light and many, many books.

For John and Judith

"Those who tell their own story ... must be listened to with caution." Jane Austen, *Sanditon*.

CONTENTS

Prologue

Edith

Evening followed morning: then, the night and the weeping. Edith's mistake was to tell them she once saw Fred Astaire. She saw at once that they disbelieved her, and tried to erase the error. "In my dreams," she said quickly, and relief looked back at her. So, not gone yet, said their eyes, meeting above her head; yet, there was a wariness still. "His name," she added, holding the gaze of the one in charge. "Fred Astaire's name: that was the last thing George Gershwin said before he died. Did you know?" There was no response. "And, when I die," she went on, striving to look bright, "I plan to spend eternity dancing with Fred Astaire, so anything that needs to be said to me should be said now, while the opportunity remains." They laughed then, and filed out, with their stethoscopes and their blood-pressure gauges and their pens and their charts. Nonetheless, Edith knew that she had had a narrow escape, and resolved to be careful. That night, however, all unobserved, perfectly still in her safely barred bed in her floral prison, Edith Barratt danced once more to the soundtrack of her youth; and there was no weeping.

Ruth

❧

Heimkehr

In later years, after the success of *The White Stormtrooper*, Ruth Deacon was sometimes heard to say that she stumbled upon the Barratt Papers: in other, rarer moments, she offered another version. One part of the story always remained the same: that it all fell into place on the 30th of November 1995, the day the Clintons came to town. As to where it started, however, that depended on the version, and to whom she was talking. Generally she said it began at the end of June 1995, at the start of her first big conference, in a week that started out so hot and summerlike that everyone went around in a haze of disbelief.

As to the five hundred North American academics, however, newly arrived for this major conference — *Re-Vision: Memory and the Fictions of History* — it was clear from the outset that they were unimpressed. Almost all used to a climate with four distinct seasons, thoroughly warned in advance by Ruth herself, in her capacity as organiser, to bring warm and waterproof clothing and footwear for the expected cool and showery Irish summer, they did not relish the prospect of spending a week wearing sweaters and oilskins in stifling halls and un-air-conditioned buses. That first night — the night Cory Latimer failed to turn up — one of them had taken Ruth to task at the opening reception.

"Dr Deacon? May I have a word?"

Anxiously — where *was* Cory Latimer? — Ruth turned to the speaker, Barbara Selby Hayworth, world authority on Edith Wharton and her circle; small, intense, warmly clad in black wool.

"Why, yes," said Ruth, unnaturally calm, "of course, Professor Hayworth. How may I help you?"

"I don't know if you can, Dr Deacon," said Barbara Hayworth, with no hint of a smile, "unless you can provide me with an entirely new wardrobe, and perhaps a very large fan, ideally with a minion to wield it in my general direction. I was simply wondering — idly, you understand — how the organiser of a midsummer conference, so confident of rain and cold that she would not only urge but urge strongly the wearing of heavy and rainproof clothing, would even possess, never mind so coolly sport, a white linen dress such as yours? Or would not think to suggest that we all bring with us something similar?" And, forehead glistening, she had turned an angry back.

Looking round the room, Ruth saw all about her a sea of equally dissatisfied, overheated faces — at which point her phone began to make its messaging sound. A slight lift of relief; and then relief itself disappeared. It was not from Cory: it was from Chris, Ruth's husband or, rather, her soon-to-be ex-husband. It was from Chris, anyway. "Hi," it said. "**Staying Dublin after all tonight. Chance of a job! Sorry about Hilde. C.**" Chance of a job? Chris? He hadn't worked in months. What was he … Ruth stopped herself. It hardly mattered. What mattered was this: five hundred disgruntled delegates; no Keynote Speaker for the next morning, the first day proper of the conference; and, now, Hilde to baby-sit. And it was still only the first night.

Though the next morning brought blue skies and the promise of another glorious day, there was still no sign of Cory Latimer; and there was no Chris to see to Hilde, though he had promised. It was the only thing she had asked of him, to take over Hilde's care during the week of the conference, and he had reneged before he started; a first even for Chris.

Yet, whatever about him, why would Cory Latimer choose this moment to let everybody down? What would be the benefit to her? She had been more than happy to take on the role of Keynote Speaker at the conference, particularly when her name was not only recommended but indeed imposed upon Ruth by the new and rigidly business-minded College President himself. The President loved business. No doubt Cory's profile, heading an international consultancy between Dublin and Europe, suited what he called his vision. Cory's application, of which Ruth had only briefly had sight, emphasised her many and wide-ranging contacts in the world of business and, even more, her ability to negotiate the labyrinthine ways of grant application. In this, apparently, she excelled. The President then went ahead and appointed Cory to the position of Visiting Fellow for the coming academic year, quite overruling in the process the usual procedure of a selection committee, and at the same time — with no consultation — announcing her as Keynote Speaker for the forthcoming conference.

There he was, Mr President, handsomely suited and perfectly coiffed, standing poised at the podium as Ruth arrived, Hilde in tow. She had no choice but to bring her. Leaving her behind was not an option: she had taken to wandering, to forgetting that gas rings were switched on, to leaving cigarettes burning on the carpet. Ruth was bitterly conscious that she had no-one to call upon — unless she counted Thomas, the only cousin, safely in London if not Berlin; or Chris, on whom she was now fairly certain she could not count.

Ruth, therefore, did the only thing she could. She caught the eye of Sandra Harvey, College secretary and a longtime ally. Sandra, always quick, responded at once: between them, they settled Hilde where Ruth could see her and she could see Ruth. Then Ruth took a deep breath, explained to the President that the Keynote Speaker would not, it appeared, be immediately present, said that she herself would take over and speak, and sat down before he had the chance to respond. A consummate performer, the President smoothed his tie, assumed his smile, and called the gathering to order. They were welcome, he said, and he hoped and felt certain they would have a wonderful week in beautiful Northern Ireland. He was delighted that the conference was being held here in Aeneas Benner College, with its long and distinguished history of scholarship; and at such a time of optimism, with the miracle of the recent ceasefires in place, with everything to look forward to, he anticipated the dawn of a new and unforgettable era in the history not only of Northern Ireland, but also of, as he put it, the free world. It was his regular speech, tailored for the present audience, yet still moderately impressive. He mentioned his vision for the College only five times, and the unfortunate necessity of income generation hardly more than three. He then turned to Ruth, most gracefully yielded the podium, and had just smiled his way into his seat as she began to speak; which she did, for the requisite forty-five minutes.

Given that she had written her remarks between two and three that morning, given also that she alone was treated to the President's increasingly glacial stare of displeasure, it may well have been the performance of her life.

No matter. It passed, it ended, and no-one seemed, as they went to take their coffee, tea or, for the venturesome, local tap water, unduly unhappy. Fortunately, that morning was cooler than the previous evening had been, and the delegates were slightly less uncomfortable. Best of all, Hilde remained docile throughout, and by the end seemed to have fallen quietly asleep. If it could only last into the second part of the morning, all might yet be well. Watching Hilde, willing her to slip more deeply into her doze, Ruth glanced over the programme, and her heart sank. Of course: Clara Anderson was next, speaking on *Heimkehr*, her prizewinning book about her mother, Anna Liebermann, who had spent her youth in a Nazi concentration camp. The book told the story not only of Anna's experiences but also of her subsequent, quite remarkable escape and later survival. Hilde should not hear this: Hilde must not hear this. Had Chris been there … but Chris was not there. Anger resurfaced. Had Cory Latimer turned up even now to perform her next task, which should have been to introduce Clara Anderson and chair the discussion, Ruth might have been able to spirit Hilde away. Instead, quite unprepared, she would have to chair it herself and hope for the best.

As Clara Anderson stood up, a respectful hush took over the room. Dark of hair and pale of skin, she was a gifted reader, and an instinctive performer. The President himself picked up, his eyes once more indicating approval. Clara's narrative was simple, her style unforced, and she chose her extracts with care. She had written an account, she said, of her mother's remarkable endurance and survival because it was a story which, in this fiftieth year after the ending of the war, needed to be told. "When I decided to give this book the title *Heimkehr*, I knew it could, and probably would be translated as *Homecoming*: but to my mother, it also means *The Journey Home,* to this country, to Belfast, which became her home. I have told it, therefore," she said, "as my mother told it to me. I can never forget it, and I hope you may not either."

The silence deepened. Everyone was with the young, gifted Anna Liebermann, cruelly torn from her parents and her home in Prague, finding ever more resourceful ways to survive deprivation and maltreatment in a series of increasingly punitive camps; everyone sat tense as she held on, just and no more, until the arrival of the Americans, only to find she still had to struggle through the danger and the bitter cold of a bleak and exhausted Europe; all held their breath as she evaded capture at the border; and there was at last an audible sigh of relief as her story concluded in, of all places, Northern Ireland.

Ruth watched Hilde all the while: yet, disturbed and wakeful though she had been the previous night, her exhausted sleep seemed to grow ever deeper. As far as Ruth could judge, she heard nothing. Clara's reading came to a close, and was immediately greeted with rapturous and heartfelt applause.

The President nodded approval in Ruth's direction; and then two things happened.

First, quite unexpectedly, a little figure, slight, finely boned, with the lithe grace of one who had been trained in dance, stepped up to the podium; and Clara Anderson introduced Anna Liebermann herself. Gasps of disbelief, followed by a renewed and even more enthusiastic burst of applause, greeted this unlooked-for but clearly welcome addition to the programme.

Ruth was as surprised as anyone. Nobody had told her

that Anna might come: in fact, she had understood that she would be unable to be present. Yet, here she was; and here, too, which had never been part of the plan, was Hilde.

It was not that Ruth lacked admiration for Anna Liebermann. It was, in fact, she who had invited Clara Anderson to speak at the conference. Anna was a living example of survival with grace and honour. Ruth had met her some months before at a book signing, when *Heimkehr* first came out, and been charmed and humbled by her dignity and, indeed, her humour. She had said two things that stayed in Ruth's mind. One she said publicly. When she had arrived in Northern Ireland after the war, she said, still unable to believe she had survived, she had thought her story would be interesting to people, that they would want to know what they had been fighting for, but it was not so. Nobody wanted to know. It was, Anna said, as if she had uttered obscenities in public.

Her words struck something in Ruth's conscience and when she had queued to have her book signed by Clara Anderson, she then held it out to Anna Liebermann. "Would you, please?" she had said and then, to her own surprise, heard herself ask: "Is it really the case that people didn't want to hear your story when you came?"

Anna raised her eyebrows. "I assure you it was so," she said, and wrote her name beneath Clara's.

Below the sleeve of her summer blouse, Ruth saw the tattooed camp number.

Anna, handing back the book, paused. "Have you seen *Schindler's List*?" she said.

Ruth, dragging her eyes from the tattoo, shook her head. "I'm afraid I lack the courage," she said, which was the simple truth.

Anna, holding her gaze from eyes still bright beneath the hooded lids, handed her the book. "You can safely see it," she said, and she shrugged a little. "The reality was much worse."

Ruth, profoundly ashamed, realised that she too would have been one of those people who chose not to know. She had never wanted to hear Hilde's story of her own youthful escape from Nazi Germany. Perhaps it was to atone a little that she had invited Clara to speak at the conference; now however, with Hilde most unfortunately in the audience, Ruth's one wish was that she had never thought of issuing the invitation. Unlike everyone else, therefore, she hoped that Anna would not say very much.

Anna Liebermann, inclining her head, with an elegance of movement speaking of her early training, executed what was in essence a half-curtsey. Then, as she acknowledged her audience with the slight but commanding raising of a hand, displaying the camp tattoo on her arm, the second thing happened. Hilde woke up. At the same moment, most unluckily, Anna Liebermann's eyes met those of Hilde: whereupon Hilde began to shake and, quite audibly, to weep. Clara Anderson, alarmed, looked to Ruth to do as the chair ought: to intervene and conclude. Ruth, however, watching Sandra struggle with an increasingly loud and agitated Hilde, found herself unable to move. Applause for Anna and Clara, first rapturous, then expectant, and finally dwindling into puzzlement, left a silence.

Then, just as Ruth, frozen, met the wise and ironic old eyes of Anna Liebermann, a figure, straight, quick, assured, strode to the podium and took the hands of both Clara and her mother, to the sound of renewed and relieved applause. At the same time, down in the audience, someone gently gathered up the shaking Hilde, her distress now drowned by the sounds of the applauding audience, and led her away. Chris had come back. And in that endless momentary gap of time and space, Ruth thought she glimpsed in the crowd a face she had not seen for many years. Dear God, she thought, let that not be Miss Barratt. Let me not be humiliated in front of the one teacher I spent years trying, and failing, to please.

Beside Ruth, meanwhile, there stood, at long last, Cory Latimer, waiting for the applause to finish, waiting for the stage to be hers — and as soon as Anna's moment was over, she seized her own. In her boyish jacket and long, sun-burnished legs, acknowledging a relieved and delighted President, dismissing Ruth with the briefest of smiles, she graciously thanked the speakers once again. Then, begging everyone's pardon for her own non-appearance the night before, she explained that, recovering as she was from cancer — shocked but sympathetic sounds from the crowd — she had been overtaken by ... by a temporary setback. She paused, looked down, then up and outward, eyes just perceptibly brimming. She hoped they would understand. Their renewed applause said they were all too ready to understand. Cory then singled out for praise the organiser of the conference, Dr Ruth Deacon, who had stepped in for her at the inaugural lecture and spoken, she understood, quite outstandingly. Applause swelled again: for Clara, for Anna, for the marvellous Professor Latimer — so brave! — and even for the gallant runner-up, Dr Deacon, who could have killed Cory Latimer where she stood.

White Samite

In the middle of the night Ruth suddenly woke and, without looking, knew that Chris was watching her. There he was, sitting on a chair by her bed; and beside him was the whisky bottle. She sat up, tugging the quilt about her in pointless fury.

"What are you doing?" she said. "Who told you that you could come in here?"

As if it had not been bad enough to go home and find the pair of them, himself and Hilde, sitting there watching television, as if nothing had happened; but to go to bed, struggle for ages to get to sleep and now wake to find him sitting staring at her with bleared eyes; to hear yet again that he was sorry, sorry, so sorry. It was intolerable. Yes, he had been with Cory Latimer. No, he had not meant it to happen, and it was only once. Yes, it was over. Could they not, please, try again? He did not want the divorce. Back and forth, back and forth, weeping and crying, he went over his litany of self-recrimination, even attempting, at one stage, to climb in beside her.

13

"Try that once more," she said, through her teeth, "and I promise you I will send for the police."

Then he sadly left, a good man wronged, shoulders slumped — a nice touch — and even as the sliver of light narrowed behind him, Ruth knew she would soon hear through the wall the sound of remorseful sobbing. Right on cue, there it was. Seething, wide-awake, she turned over; but it was hopeless. No rest, no sleep would come; just that sound, that noise, and a collage like a film on a loop, over and over: Hilde, Anna Liebermann, and those two bouncing in like Batman and Robin to save the day. And Miss Barratt. What was she doing there? Was she even there? Ruth went over and over the whole thing: and she was nearly sure that when she looked again there was no sign of the person she thought had been Miss Barratt. Was it her? Or was it her imagination?

Whatever it was, there was no more time to think more about it, no time to grapple with any further possible miseries roaming around the bedroom, because within what seemed like minutes — perhaps Ruth was dozing, perhaps not — Hilde began. Perhaps Chris woke her, perhaps she would have wakened anyway, but the end result was that the police were indeed called.

The new neighbours at the other end of the road did it, seeing Hilde wandering about the road in her nightdress, crying for her mama. So the police did come after all, though not for Chris. In the end, between them, Ruth and Chris spent most of the rest of that night reassuring Hilde that she would not be sent to a concentration camp, and part of it in bitter argument about who left the door off the deadlock in the first place; and it was all so very hectic that it was not until the next day that Ruth realised that she had bled again. This time, she had ruined not only her nightdress and the sheets but even the very mattress. Her penultimate thought before slipping into the shortest and most fitful of sleeps was that at least it wasn't the white linen dress. "Clothed in white samite" was her last random thought, falling down the whirling slope: and then she was gone.

Something in the Air

Everything passes. That endless first day of the conference galloped into a succession of energetic days and active evenings, giving little time for introspection. Then, quite suddenly, it was over, and the delegates were gone. All of them, all five hundred, off home or setting out to explore the charming wonders and inexplicable strangenesses of Ireland. Beyond advising, as best she could, an intrepid few to resist the temptation to involve themselves in the political demonstrations of loyalty or otherwise shortly expected, Ruth saw them off with relief and, inexplicably, a kind of sadness. Then she filed away her notes and the newly gathered business cards, wrote her letters of appreciation, and finally revelled in the delicious, almost tangible silence.

When Sandra dropped by to collect the various documents to be signed off and filed at the end of it all, Ruth was, as she hastily told her, just about to leave.

"Oh, you made that appointment, did you?" said Sandra, leafing through the papers. "You should have done it long ago."

"Yes, well, I more or less had to," Ruth said, gathering her bag and her keys. "It's got much worse. Right through to the mattress last night."

"That's good," said Sandra, clearly not listening, eyes on the papers Ruth had handed her.

Irritated, Ruth stopped at the door.

"What is it?" she said. "What's the matter? I have to go, so tell me quickly."

"No, nothing," said Sandra, looking up, "or rather, I don't quite know. There's something in the air, but I don't know what it is."

Ruth shrugged. "Let me guess," she said. "Mr President. One of his big ideas. His Vision. But nothing will happen over the summer. I mean, nothing ever happens over the summer, does it?"

Now, it was Sandra who shrugged.

"Well," she said, "nothing used to, that's true. But now ... I don't know. There's something coming."

"Look, I have to go. I suppose there'll be a memo. He'll get his secretary to send out The Memo, I suppose."

"I suppose," said Sandra, looking down again at the papers. "But, Ruth, listen. You see this list of all the people who were here? You could use it. Go through it and identify useful contacts for, you know, Fellowships and future conferences, that sort of thing."

"I could," Ruth said, exasperated, "but for the love of ... I mean, I've just killed myself for a week, and nearly bled to death in the middle of it. Not to mention this past year planning it. My God, can I not take a break?"

"Well, I'm not taking one," said Sandra, and this time it was she who sounded exasperated. "At least not till I work out what's going on, and you should do the same. If you take my advice, you'll get your insides sorted and organise some sort of publication PDQ."

18

Ruth turned to go again.

"I've some mail for you, here: do you want it?"

"No, I don't," said Ruth. "Does it look important?"

Sandra looked. "I don't know," she said. "One looks like a memo from his office, and the other is handwritten. Don't know who it's from."

Ruth was halfway out the door.

"What did I say? A memo. But listen, I don't have time. Just put them on the desk, or keep them for me down in the office. It'll all do tomorrow. Lock this door for me, will you?"

"I will," said Sandra, "but look …"

Ruth, already late, one hand on the front-door handle, half-listened as the voice floated down the stairs.

"I've heard he's on the warpath for publications …"

He seems to be on the warpath about something new every day, thought Ruth, as she sprinted down the road, just missing the bus that would have brought her comfortably to the specialist's door.

More sprinting resulted in a breathless and undignified entrance; yet, though she was on time, he was not, allowing her the chance to calm herself amid the deep sofas and soothing prints of his elegant waiting-room.

She was perfectly calm throughout the examination, reasonably calm as she waited for him to assess the results, and far from calm as he told her he was bringing her straight into hospital for exploration and, possibly, major surgery.

Nights of July

There was surgery. They kept her in. "Is that usual?" she asked, when they said she would not be going home immediately. "I thought I'd only be here for a day or two."

The nurses gave nothing away. He told her eventually, her specialist, that the surgery had been major. Keeping her there a while was just a precaution, and quite normal; and in any case, he said, since she was there, why didn't she take the opportunity to relax? He had a point: what was the use of paying into the College's supposedly generous, certainly expensive health insurance, if not to relax, given so rare and unlooked-for an opportunity?

She settled back, then, sedated, in deep white pillows and decided it was not so bad. Indeed, it became almost pleasant, this private clinic world of quiet voices and tea in proper teapots, and little dainty sandwiches, if one should so desire. It was rather lovely to drift in and out of sleep without responsibility for anything, not even Hilde, now Chris was back; and the distant noisy crashing of July's divisive celebration belonged to the far away outside, nothing to do with this haven of peace.

Day one, day two, days three and four: all of these passed more or less without incident. Chris came in the afternoons, apparently sober, reported on Hilde, told her scraps of the latest news in the paper: there was trouble at Drumcree, bad trouble, he said, in case she wanted to know. "I don't," she said. "Don't come in here and tell me stuff like that. Just look after Hilde." No-one else came, not even Sandra; but then, as well she knew, people who could not get out of the city in July tended to stay off the streets.

Then came the fifth day, the danger day of which her surgeon had warned her, the day when the blues arrive; and arrive they did. The staff let her be that day, did not make her try to sit up, or walk, or eat what was good for her: for that day, and that day only, she could lie in darkness, and see nobody if she so wished. She so wished. Chris, they told her, had come, and had telephoned; not that Ruth cared. Sunk in misery, she could think that day of only one thing: a long section of her adult life, a fundamental part of her entire being, had gone with those tired and malfunctioning organs; and she felt profound and unforeseen grief. For what? That she could not have said.

They gave the evening medication about nine thirty: the whole little world of which she was now part settled down to low voices and shaded lights. She was just drifting off when the commotion began. She was already in a pleasant, dim darkness when she heard the raised voices. That sounds like Chris, she thought, but it can't be Chris: he's with Hilde; and she slid on down into sleep.

It was indeed Chris, as she found out next morning. She found out also that he had reckoned without Sister, who let no-one bend her rules; and that he wanted to tell her that Hilde, distressed by the noise of the drums and the television coverage of riots, had run out again on to the street, and this time tried to hail down a car by standing in front of it. He wanted to tell her that Hilde was in hospital with a suspected fracture of the hip, and that he was sorry. He did not get the chance, however, because of Sister; and by the time he did, all Ruth wanted to know was, as if she could not guess, what he had been doing when Hilde got out this time: and then to tell him to get out of her house and her life.

He did neither, of course, just as Ruth had known when she said it he would not. He was there when, two days later, the taxi dropped her off at home. He made her tea. He coaxed Hilde to talk to her when Hilde, resentful as an abandoned child, turned her head away.

"Look," he said, placing the tea in front of her, "I know you don't want me in the house. But why not let me stay for Hilde? You can't lift her or see to her. I can. Let me be her carer. I'll keep out of your way"

I'm a fool, Ruth told herself, even as she agreed, cravenly glad not to be alone, or truth be told, not to be alone with Hilde. So long, she told herself, as he looks after Hilde; which he did, more or less, except when he did not; except, as it turned out, when it most mattered.

The nights of July were long. That cool spell, so welcome after late June's heat, had passed; and with an odd synchronicity of things, the weather of politics heated up, even as the marching and the rioting and the short tempers of those who had little patience in the first place saw to it that night after night was hot in more senses than one.

Ruth never did find out where Chris was the evening it all came to a head. Glass breaking on the road outside seemed to spark it; and Ruth, hearing the wailing, the torrent of German from her room, and the heavy thump of her fall, knew before she looked that Hilde must have managed to move the protective rail and tumble out of bed. She knew, also, before she looked, that Chris's room would be empty. She knew as she tried to lift the sprawled and weeping Hilde that she should not do it; and yet she did not know what else to do, the little, unexpectedly heavy body being so obviously in extreme pain.

When Chris finally checked in next morning, he found them both passed out cold on the floor. Two ambulances went to two different hospitals; and this time only Ruth would return, after yet another week of recovery, to her home, with strict instructions to do no more lifting and to rest as much as possible for at least another month. For Hilde, however, much as Chris might have wished it to be otherwise, home, after hospital, was to be in nursing care.

The Memory Book

❧

That Girl

I'm supposed to write things down, as therapy, to make sure my faculties stay intact as they can. I do it because I have no intention of becoming one of the sad, bent and huddled in what they like to call the Day Room. It's not day in there: not day or night, nor age nor youth. I have always been independent, and I have always said I would not leave my own home until I was carried out in a box. And then, to fall like that; so unfortunate. I was only on that stool to look for papers. Lying so long, they said, was the problem; and the fact that it was holiday time. Holiday time! The noise and the banging and the crashing told me it was the Twelfth of July, and no holiday. That business at Drumcree: what are they thinking? Will it never stop? That was the reason I was looking for my old papers, not simply to divert myself from the noise and the fact that I would be for days a virtual prisoner in my own house, but also to remember another time, when we all pulled together in this town. If these people had gone through the war, they would have less to fight about.

At first, in here, they called it respite. I was in respite care: that was all. I doubted it then: I am certain now this is no place of respite, and that there is no respite from disability. I seem to have been left with somebody else's legs; hence this cumbersome wheelchair. Before I came in here, I did make an attempt to sort my papers, as my solicitor advised, and I found so many things: letters, manuscripts and something I had almost forgotten, a diary from 1938, when I was not yet twenty-three. Some of it was in German: not very good German, I would say. I think that's when I was still engaged in my fairly ill-matched struggle with German. I could call it *Mein Kampf*, because I certainly did my share of kampfing with it, but I'd better not say that out loud, not near my little neighbour anyway. I'm inclined to think she's German, and I'm nearly sure she's Jewish. I rather like her. She's quiet, and she doesn't trouble anyone, and she is visited by a young woman — well, not all that young, but younger than us, so practically a child in here. "The wee girl," I heard one of them in the other corridor call her. I did ask one of them if she could quietly find out her name for me. Quietly! What was I thinking?

"What's the name of that girl goes in to see Hilde?" one of them shouted all over the corridor. "Edith wants to know!"

Oh, heavens: that was their idea of asking quietly.

"Aye, her, the one with all the books and the specs and the duffel coat!"

"Ruth!" came back the answer.

"Ruth What?"

"Deacon!"

Then one of them put her head round the door: "Ruth Deacon, Edith. Okay?"

Discreet enquiries had been made.

26

Well, it was worth a letter to the College where, according to her book, she is or was based; and if she did receive the letter, and if she comes in again to see my neighbour, perhaps she will look in. I hope so. I need to get the thing organised. No-one in this place is organised. No-one can be trusted.

My neighbour and I seem to be chosen to sit together: two oddities, I suppose, at these dreadful singsongs and get-togethers they make us attend. I suppose it is because we arrived on the same day, spilled out from hospital in our matching wheelchairs. Still, just because we can no longer walk, I wonder why they think we are incapable of listening to anything more challenging than "The Mountains of Mourne" or, Heaven preserve us, "Happy Birthday". We are not six years old. It could be worse, I suppose: it could be "Roll Out the Barrel", and I daresay before long it will be. After all, why not? The gang's all here, if by the gang we understand the old and the dispossessed.

I must see if I can find out my neighbour's full name. We only do first names in here. I'm Edith to everybody, after being Miss Barratt all my professional life. She's Hilda — or is it Hildy? I'm not sure.

The entries in that little diary are short. The thoughts of youth may be long, long thoughts, but they do not always commit themselves to paper. The entries are useful only in that they tell me what I was doing then. What I had written was "*Ich will in Berlin gehen*" which, if I remember, means "I intend to go to Berlin", or else that is what I meant it to mean, because according to this diary, in late August 1938, that is what I had intended. How could I have forgotten? After all, I did go. I went.

They saw me writing this down, and said how nicely I write, or some such nonsense, and now they give me no peace. This book I have in front of me is the one the therapist brought me, quite a nice one: heavy paper, smooth, the kind I always liked. On the front is printed the word *Memories*. Very well then: this can be my memory book. I have a pen I can hold without too much difficulty. Arthritis, my last but relentlessly faithful companion, makes constant and painful demands on my attention. They say I have my marbles. I can see I had better try to hold on to these useful marbles.

There is no point, however, trying to recall last year, or last week for that matter; it slides away, and it can, as far as I'm concerned. Drumcree. Ah, but the high and far-off times! They want me to remember the war. Fifty years, they tell me, since it ended: so hard to believe. I'll happily remember that war, because it came to an end. These days, though they talk of ceasefires, the war never ends: it simply continues — nasty, dirty, covert, unceasing. Listen out there: bang, crash, crash, bang, all summer long. They call it the Marching Season. We have autumn, winter, spring and the Marching Season. Drumcree. John Mitchel was married in that church. I wonder do they know, the marchers? Mitchel, the Young Irelander: transported for his part in a futile bid to overthrow the government. They might be less keen if they did know. It's ludicrous to those of us who lived on the other side of time.

Fifty, sixty, seventy years ago, I remember clearly. I remember being twenty-three, and determined to get to Berlin. Paul: I remember him, because I cannot forget. I tried for too long to forget; and the effort was greater than letting it come. I was like a child at the edge of the sea, digging in the sand with my spade, angry at the water's return each time I emptied it out with my little bucket. Let it come: let it fill up. I cannot fight it now.

So I told her, the therapist, whatever her name was, that I would dutifully keep a memory book, but that no-one was to read it without my express permission. She shrugged. "So long as you write in it," she said. "Tell you what, why don't you write down all about you and Fred Astaire." Then she laughed, and left. The thing is, that is true. I did see him, once, long ago; and it's true about George Gershwin as well. At any rate, I read that, about George Gershwin, and I choose to believe it was so.

There won't be much writing today. I am tired. Those flighty curtains hardly keep out the thinnest of suns, flirting at the side of my eye, and then the waving black lines begin; it is tiresome, yet I have neither the capacity nor sufficient will to do something about them. They might come in soon with yet more tea; or that girl might come, if she is the girl I think she is.

At last, a blessed cloud has dulled the glare: the bliss of cool shade behind my eyes. If that is the sound of rain, I'll think no more for the moment.

I may tell that girl, if indeed she is the same Ruth Deacon I remember. I'll think about telling her, and giving her the task, if she is up to it; and, indeed, if she will undertake it. I may. I know what I would say: and if I forget, or something prevents me, at least I will have written some of it down.

The Morning After the Explosion

I was just thirteen when I saw Fred Astaire, with his sister, in London. It was December 1928, and it was my Christmas treat to be brought to see them in *Funny Face* at the Princes Theatre. Ah, the magic of that, even now! It seemed that they scarcely touched the earth. They skimmed it, air sprites that they were. Later, when I knew more, I would think of Ariel; or rather, he was Ariel. She, Adele, was more Tinkerbell. She was light-hearted, almost vulgar, chocolate-box pretty; but he, he was of another kind. His was a face made for seriousness. Think of that dance in *Swing Time*, the two figures, black and white, spiralling across the marbled floor, spinning up a curving staircase, whirling to meet in a final stillness, the poised moment, then the break, the separation. I read that Ginger Rogers bled then through her shoes, the pearl turning pink, and that he did not notice. He would not have noticed if his own feet had bled: he expected the same of his partners. You see that serious stillness in his later work, too: *On The Beach* and that terrible film, *The Towering Inferno*, terrible,

31

apart from him, and improbable in every other way.

Yet, improbable things happen; like the explosion that happened in the early hours of the following morning. Gas, I remember: a disused tube tunnel under High Holborn, many people gassed, one man dead and a great cavity blown in the road just outside the Princes Theatre. We were so close still to the memory of the war, and suddenly we were all hurtled back; a faint, terrifying miasma of gas floating all around; the theatre closed until further notice. And there they were: Fred and Adele, just sitting on a wall, their heads in their hands.

I saw them, and I pointed them out to my parents. He doesn't have as much hair as you would think. He didn't, I mean. My mother said: "Those poor young people — their careers will be ruined."

My father said: "They're lucky. And so are we. This could have happened last night."

"Hush," said my mother. "The child."

The child didn't care. The child was still entranced. There they were, on that wall. Little Adele, like a fallen angel: epicene Fred, with his high forehead and his pale thin hands, still touched by light; behind them, through the gaping bricks, a blackened ruin that had been the gateway to their enchanted space. Still, even then, even on that broken wall, it was Fred who entranced me, even sitting with his head in his hands in a kind of despair.

Is that what I saw? Was it some kind of tragic capability I saw on his face in 1928? Adele, so soon to leap into the aristocracy of England, looked upset: not he. His face showed a devastation I did not yet know but recognised. I would see it, and feel it, and it would be over another man, a soldier of the German army, and he would be an enemy, and I would love him.

They had a particular dance: "The Babbitt and the

Bromide." I still don't know what that means, and I can hardly describe it, but there is film of him on roller-skates, with Ginger Rogers, that one where they go round in circles, dizzying, decreasing circles — it's the same dance. That film: was it *Carefree*? Later, he sings to her, hazy in fog, his face a mask of sadness: he is losing her forever, but they can't take away the memories he begins to cherish, even then, while they are still standing, grieving in anticipation. He knows. He knows.

I know, too. They can't take it away from me, either: they can't erase the way we danced. They play that song to me sometimes in here; the kind ones do. They know I like it. Or rather, they think I like it, but it isn't that. I don't like it at all. I live it. I am there, and I can spin and dip — and then I can't. They don't stay long enough to know that; and why should they? I don't belong to them. I pay my way. That's all. Besides, they have others to see to, and some of those are dying; some are distressed. All it is with me is that I can't function as I used to; reading is tiring, and the lines have begun to wave.

I have tried to read that book that won all the prizes, *Heimkehr*. One of the last things I went to, before I came in here, was a reading by the author from the book, based upon her mother's wartime experiences. The book is heavy, too heavy for me to hold; and the content itself is a little too heavy for me as well. The mother was an interesting speaker, better than the author. A memoir, an autobiography, might have served better; though whether I quite accept what she claims, I am not sure. The daughter is what I think they now call a revisionist. I also think I saw Ruth Deacon there, too; that is, if it's the girl I'm thinking about. It's my eyes. I just can't be sure. At any rate a Ruth Deacon was one of the speakers; and if I'm not mistaken, my neighbour was there too.

I get up and walk around at night. What am I saying? I don't get up: I can't get up. In my mind, I get up and walk round and explore this place: and it's not much, for all their brochures. Yet, when they put that song on, on this machine beside me, I am dancing in the Ballhaus in Berlin, and I am young, and my life is full.

The Ballhaus in Berlin: the mere sound of it is enough. Clärchen's Ballhaus. Little Clara's Ballroom, Auguststrasse 24. It may not look like much from outside, an ordinary tall building, yet it survived two wars. We bombed it. We, the allies, bombed it. They say it survived, and that today it could be anything, even an official residence. In my mind, I travel there. I stand outside. It looks very quiet. Even on a still evening, no sound comes from the Ballhaus: but once past through the doorway, the sound reaches out and wraps around, and it is impossible to do anything but go forward, go inside and become part of it. Perhaps it is a waltz, or maybe a tango, and the place is dimly lit. Are there candles? I remember candles, mirrors, the *Spiegelsaal*: yes, upstairs, the *Spiegelsaal* — great mirrors like a hidden Versailles. They say duels were fought here, the flashing brilliance of silver steel against those intricate garlands, those blank-eyed cherubs, impassive, impervious baroque. There are bullet-holes. I remember the music of violins: was there an accordion? It hardly matters. All around are dancers, swirling, shimmering like the shadows of leaves on the trees. There is no hurry in the Ballhaus: there is only the dance, and the sitting down at little tables at the side, for a glass, or coffee, or just to rest for a little before the longing takes hold, that irresistible urge to be swept away in delight.

That was where we danced, and where I dance still, in myself. It survived two wars; two wars, and for all I can tell it is there yet. Paul said it had been commissioned by Kaiser

Wilhelm's butler. I thought it was a joke, but Paul did not joke. It was the one thing that jarred; or maybe it was one of several things. There are always things we do not like about the ones we love. He, Paul Herrold, was the one I loved; there, I have said it. After all these years of denying it, forgetting it, burying it, there it is. And still, it wrings my heart to say it, think it, write it.

I used to play a game, just by myself — it may be a habit characteristic of only children — I would say a word, or a group of words, "rain", perhaps, or "world without end" over and over again until they lost their meaning, and I was in a state of blissful nothingness within the sound, the feeling of the sound. He was the one I loved. I don't know what that means any more: I just remember the dance, the feeling of the dance, the sound and the smell and the joy of dancing in Clärchen's Ballhaus.

My parents or, I should say, my mother loved the theatre. The arts, I suppose one could say: she loved the arts, all of them. I think it is why she put up with Kitty, because, whatever Kitty's faults, she was a member of an artistic family. My father's tastes were more conservative, but he did not sneer at the new, like some of my teachers, indeed like some of my lecturers later on. He enjoyed the popular as well as the classical. I used to hear one or other of them singing. "Voi Che Sapete", she; he, "I Dream of Jeannie". I think they were happy. They were certainly united. Indeed, if anyone was out of tune, it was myself.

I believe I was always more in sympathy with my father than my mother, which may be why that last episode was so upsetting. Seeing them all round me, that was the trouble: nurses and care assistants and in the middle of it my parents, and Paul, all talking over one another, all those voices, the living indistinguishable from the dead, all their shapes shifting and going through one another, walls as if they were doors, windows as if they were water, and everything moving as if we were in a ship. I was nauseated, humiliated in front of them all, and the pain, that sick pain dizzying in my head; then it was quiet and dark, and there was just Louisa. Those kind girls from the Philippines: I wanted to say thank you. I know I said thank you, but she did not respond. She called Natalia: not so kind, but certainly efficient. Natalia held my wrist and she looked at the watch on her pocket, and she looked at me as if I had not spoken. "Don't worry," said Louisa. "It'll come back." Then I knew: I was speaking, and no-one could hear me, and no-one knew I was talking away in here, in this crowded space inside my head, where they had all moved in: my parents, and Paul, and Fred and Adele Astaire. Oh, Fred. The way he danced!

It's strange to think we might never have seen him. If his parents had stayed in Austria, what would have become of him, born in 1899? Friedrich Austerlitz would have had to go to war. He would probably have died, or lost the limbs that would make him famous, the dancers' dancer. Austerlitz: was that not a battle in the Napoleonic wars? I think it was. Mary Parker's the one for history. Mary will know.

I was going to write: *I'll ask Mary Parker in the morning.* Then, a bird flew past there, outside the window, and I remembered. This bird, like an omen, reminded me: I have no class in the morning, no job to go to, no home, nothing but this room where I will probably die. And Mary Parker, who liked to go for coffee in the Abercorn, is dead, long dead. Yet, there *was* another bird, somewhere, wasn't there? A little friend. *Amico.*

Friedrich or Frederick Austerlitz: it was one or the other. And, was there something about the father? Did I read that somewhere, that his brothers did well in the army, but that

36

he left the country, or had to leave? If he had not, Friedrich would probably have been a soldier in the army of the Kaiser. If his father had not left Austria, he would have been old enough. Then we never would have had Fred Astaire, unless we stumbled on a grave marked Friedrich Austerlitz, a young soldier dead at sixteen, or seventeen. For whatever reason, good or bad, the father took ship for the New World, and the brothers stayed behind. Omaha, Nebraska: that was where they went. I saw a photograph of the house where he was born, a little white clapboard house, modest, unassuming: straight out of every down-home film ever seen, the emigrants' dream. He was a dancer from the age of four: his mother's doing. The father seems to have been left behind in Omaha when his wife took the children to New York, and she saw to the children, bringing them on, teaching them, putting them on the stage, astutely Americanising the names, Friedrich to Frederick to Fred, Austerlitz to Astaire, giving him his chance of immortality.

Paul and I used to talk like that, when we first met, about the ones who were killed, the ones who could have been, the talent that was lost as well as that which was saved, like Fred Astaire, like Erich Maria Remarque. Paul felt the waste, in those days, of that war. Remarque, in his view, had given the world a great, disturbing examination of truth in *All Quiet on the Western Front*. He called it *Im Westen Nichts Neues*: Nothing New on the Western Front. It was quite a different title, he said: that for the war-makers, those in charge, there was nothing new, nothing worth bothering about in the negligible thousands dying at the front in boredom and in filth. I can hear him reading: "*We are at rest five miles behind the line ...*" No, no, that came later. That was at our house. I mustn't get mixed up. I must keep my head clear.

The book — the book was certainly burned in 1933, as was the film. If in 1915, when I was born, Friedrich Austerlitz had lain dying on a battlefield in France, there would still have been nothing new. *All Quiet* would still have been written, still have been burned in 1933. But in 1932, when first we met, Paul could not have known that. I could not have known that. I still did not know that, or did not think of it, six years later, dancing with him in Clärchen's Ballhaus.

Yet, even those six years later, the music swirling in my head, the thought remained: but for chance there would never have been a Fred Astaire; but for chance I would never have seen him with his sister, sitting with his head in his hands outside that theatre in London in 1928. Paul, to whom I voiced these thoughts, said he did not believe in chance. Was it chance, I sometimes idly wonder now, that the date on which Remarque's book would be burned in 1933, was May the 10th, Fred Astaire's birthday?

The Half-Said Thing

The first time I saw him, he was in a hospital bed. That was the time I had got a notion in my head about learning German. I don't know why it had to be German: at that time it could have been anything. I was not far off seventeen, still enjoying that abundance of youthful energy which so quickly dissipates itself. I wanted a challenge, and I decided, however it happened, that I wanted to learn German. There was a teacher then — what was her name, did she enter, did she become a nun herself? "Travel, girls, travel: that's the thing" — that was her. The name is gone. Anyway, she gave me a book to start me off. "But," she said, "you need to practise." She said: "I was over in the hospital earlier today. There was a young man there, a German, a tourist. He has been to the Eucharistic Congress in Dublin, and was touring Ireland. Unfortunately, the poor young man has been involved in an accident, knocked off the motorcycle he had hired. God must have looked kindly upon him: he is lucky not to have lost his leg."

I listened, with sinking heart: I thought I was about to be

lectured about the Eucharistic Congress, about which we were then hearing, in my view, far too much. Sky-writing seemed to me then, as it does now, excessive, even if its message is holy and wholesome. What was it they wrote in the sky over Dublin? "*Gaudeamus, adoramus*"? I struggled to remember, even at the time.

Then, I heard: "Are you listening? I said, I want you to go over and visit this young man, and then you can recount what you learn about the Eucharistic Congress to the rest of the girls. There is nothing like hearing a first-hand account; and then you can write it as a paper, and that will be good for you, too. It will also, of course, be an excellent opportunity to practise your German."

I said nothing, for nothing about it appealed to me.

She sighed. "Edith," she said, "at the very least you can think of it as a corporal work of mercy."

We were meant to carry out corporal works of mercy, including visiting the sick, probably in order to avoid the Jansenist doom which was certainly waiting for us. Nobody thinks that way these days, but we did, so I agreed, though I was in no mood for it.

She must have seen that. "Bring somebody with you," she said, as I was leaving. "I am certainly not advocating that you visit strange men alone." She did become a nun. I remember now.

So I asked Kitty, my on-and-off friend or, as my father called her, my sparring partner, mainly because she was still in the cloakroom when I went downstairs. I was far from pleased, and I half-expected that she would laugh it off as a joke, and then I could say there was nobody to go with me, and just leave it there. I did not expect what did happen. Without a word, she pulled on her Burberry, fluffed up her hair and — this was Kitty — producing from her pocket a powder compact and a bright red lipstick, dabbed her nose, snapped the compact shut, glanced at herself in the mirror, slicked on the lipstick, flipped up her collar and said: "All right then. Let's go." Kitty was a great one for impulse.

The hospital was just over the road from the school. It was a good school, famous then and later for sending out strong and independent women. *Veritas,* our noble motto: another word I think about until it shimmers and disappears. We wore rather jaunty jockey caps; we thought we were a cut above. People looked at us in the street. I considered myself already strong and independent — though, of course, in danger at any moment of falling into perdition. It is quite hard to explain that to people these days: the near-thrill of balancing, every day, in every activity, on a tightrope over the mouth of Hell. I was anyway; I doubt that Kitty was, but then she hadn't really been steeped in it as I had. She had her own demons, however: her father, by all accounts a most talented musician, seemed to spend his life giving concerts abroad. As to her mother, rumour divided itself between the story that she had died when Kitty was born, and the two far more prevalent and interesting theories, one that she had been a dancer, possibly a chorus girl, and that the marriage was so scandalous and shocking that there was a rift between Kitty's grandparents and their son, or else that she had continued to be scandalous and run away and abandoned them both. Kitty did not enlighten us, if she knew; in fact, I always thought she enjoyed the speculation. What was certain was that her guardians and only company, apart from all of us at school, were her two elderly grandparents. English was not the grandparents' first language. I didn't know what their nationality was.

At school, she was known as Kitty Brown. Her looks suited her name: hazel-brown eyes, dark-brown hair, a permanently golden skin that took the sun. That was all we saw and, as girls, we openly envied Kitty those effortless good looks and seemingly natural grace. All my father would say about her background was that it was no wonder she was inclined to go a little off the rails. It seems he thought that I could be a steadying influence; though I had once heard my mother make a remark about Kitty which I think may have been nearer the truth. I had admired, probably irritatingly and too often, their lovely house up near the zoo, looking out over the lough and its silver ships, and beyond, the misted blue hills. Light filtered in reds and blues through a stained-glass window her grandfather had designed himself, and everything about their life seemed bright and desirable, in contrast to the safe predictability of mine. I envied Kitty her freedom to do practically anything she wanted. "The trouble with Miss Kitty," said my mother, "is that she is both neglected and spoiled." Perhaps she was. I liked her, all the same; except when I didn't.

In any case, she and I went across that afternoon, and there he was, the young German, in that narrow metal bed, propped up, a lock of hair falling across a high forehead; and something about him was instantly familiar. He looked like a schoolboy or, maybe, a student, yet he told us he was twenty-five. What most struck me, though, was that he looked like someone I knew, or had known. I could not understand this. I looked at the name. Paul, it said: Paul Herrold. I still could not understand.

He spoke a clear and grammatical English, but was obviously experiencing some difficulty with the vernacular of our town. Once he learned, however, through my halting, embarrassed explanation, that I hoped to practise my spoken German, he switched, and for five painful minutes I stumbled. He let me stumble, and Kitty was no help. She just sat and looked at him with that opaque inscrutable insolence that was peculiarly hers. It enraged, at some point, every teacher she ever had, and I can understand why. Our German patient went between watching me make a fool of myself and glancing with amusement at Kitty. There was no sound, apart from my risible attempts. Kitty just sat there, looking at him, with that little smile of hers, making no attempt at conversation; and she was the one who was supposed to speak German. After a while he relented, and we went back to English, and I thought we were on safer ground; and then Kitty suddenly got up, said she would see me later, and left, just like that.

He said nothing when she stood up, but he watched her walking down the ward, and I could not read the expression on his face. Was he offended, amused, puzzled? I did not know. Then he looked at me, and, just for a second, it was as if he had forgotten I was there. It was awkward. Kitty made it awkward, leaving like that: but then, for the first time, he smiled. He did not know my name, he said.

"It's Edith," I said.

"Edith," he repeated, though it sounded to my ears like *edit*. "Is that a family name?"

I told him I thought not. As far as I knew, I was named for Edith Cavell. It was out before I thought and, as I said it, I grew hot and embarrassed again, remembering the circumstances of her death, shot by the Germans as a spy. It was too late to retract it, yet he did not seem either annoyed or surprised.

"Edith Cavell," he repeated: "A volunteer nurse. She nursed our people too. Did you know?"

I shook my head. "I think she died near the time I was born," I said. There was so much I did not know.

What I did know, and did not say, was that my father

fought in that war, because our family was Redmondite in politics. I knew that my father and my mother's brother Patrick joined up because John Redmond said it was the duty of conscientious Irishmen to do so; and that though my family believed in Ireland's right to Home Rule, they accepted Redmond's decision to let it be delayed for the greater good. Though Home Rule never came, they did not blame Redmond; and they saw no contradiction in their sense of Irishness and their loyalty to the Crown. I knew that my father was invalided home after Gallipoli; that my Uncle Patrick, having barely survived Passchendaele, came home with shellshock to live, a permanent invalid, with us. I did not tell Paul that, despite everything he had endured, my father maintained a cautious compassion for all who had taken part in the war; that he almost never spoke of it, except that I heard him cry out sometimes in the night. Later my mother told me his dream was always the same: swarms of flies all around, day and night, in the baking Turkish heat. I know he hated the sound of swarming insects. I did not tell Paul, either, that to my Uncle Patrick, all Germans were still the filthy Hun.

I remember when I was little — before I had even started school — hearing one day a terrible clamour, a cacophony of sounds, and high above it the clanging of a bell, monotonous, relentless. Everyone stopped, and I did too. Then, like something from a terrible tale there came flying, flashing past us, with a great roar like thunder, a huge machine, scarlet and shining with brass, and it was surrounded by men, silent, purposeful men with broad pointed helmets, just like the Kaiser's — the Kaiser was always wearing one in *Punch* — and one of them at the front was pulling a rope and clanging that insistent bell, throbbing on all our eardrums. I clapped my hands to my ears, but I could still hear it and I heard dogs howling, and cats crying as they ran from it; and I looked up at my uncle, and he was white, and shaking, and as terrified as I was, and I knew what was happening: the Germans had come back, and they were coming for us, for him, to take revenge on him for having fought them off. When we made it home, my mother told me it was just a fire engine, nothing to be afraid of, something to be glad about, really; but I did not sleep well that night, and it stayed in my nightmares for a long time. Uncle Patrick had to go into hospital, I remember, for quite a while after it. I could not have told my uncle, ever, that I was learning German, much less that I was visiting a member of that nation.

Now here I was, conversing with a German, practically fraternising with the enemy.

"Are you a teacher?" I asked.

He hesitated.

"You don't have to tell me if you'd rather not," I said then, too quickly, giving him no time, but he just shrugged.

"Ah," he said. "Does it show?"

"A bit," I said, because it did.

"I am," he said. He shrugged again. "And there's nothing to be done about it."

Then I asked him, as I had been instructed, about the Eucharistic Congress. He smiled again: a tired smile this time.

"Are you supposed to ask me that?" he said.

I remember nodding.

He indicated the locker beside him. "Pass me that book, would you, please?"

I looked at the slim pamphlet, hardly worthy to be called a book: *Prayers and Reflections for the Eucharistic Congress*.

"There," he said. "Take that back to your school."

I thought I was being dismissed. I leaned my hand on the

bedspread, and reached down for my belongings. As I did, I thought I felt his hand rest, just for a second, on mine. All I could see was the starched white counterpane, and the grey hospital floor; all I could feel was a jolt, like electricity, which I did not understand. I sat upright, intending to stand. I found I could not. His eyes grey, light-filled, holding mine: a split second. That lock of hair.

"I blame Kuno Meyer," he said.

I did not know where that came from.

"Meyer, and Douglas Hyde."

"Wasn't Kuno Meyer German?" I heard myself say. Shamefully, it was then all I did know.

Again, he shrugged, and this time, a lovely, becoming smile lit up his face.

"Germans and Irish," he said, "have much in common."

Did I not know about Kuno Meyer's translations of Irish poetry, he asked me then. I shook my head. "The half-said thing of them is dearest," he said, and to my shame, I did not know that he was quoting. He said I should read the work of Goethe, and Schiller, and Heine, and Rilke, too, yes, Rilke, especially, if I could find a copy with a translation, as with Douglas Hyde. He knew by heart passages from Yeats and Synge. We spoke of Sligo: he had planned to go, he said, had been setting out, when he had had his accident. He had hoped to make some sketches, perhaps some watercolours.

"Are you a painter, then?" I asked. "Is that what you do?"

"If I could be," he said, and he smiled a little sadly, "that is what I would be."

Did he mean he had no gift, or no opportunity? I did not know, and could not ask.

"We're going on holiday to Sligo," I told him, to fill the silence, "as soon as school ends," and then, from nowhere,

I heard him say: "I should like to see Knocknarea," and I felt my skin go hot; but he could not have meant he wanted to see it with me, unless he did mean that. How could I know? I was still only sixteen, and I scarcely understood what was happening to me, or even what I was saying. I have no idea why, for example, I said: "When you get out, maybe I can show you some of the places we have near here," or why he answered, quite normally, "I should like that very much."

"I could take you to the place the Brontës came from," I heard myself say. "You could sketch that." What was wrong with me? How I was going to do that I did not know. I was babbling, and I could not stop. "Their father was from here, from County Down. That was their home place."

"Here? They were not English?" he said.

"Only half," I heard myself say, "and Cornish rather than English. And Emily was learning German: she kept her book propped up against the baking bowl while she made the bread."

"The home place," he repeated, and I thought for a moment he was laughing at me. "I should like to see the Brontës' home place," he said. "I like that. It makes me think of our word, *Heimat*." He smiled, and I knew he was not laughing at me.

I was so busy thinking about *Heimat* that I almost missed the words he said after it, beneath his breath. "The half-said thing," I heard him say, for no reason, to no-one. I went away that day confused and faintly delirious, because it was all so unlikely and yet so exciting. I looked back at the door of the ward. He did not glance up: head down, he seemed to be writing on a pad, or sketching perhaps; and I went hot to my scalp at the sudden thought that he might be sketching me. I fled then, confused, as

47

quickly as I could; and only later found that I had forgotten the pamphlet about the Eucharistic Congress.

As it turned out, I never did show him the Brontës' homeplace or anything else. He had sustained a bad break, and indeed, it was as my teacher said: he had been lucky not to lose the leg. In fact, it emerged, if a young Canadian surgeon, newly qualified and spending a short time in the hospital, had not been on duty the night he was brought in, the leg would have been amputated. Thanks to him, though, the leg was saved. Paul was pronounced unfit to travel, and was told he needed somewhere to stay, to recover his mobility. He could not be discharged otherwise and, for whatever reason, it took some time before a place could be found for him at a nursing home. I remember telling my parents this: and they suggested he be invited to have tea with us when he was discharged.

My uncle was not with us just then. I think, by some ironic twist, that it was one of the times he was himself in hospital, still thinking he was in that other war. My father, used to caring for others, may simply have missed another male about the place, someone to talk to, to argue with, to be companionable with — or, however stable their marriage was, my parents were long past the time, it seemed, when they found pleasure only in the company of the other. My father found the idea of what he called "Edith's German" quite intriguing, and I think my mother was both nervous and curious.

As it was, he got on so well with my father that I felt almost excluded, especially when they started discussing the true title of *All Quiet*; that was supposed to be mine. That was when Paul began to read to us from it — all of us, not just me. I sat like the child I suddenly was, jealous and resentful, as they talked about prejudice between nations and between religions, and I heard my father explain to him, to his surprise, about the divisions of our country, and the hatreds that soured our relations. He told him — and this took me by surprise, because he was always so circumspect —about a family we knew. The father was in the Civil Service. Having been dispatched after Partition from Dublin to the North and, needing to find somewhere to bring his family, he had taken and moved into a house that no one wanted to live in, though it was a fine house in a good district of the town. I remembered that house. The civil servant's daughter was my friend at our first school. I remember going to play in the house. It was only once. We were sent into the front room, the good room, which no-one used; but we soon asked to play outside, preferring, without understanding, the cold of the autumn air to that room, where the chill had a deeper and a darker smell. I was never there again: the family moved away shortly afterwards.

It was only because my father told Paul the story that I learned that murder had been done in that dank room. A whole family had been wiped out, a father and all his sons, even the littlest, who tried to hide under the sofa and was dragged out to be killed, because a policeman had been shot by the IRA. I remembered, then, overhearing the word "reprisal", and receiving no answer to my questions. Neither the man, my father said, who was a publican, nor his sons had any connection with the IRA: their mistake was to be perceived to be of the wrong religion at the wrong moment in the wrong place. Bigotry, my father said; bigotry and intolerance were to blame for that appalling crime. Paul shook his head in wonder. It was, he said, a horrid tale; I remember that he used the word "horrid". Yet, he added, history, not least the history of his own country, was full of such terrible tales; and they began to exchange them, man to man. What did he make of this man

Hitler, my father asked. Would he last, did Paul think, or would he be another flash in the pan?

I wasn't having that. If they started on politics, especially international politics, I would be completely excluded. I racked my brains, thinking furiously of our conversation in the hospital, and it came to me. The Brontës: I imagined that he had not read *Villette*. If they wanted blind bigotry, I said loudly, quite consciously interrupting, if they wanted to see cold revenge, and if they wanted a narrator who did not understand what was plainly before her, a narrator who did not know her own heart, or her own capacity for self-delusion, that was where they needed to go. They looked at me, Paul in something like wonder and surprise, my father in mild disapproval at, I suppose, the interruption; and then they went straight back to German military history, but not, at least, international politics or the new man, Hitler. Instead, they veered into legend: Tristan and Isolde came up, and I struggled back in, and tried again. I said: "Like Diarmuid and Gráinne," and — I think with a look between one another — they thought it best to concede that much to the child, and Paul smiled his lovely smile and said: "*Frisch weht der Wind der Heimat zu, Mein Irisch Kind, wo weilest du?*" and it seemed for a moment like a promise to me, a hope of something I could neither name nor understand. "*Fresh blows the wind towards home, My Irish child, where dwellest thou?*" It was just a moment, however, for my father started straight away on Eliot's use of the second line, and Paul looked away, and they were off again.

Once more, brazen child that I was, I pulled them back. "You can see where their story ended," I said, "in Sligo. And nearby, Knocknarea, where Queen Maeve sleeps with her knights, awaiting the call to her country's aid." I had him then.

"Like Barbarossa?" he said. "There is a mountain in Thuringia where he sleeps with six of his own knights. When he rises, Germany will be the foremost kingdom on the earth — just as soon as he winds his great red beard three times round the stone table where he sits."

"I think Maeve has more than six," I said, and they laughed, and I do believe I was so much back in the conversation that by the time the afternoon ended I heard my father suggest that, if he should be well enough, Paul might consider making his trip to Sligo at the same time we did, and I was almost deliriously happy. I had carried my point, and my friend belonged again to me. The thought of it sustained me, to such an extent that, even though it did not happen, I thought so much about it, planning it, dreaming it, that I began to think he did come with us, and when I was in Sligo with my parents, looking up at Ben Bulben, where the end came for Diarmuid and Gráinne, I dreamed him beside me. When I looked across at Knocknarea, the mountain of the birds, where Yeats's Sidhe gathered, where Queen Maeve sleeps waiting for the call to rally her knights and return, I had my Tristan at my side, and I was his Irish child; and in Dromahair, where the fairies danced, I was the stolen girl drifting into fantasy.

In reality, of course, he just went away. He was discharged and he went home to Germany. He had said that day he came that he would keep in touch with us, and he did, twice. I do not know what happened to the letters, though I do remember them as if they were here in front of me. They were addressed to my parents: the first a bread and butter letter to say thank you. He also sent greetings from his wife, and a photograph of them with their little boy Rudi, just three years old, and said he hoped to bring them with him on his next trip to Ireland. I remember the shock of that. What wife? I knew of no wife, or son.

"Of course you did," I heard my mother say. "He spoke of them when he was here. If you paid attention to what was going on around you now and again, instead of wandering about in a dream, you wouldn't make so many silly mistakes." Her voice was so sharp.

Perhaps she was right. After all, I had not even been conscious of speaking those words aloud. Had I known that? Had he spoken of them? I had no memory of it. Yet here in the photograph was the evidence: the slight, fair man, arm about his round-faced wife in her floral tea-dress, shading her eyes, and between them, a little blond boy with the sun in his eyes and a frown on his face. "*Paul, Freda, and Rudi*," it said, "*May, 1932.*"

His second letter to my parents arrived, barely a month after the first, telling that his wife and his little boy had been killed in a car accident. Once again, I was shocked: not just because of what had happened, although I knew that it was shocking, but because my first thought was that he was now free, and the fact that I thought that shocked me more.

"Poor young man," said my mother, and I noticed she looked quickly at me. I kept my face blank. "You'll write, of course," she said to my father, still with her eyes on me.

"Of course," said my father, shaking his head. "A terrible thing. I'll go over to the Monastery and see that a Mass is said." That was an end of it, as far as they were concerned.

It was 1932. I was not yet seventeen. I knew so little; but one thing I knew. As soon as my German improved, I was going to write to him, myself, and I was not going to ask anybody's permission, or anybody's help. And I did. It took me some months to be reasonably competent, but I wrote to him that Christmas, and I sent him a gift. I did not want to part with it, which is why I did: what is the use of a gift one would not rather keep? I had one book on my shelf to which I often returned, a book whose author understood the cruelties of chance, of the moment missed, and the loneliness and regret that follow them. I sent him my own much-loved copy of the poems of Thomas Hardy. I missed it, from my heart; but I did not regret sending it.

Ruth

❧

Earth to Thomas

Ruth Deacon to Thomas Bowers, by email

Earth to Thomas! Joke. Good to hear from you. About
Hilde, you said in your email you would like me to tell
you why, as you put it, I dumped her in a nursing home,
and why I chose a convent. Well, first of all I didn't dump
her. Secondly, she's not in a convent. They had no room;
and anyway, it hasn't been a convent for years. Thirdly, I
didn't do the choosing, at any rate where the convent was
concerned. That was entirely her notion. I'm not at fault,
any more than you.

First, yes, Hilde is indeed in a nursing home, for
temporary respite care, and so far I have been doing my
best to go in every day. As I said, she chose to go in. She
did choose: Chris would say otherwise, but he has his
own agenda, and you know as well as I do that Hilde
always made up her own mind. After all, would either

55

you or I even have thought of a former convent for her? That was all her. I thought it would be a mistake. I mean, food, for a start. You'll recall, I'm sure, that she always found difficulty digesting food that was not kosher, and that was hardly going to alter. Her system, she said, could not make so radical a change. Her speech — do you remember — was like that, always quite formal: "so radical a change." I think she was always translating, like the stranger she always felt herself to be. My mother didn't — I think your father didn't — but Hilde did. Maybe it's just that the other two got away before her. I don't know.

But the convent thing: you may remember I was educated at a convent, because it was my father's wish. After my mother died, and Hilde came to us, she didn't like it, and said so constantly, as if it was any of her business. And then she went and chose a former convent for herself. All I did, after the business of the conference, and my own spell in hospital — really, it was then that it came home to me that I couldn't do my job and care for her at the same time — was to leave it up to her to decide where she would like to be looked after this summer. When the convent had no room, then, yes, I did the deciding, from the list of available places. I did the best I could. That's all. Take it or leave it.

What's more, I've been doing my best to visit in the afternoons, or at least when things are quiet. I suppose you read about the trouble at Drumcree? You can guess, it's made the summer pretty tense. It hasn't helped Hilde's nerves much either. At any rate, so far as anyone can judge, the ceasefires seem to be holding, both Republican and Loyalist, so we may all go on another bit.

You asked me about work. I haven't actually been back since I was ill — still on sick leave, and I'm in no hurry to return. As far as I can gather, it's all going to become harder: we have this new President, with his own inner circle. From September, we'll have no Common Room any more, for instance: it's to be let out for what are known as "functions" which, I gather, translates as money-making parties. So, while we are endlessly exhorted to display a collegial spirit, we shall have nowhere to display it. And we have more and more students to supervise. I've got one young American called Sky, for Heaven's sake, and God knows how she got funded; but she did and I have her. As long as they're funded, nothing else seems to matter. On top of everything else, there's talk that we all have to get out a requisite number of books and articles within a very limited time. How limited, I don't yet know; but I expect to find out. Meanwhile, to ease myself back in, I'm about to go and speak at a conference in Italy. It was all arranged, and I'll enjoy it. I think I'm entitled to that. And, while I'm perfectly sure you're not interested in any of this, I'm telling you so you know why Hilde's in there.

Anyway, so far, it's been more or less all right. With the summer, we've been able from time to time to get out in the grounds. The air seems to improve her spirits, but returning to the room is always difficult. She's bewildered, like a refugee wondering when, or if, she might be going home. Yes, you'll say: as Hilde and her siblings were themselves. But it was different for my mother and your father: you know it was, and therefore different for you and for me, which is part of the problem. We have no experience and only limited patience. We don't know how to cope.

Back in the Thirties, there was just no going home for any of them: and there may be no going home this time either, not for Hilde; not with what ails her. This is why I need to talk to you. The problem is that she wants to go home, and I don't mean to my house. She wants to be back in Berlin. She wants it all to be as it was before she had to leave. If she is to be anywhere but the nursing home, then I need some help, and I have no-one but you to ask. As to your query about Chris and me, things are not good at the moment. I'll tell you about that again. I can't go into it now.

Hope to hear from you soon and it would be nice if you could get over to see her. Hope your next trip is also a success: but it will be, knowing you.
Ruth

That's all he's getting, thought Ruth, pressed "send", and instantly regretted it. It was not right. Why antagonise him? She thought again, and wrote another:

Dear Thomas,
I should have said I am actually leaving today for Italy and, since Hilde seems fairly settled, I'm going to take a short holiday once the conference is over. I'll be at the Hotel Porto Rocco at Monterosso, in the Cinque Terre. If you get finished in Basel, do you think you would be able to come and meet me? Think about it. It might be nice to catch up and, of course, as I said, I'd really like to talk to you about Hilde.
Best,
Ruth

Better. That was better. She pressed "send", then finished

her packing, as quickly as she could, tidied the house — so much easier now that Hilde was gone — and rang a taxi for the airport. She did not notice as she set off that she had forgotten her mobile phone, which is why she missed the message from Chris, telling her, among other things it might have been useful to know, that he himself was leaving for Italy.

The Memory Book

❧

Castel Gandolfo

It was some six years later, in the summer of 1938, that Kitty and I went travelling in Europe. There were not many jobs for young teachers at that time, but I had picked up enough substitute work here and there to have enough for a holiday. Kitty wasn't really doing anything just then: she was just as bright, funny, and fond of a good time as she had been at school — a terrible flirt, in fact, what my mother called "advanced" — and her family, unlike mine, had money. Kitty did not have to save. We got on well most of the time and, of course, a girl could not easily travel alone, in those days: at least, not according to my parents. So when Kitty said she thought she might travel for a while in Europe, perhaps meet her father, I saw no reason not to join her. My mother thought it unwise; my father thought it a good opportunity for me. I need hardly say which opinion I heeded.

It was partly selfish, perhaps, because Kitty had developed a real facility for languages, including German,

61

which I always suspected she spoke at home. She also had more than a little Italian, certainly more than I did. Her people may have been Italian somewhere: wasn't her mother, among all the rumours, supposed to be Italian? Had I heard some of them were Jewish too: was it her grandparents? Did she tell me that herself? I can no longer remember. In any case, she knew enough Italian to see to us both, and I had enough French and Latin to feel I could manage. My plan, if we managed to get as far as Germany, was to try out and perhaps improve my still fairly rudimentary German, and rely on Kitty to carry us both through any difficulties. Honestly, as I write that, I wonder where my head was. Rely on Kitty! What was I thinking? I soon realised my mistake.

By the time we reached Rome, I had grown very tired of her behaviour, well, of Kitty, really. There are courtesies, conventions, which should be observed, and she did not seem to understand that. She did not pay her way, for a start: so much for her family being well-off. I was forever picking up the bill, to be squared up later, which meant never. Then, there was the hotel. Our hotel was full of a large inter-related family of Germans, tourists called Schmidt. It was an ordinary name, and they were an ordinary family, large, kindly, expansive, from a town named Ulm. I liked them, all the sisters and the cousins and the aunts, even the opinionated Uncle Ernst with his carrying voice, and Kurt, the gangly boy with a crush on Kitty. I couldn't work out which branch of the family Kurt belonged to; there were just so many of the Schmidts, practically taking over the whole hotel, not that it was so very large. Even Kurt had his own guidebook and camera and a list of essential Italian phrases, though, to be fair, we had all of those, too. The family was, by and large, earnest, and thorough, and kindly; but Kitty, pleasant enough to their faces, mocked them cruelly as soon as they were out of earshot, especially poor Kurt, sadly smitten by her. I remembered her mischief when we were at school — goodness knows she got me into enough scrapes — but I had somehow overlooked her tendency to malice. "Tell that smart piece nothing important to you," I recalled my mother saying when we were at school. "And, remember, your friend today is your enemy tomorrow." Wise words: I often think of them now. At the time, I scarcely understood what she meant, but certainly I saw that Kitty was most unkind to and about poor young Kurt, his voice hardly broken, struggling with first love.

The Schmidts were Protestant: yet, and this I found both interesting and curious, they carried letters from a priest in their home town, asking that they be admitted to an audience with the Pope. It was more than we, two Irish Catholics, had; not that Kitty wanted any such thing, and it was never certain that she would have described herself as either Irish or Catholic. Her curiosity was for Mussolini, *Il Duce*, not the Pope. So, when she decided to do her sightseeing by herself, I readily agreed. I hardly needed her, anyway: the Schmidts had taken to me, and invited me into their party. It seemed each of their letters admitted two, and they had one place free, and I accepted it.

At the Vatican, I think the Germans were a little disappointed to find that the admitting priest, seated at a long table issuing the requisite cards, could not understand their version of Italian; and he spoke no German, which was even more disappointing, and resulted in their having to ask me to act as interpreter. He wanted to know if any of us were newly-weds because, if so, we would have a special audience before the reception accorded to the public. My Germans, almost all long and happily married, or long beyond any such intention, smiled at the idea of being taken for newly-weds, except for teenaged Kurt who seemed wretched, and I wondered, briefly, about the depth of his passion for Kitty. What I remember most, though, is how hot it was. I should have liked to leave: I looked about me for an escape route. Yet, since the kind Schmidts had given me their invitation, and the careful priest had so laboriously and elaborately copied out all our names on to great invitation cards, vividly rendered in violet and black, there was little to be done but join in and hand in the perforated strip. The Schmidts, delighted, kept their cards as souvenirs. I do so wish, now, that I had.

Two days afterwards, we all set out on an excursion, by tram-car. I mean the Germans and myself. I asked Kitty if she wanted to come along for the ride, but she said no, as I rather hoped she might. She probably had what she liked to call a date: she had many late nights while we were in Rome, and quite a few of them turned into morning. Some of them even started in the morning, as far as I could judge, and went right on to the next one. Well, I thought, as we rattled along, she can go her own way, and I was glad to be without her, for the journey was quite wonderful.

We travelled the Appian Way, where St Paul entered Rome — and, I think, where Julius Caesar crucified his opponents — and then over the Campagna, with its broken arches of the aqueducts built by the Caesars. On we went, hot and pressed together, all that long drive through the shifting, shimmering heat of the day, until at last we came to a dusty halt in the little town of Castel Gandolfo, in the district of Albany. Beyond the blue line of the sea, a mere twelve miles away, lay the stifling press of Rome; but it was here, with the salt sea blowing towards them, that Pompey and the Emperor Domitian, and so many of the Popes had chosen to spend their time. It was not difficult to see why.

Yet, the market-square! We were right back in the world

of getting and spending. There was noise, movement everywhere, booths selling everything: near the sea, cheap souvenirs, postcards and ices and lemonade; beside the papal residence, rosaries and statuettes and missals. Such a strange combination, repeated in the bearing of that crowd: they were darkly, even soberly dressed, as was proper for the pilgrim, yet they were also noisy, vociferous, with a kind of feral, infectious energy. I spotted a café near the sea wall, with one or two lucky people already in its cool shade. For a treacherous moment, I thought of abandoning the Schmidts, but I overcame the impulse, and I stayed. If I had gone, though, if I had gone ...

Some groups had begun to form on the steps, leading up to an enormous door, studded with iron. As the door slowly opened, the excitement gathered; only to subside in groans as it became apparent that only the young married couples were being admitted, disappearing behind the fastness, two by two, as if into the Ark. I almost left then. That café beckoned. It was hot; I felt unreasonably deserted, though by what or by whom I could not have said. There was no indication of how long we might have to wait.

Then, just as I was about to give in and go to the little café by the wall, the door opened again, and we were all ushered onto an inner courtyard, paved, cool, lined with wooden benches. We sat again: priests and nuns, young men in shorts, hikers, I suppose, happy wanderers; Italian women swathed in black; African students. Eventually, we were called to step into line at the foot of the staircase, and up we all obediently got. Yet, I've often noticed that when a crowd tries to get into line, something happens. Perfectly sensible people become convinced they won't get a place, a quiet panic sets in, and a kind of genteel but determined jostling takes over. However it happened, between the hikers and the nuns — some sharp elbows there — I became separated from my German friends. I couldn't see them on the long staircase to the reception hall; it was so steep, and we were so many, that I had to concentrate on my footing. Then, when we did arrive, there was nowhere to sit. I don't mean I had arrived late: there simply were no seats, and through the high windows the sun beat down directly upon us.

I do remember the Swiss Guards, for one of them, like a gaudily striped circus acrobat, sprang out of his place to stop a tourist, one of the Germans — that was where they were! — from taking a photograph. It was loud Uncle Ernst; how proud he had been of his Zeiss, and now they were trying to take it away from him. I did feel sorry for him, or rather I started to, because almost immediately I saw something else. Beside him, a restraining hand on the arm of the Swiss Guard, was Paul — Paul, whom I had not seen in almost six years. I had a moment of clarity. Of course, I thought: he was a Catholic. Hadn't he come to Ireland for the Eucharistic Congress? Why shouldn't he be in Rome?

Then the noise began, the roar of the crowd, clapping and cheering as a procession began, two red-robed cardinals, some white-clad dignitaries, and then, in his *sedes gestatoria*, carved and golden, the Pope himself, borne in to the cries of "*Il Papa! Viva il Papa! Viva! Viva!*". I watched it all in a kind of dream, not sure if any of it was happening, wondering how I came to be in this curiously anachronistic set-piece, wondering if I had really glimpsed Paul, for in the silence that followed the very simple raising of the hand by the old, frail man in the chair, I lost sight of him, or of the person who resembled him. I could see my Germans, for one of them stepped forward, to let through a party of German–Americans, and their leader, a priest, was invited to receive a special blessing.

After the priest had backed away, everyone received the papal benediction, and it was over, the tension broken, and the whole flock pressed down the stairs once more, out through the blessed cool of the courtyard, and then back into the pitiless sun.

It took some time: no-one was in a hurry; and quite a few were trying to reconnect with members of their parties, lost in the downward surge. I still could not see the Schmidts, but I remember wondering how they reconciled this visit with the rise of National Socialism in Germany — for the Pope, old and fragile as he seemed, was deeply and outspokenly opposed not only to the German régime, but right there, in his own country, to Mussolini. In those days, such idle wondering, unaccompanied by any logical extension of thought, represented the sum of my political awareness.

Once again, there was no sign of the Schmidts. I followed my earlier instinct, and, though the crowds necessarily rendered our progress slow, I threaded my way through them as best I could, thinking only of the little café. I reasoned that, from there, I would see them in the crowd and, as it was near our tram stop, I would surely catch them.

I saw an empty table, could hardly believe my luck, and began as fast as I could to get over to it, making it just in time. I had hardly sat down when I thought I saw Kitty. I looked again. It was Kitty, sitting by herself at a table just a little away, staring at me in disbelief clearly as great as my own.

"Kitty!" I said, when I could speak. "What...? You changed your mind?"

She said nothing for a moment. Then she sighed. "Well," she said, "I suppose it was inevitable."

"What?" I said, baffled. "What was inevitable? You've

gone out of your way to avoid being anywhere I am almost since we arrived in Rome — yet here you are."

She said nothing, but she took off her sunglasses. Her eyes, those famous hazel-brown eyes, had turned dark and opaque, never a good sign with Kitty.

"I'm glad you came," I said, "but I don't understand. What are you doing here?"

She paused, seemed to gather herself, and shrugged. Slowly, almost reluctantly, she rose from her seat, elegant, feline as ever, and insinuated herself into the seat opposite me. Her eyes were hidden: the glasses were back in place.

"Maybe I thought I'd join you," she said, with a shrug. "There's more than one tram, you know. Anyway, I've decided something, and I thought I should tell you."

I should, perhaps, have spoken then. Maybe I should have told her about thinking I had seen our German patient. I thought it, in my head; I had been planning to drop it on her at the hotel: see what you missed! Yet, though I don't know why, I said nothing. Call it instinct. Tell that smart piece nothing, said a voice in my head. She said nothing either. The moments passed. A basking lizard on the wall watched us, neck pulsing, eyes unblinking.

I was the first to weaken. I did not want to. I had an uneasy feeling, as if there was something I had known and had refused to know. "Kitty," I said, "what was it you wanted to tell me?"

She hesitated. "Oh," she said, eventually. "Well, I'm going to... that is, I've decided to leave."

The basking lizard darted into a hole.

I leaned back in my chair and looked at her: she was making no sense.

"Don't be silly, Kitty," I said. "We've hardly started."

She shook her head. I don't think she was paying much attention. She sat looking out at the sea; far out, a lone swimmer, a tiny dot, carved his way like a small white seal across that unfathomable blue. When she turned back to me, blank-eyed still behind those dark lenses, it was clear that she had made up her mind. She stood up. I couldn't see her face against the light.

"Look," she said. "It's simple. I've decided to meet my father, and travel with him for a while. I just want to get out of here." She shrugged her shoulders once again. "I'm sure you'll be fine," she said, "with all your new friends."

And with that, she just walked away, and I was left there, thinking all sorts of confusions. She didn't turn back.

I don't know why I didn't just get up and go with her, and make her tell me what this was about. It would have been the right thing to do, I suppose, but in another way it made no sense, and anyway I was tired and hot, so I just pushed away some earlier customer's glass, and signalled to the waiter. I looked out over the sea, and there was the lone swimmer still, tiny as a dot, carving his way across that infinite blue, little white horses playing about his feet. I thought for no reason of Icarus and, inexplicably, for it was still very hot, I shivered as if a shadow had fallen. I turned round; a shadow had indeed fallen, and a dark silhouette stood above me. I thought: Kitty. But the shadow moved, and the sun and the day returned and shone about it like a halo, and a little bird flew down and perched upon my hand.

"Look," said a voice I had not thought to hear again. "You have a friend. *Un amico*."

A Little Bird

It is strange, but as I sit here reading my old diary, I seem to be back there, in Rome, that glorious summer day in 1938. I was twenty-two, not far off twenty-three; yet, I was still a girl, with a full set of girlish expectations.

I did not expect, for example, that my travelling companion would decide to leave me in mid-journey; though, knowing Kitty, I should have done. I found myself sitting alone at a café in blazing heat; and then suddenly I was not alone any more.

There was a little bird: I do remember the little bird. He had injured his wing, and, yes, I can recall the tenderness with which Paul handled him, and my question: "What happened to him?"

"Somebody hit him."

"Why would somebody hit a little bird?"

He shook his head, and cradled the little creature.

"An angry woman," he said, and his face reddened as he said it, as if he were angry himself. "An angry, careless woman hit him as he perched on a chair."

71

He shook his head, and said nothing. The lizard came out again and watched us both.

"I saw you in there," he said, inclining his head towards the papal residence. "I tried to catch up with you, but I ..." He stopped, shook his head again. "So many people. Impossible. Then I saw you over here. I could hardly believe it. Little Edith. '*Woman much missed.*'"

He remembered. He remembered the Hardy poems. My heart began to beat fast, a painful, breath-taking pulse. Could I be the woman much missed?

"Kitty was here too," I said quickly, God knows why. Why should he care about Kitty? I needed to talk, because I wanted to listen. "You remember. The first time we met. In the hospital? Didn't you see her?"

He did not answer, and went on stroking the little bird.

"You shouldn't sit in that full sun," I said then, still too quickly. "You're getting very red."

He was. His skin was too fair. Even as I spoke he grew redder.

"Oh yes," he said. "Your friend. But I'm not sure we spoke much."

He was right. I had forgotten that.

"That's true." That was enough of Kitty. "Anyway, she's gone."

He had moved out of the sun, and his face was in shadow. "Gone?" he said. "Where?"

I realised I did not know. "Back to the hotel," I said, "I suppose. She says she's going to meet her father. He's somewhere about, apparently." I must have sounded angry myself; well, I was.

"I ... " he began, but he did not finish his sentence, because the Schmidts, led by the uncle, had spotted us.

They hailed us and joined us, noisily and merrily. Before I knew it, Paul was backing away, making his excuses to them. Yet, just before he left, while the Schmidts were calling for refreshments, he bent over my hand and, softly, gently, kissed it. No-one had ever done that before. I was enchanted.

"*Mein Irisch Kind,*" he said. "*Wo weilest du?*"

Yes, yes, I recognised it, of course I did, and maybe it was chance rather than his reiteration of that long-ago moment: but I do believe he meant it. In fact, I know he meant it, because he said "Where are you staying?" so quietly. I told him the name of our hotel, and the length of time I had planned to stay, and an expression that I cannot describe came over his face. I felt certain that he was going to invite me to ... I don't know ... something, lunch, dinner, dancing, something, but all he said was "Ah, yes." For a moment he frowned, as if he had something difficult on his mind; then his face cleared, and he smiled. "I know the address. You should stay with your friends."

Surely he was going to suggest something more than that?

"But ... Kitty ... I may not stay now. I don't know ... I don't know."

"Stay there," he said, in the same low tone. "Stay there for a little."

My heart leapt: then, with his next words, lurched.

"I have to leave tonight, but I want to write to you. Stay long enough for me to write to you at an address I can know. I want to do that." When he smiled, creases, new, not there when first I saw him, appeared at his eyes: "I shall see to our little Amico here, and tell you how he gets on."

Then he was gone, slender and straight, the little bird still cradled in his hands; his walk, despite that slight, slight limp from the accident, a dancer's walk, weaving a skilful path through the heaving midday crowds. He could have been Fred Astaire.

A little stunned by it all, I turned to the relative quiet of the sea beneath me. The lone swimmer was gone. There was only a vast expanse: above and below the hazy horizon, an infinity of blue.

Ruth

❦

The Backward Glance

Ruth, treading water in the clear blue-green surrounding the Cinque Terre, was content. There was a time, came the peaceful thought, when no-one could get here, unless by boat. If only, she thought, swimming lazily back to shore, it were still so. Yet, even here, even beneath the line of neat, bright umbrellas on the tidy shore, mobile phones rang, were answered — *"Pronto!"* — and rang again. Nobody was safe any more, except herself, blissfully without her mobile and determined to stay clear of all communication, except through the hotel. Sandra had the number, so did Thomas, so did the nursing home. No-one else was given it: no-one else needed it.

And, she added to herself, walking towards the hotel in the gentle warmth of the late afternoon, the system worked. Thomas had reached her; they were meeting this very day. The nursing home had also got her, and told her of Hilde's increasing agitation: it was the right time to discuss it with Thomas. Even Sandra had managed to get through, with a worry about what she called "restructuring" within the College. The connection was bad that day, and she had some difficulty making out all that Sandra was saying; yet, to Ruth, warm and relaxed in the Italian sunshine, it seemed that Sandra was overreacting. What changes could they make with everyone away? Who was even there to make them? Whatever about the rest of it, work could wait until she was home.

As to Hilde, however, something had to be done. Thomas must help. She could not and should not have to handle this alone. It was not fair that, so soon after her mother's death, Thomas's family had offloaded Hilde on to hers. It must have been obvious that, after living with that family for years, Hilde would naturally have hoped to be allowed to stay. This, like *Kristallnacht*, like the *Kindertransport*, was one of her themes: Thomas's father, her own brother, had not wanted her any more. Once she started, there was no stopping her: there were no shortcuts, no abridged versions. Had there been one, it would have been that her brother David, at fifteen, and Ruth's mother Miriam — Mimi — their parents' little afterthought, not yet five, had got out of Berlin to England just in time, in March 1933; and that David and Mimi, secure in new lives, then affected not to know about the persecutions endured by those who, like Hilde, had to stay. Perhaps, Ruth had occasionally suggested, they did not know. Perhaps no-one, until Hilde arrived, ever told them. Surely Mimi, having been so young, would hardly remember anything; perhaps, as the new life clarified into a better future, neither David nor Mimi chose to remember. Living in England, how could they not become English? Mimi scarcely knew what the other life was like, and David, seeing that adaptation was a necessity for survival, was wise to put the earlier life behind him. Was it not true, Ruth had asked Hilde, that he had fought on the side of the British in the Second World War? And was it not the case, she tended to say to Hilde, knowing she was needling her, that David had anglicised his name, his speech and his attitudes? For that Ruth knew, not from Hilde, but from her own father. David Bauer had become David Bowers, a Cambridge graduate, marrying in his early twenties an English rose, whose name, in fact, was Rose. Thomas, their only child, born in the year before the ending of the war, had grown up convincingly English, notable for his good looks and an admirable facility for languages, including German; all of which made his career at school, at Cambridge, then at King's Inns, a great deal easier as relations between Britain and Germany gradually thawed. Mimi, her father had told her, had captured his heart when David brought her one summer day to visit, and gave her tea in their shared college rooms. "This," her father wryly reported David saying, "is Michael Deacon, my wild Irish friend." And in due time, when Mimi accepted this not particularly wild Irish friend, it was to Belfast that she eventually came as Michael Deacon's bride, and where Ruth, their child, had grown up.

Hildegarde — Hilde — she knew, had been less fortunate. She knew because Hilde told her so, until Ruth did not listen any more. Both she and her father heard many times how, at nine years old, Hilde had not been fit to go with the other two: taken unexpectedly ill, running a high temperature, liable for quarantine, she was too unwell to board the train and had to be left behind. Shortly afterwards, after an uneasy time of waiting, her father was one brutal night taken away, never to be seen again; they knew she had lived with her mother in anticipation of more hammering on the door, until she was fifteen. Most importantly of all, they knew Hilde had eventually and dramatically got out on one of the last *Kindertransport* trains to leave Berlin, and that after a long confusion of being shunted about from this family to that, she had, towards the end of the war, been reunited with the brother she had not seen for years. She had been deeply grateful, she said, to be taken into his new home with his bride. English Rose, however, had never become reconciled to the presence of Hilde. Yet, as she proved useful when Thomas was born, she was permitted to stay, a second mother without privilege throughout his growing up; until she was no longer useful, and then she was out. Thomas was bound to know all this. He must know that she, Ruth, had done her bit and that it was now his turn. If he did not, he soon would.

Thomas, waiting for her in the foyer, rose to his feet as she came in. At his feet sat a briefcase, slender, expensive; and resting idly against it, a sleek, handsome overnight bag. Thomas stayed nowhere very long.

"How are you, Ruth," he said, inviting her to sit while, one elegant hand very slightly raised, he summoned a waiter. There was no other greeting; no kiss, no contact. Had there ever been? They had, after all, little in common but Hilde; and nothing about Thomas's demeanour suggested that he was anxious for more.

The waiter came.

"Ruth?' said Thomas.

"Limoncello," replied Ruth, to her own surprise, having intended to ask for Martini. He ordered two.

"You wanted to see me," he said.

So, no preliminaries: straight in.

"Well, yes, Thomas, I did. It's Hilde — whom I did not, as you put it, dump — but who does need care, and even more so now, for she has begun to be confused."

"Are you surprised?" he said. "You've abandoned her. Of course she's confused."

Ruth opened her mouth to protest, watched his face shut

78

down even further and, instead, composed herself.

"I did not abandon her," she said. "I feel badly about her. But I can't deal with her by myself."

He said nothing.

"I'm sure you know what I'm talking about. I don't know how you felt about all that — the obsession with Berlin before the war — though you must have heard as much of it as I did when she lived with you. All I saw, after she came to live with us, was that she could never allow herself to be happy, and she didn't want anyone else to be either."

Still, silence, except for a curt word of thanks to the waiter.

"As far as I could see," Ruth started again, "everything went back to that thing of hers, *Kristallnacht*, the smashing of their neighbours' houses. I can understand that there would have been a frantic effort to get out if possible; and it must have been very hard on her not to escape when the others did. But, by the time she came to live with us, you know, years had passed; and my father and I had just been through my mother's death. We really didn't need Hilde's stuff on top of that. You may remember that time."

Ruth stopped, and let the silence gather. Yes, she thought, I daresay Thomas does remember that time. But he said nothing, and the silence deepened. She broke first.

"Are you staying here tonight?" she said. "It's very pleasant."

He looked at his watch. "No," he said. "I've a train in about an hour. I'm booked on a flight late this evening. I can't afford to take time off — and I don't see how you can, if things are as you say at work."

Ruth was stung. "I haven't had a holiday in ... I don't know how long. I've been ill, you know, as well as trying to see to H—"

He interrupted. "You did say there are changes going on

in your College, didn't you?"

"Well, yes," she said, reluctantly. Why would he change the subject? "Restructuring, whatever that means. But, look, about Hilde —"

He held up his hand. "Restructuring?" he said. "You don't know what that means?"

Ruth shook her head.

"Job losses," he said. "That's what. Listen to me. You need to get back there, and make sure it's not yours they ditch."

He drained his limoncello. Her own, sour-sweet in her mouth, had left a sticky residue on the glass.

"Would you like another?" said Thomas, lifting his hand to summon the waiter.

Ruth shook her head.

"What would you like?" he said, then. "What do you want, Ruth? What is it you want from me?"

"I ..." Ruth, when it came to it, did not know what to say. "Well," she tried, "for a start, I don't know why you don't help with her. She has no-one now but us, and, I told you, I can't cope by myself any more."

"You've put her away," he said. "You don't need to cope any more. What is it you want?"

Suddenly, Ruth knew.

"I actually think I want to know why I can't like her. She's old, frail and alone; and she went through hell. Why is it so hard? Why do you find it so hard? You don't like her either."

'I never liked her," he said, "but I had no reason to. She was and probably still is a fantasist, a mischievous liar. As to whether you have to like her, you don't, but you may have to try. You've got her."

Ruth heard her own sharp breath.

"What?" she said.

"You heard me," he said. "I'm having another one of those lethal lemon things, and then I'm going for my train.

80

Are you sure you won't have one?"

She shook her head. "No, thank you. But ... fantasist? Mischievous liar? What do you mean?"

The waiter brought the drink, and Thomas set it down in front of himself, twisting it round.

"I suppose she told you all about how she was left behind, high fever and all that, while the others got away?"

"She did."

"Pack of lies. She had no fever. She was to go too, and she kicked up such a fuss, didn't want to go, that she nearly made them all miss the train. Then, at the station, she pulled back, wouldn't go on. My father had to step off the train to try to get her on. Wouldn't go. The train started to move: he saw his little sister, your mother, crying at the window, and he had just managed to get back on the train when Hilde pulled against him, nearly dragging him under the wheels. She was caught by a passer-by, someone who knew them. This person handed her back to their mother, and she, of course, was distraught, because she was going to have to start again. That's how and why Hilde didn't get out with the others. Nobody told you that, I'll bet."

Ruth, slightly stunned, was unable to respond. He drained his drink.

"It doesn't matter whether they did or not," he continued. "I'm not going into the whole thing. I haven't time. My father did get to England, but under very different circumstances, I can tell you, from whatever Hilde described to you; and he was not well-treated when he got there. Only little pretty Mimi was adopted. Not a tall, blond, German youth. For him, it was suspicion and holding camps and even corrective institutions and eventually — eventually — the army. Yes, he fought on the British side. He also served with them in India, and what he saw there, the treatment meted out by the British

81

themselves, seemed to him all too similar to the brutality he had been obliged to escape. He did not become English because he admired them: he did it to fit in, to become anonymous. Above all, to stay safe."

Ruth found herself still unable to speak.

"His own efforts made his life in England tolerable, got him to Cambridge after the war, enabled him to retrieve something of all he might have had in a fairer world. He learned, and he taught me, that it does no good to hold on to the past, or to dwell on wrongs done. Life, he said, is too short for the backward glance: it is there to be lived. Why should he, or my mother or I welcome Hilde with her own version of their history? But we did. Don't forget, my parents gave her a home for a long time."

Ruth's arguments fell away.

"But, she was genuinely grieved," she began. "She —"

"Hilde caused grief," he said, cutting her off. "She spent her time complaining, as if no-one else had ever suffered. And she demanded attention, endlessly reminding my father that her claim on him should be greater than that of my mother. How do you suppose that was for my parents? Or for me? She's the reason I asked to be sent away to school. And she almost split them: did you know that?"

Ruth, shocked, shook her head.

"Of course you didn't. When she was asked to go and help out when your mother died — did you know your father asked her? — we were glad to see her go. We didn't make her go, but we were all glad. We'd done our time. Why shouldn't you?"

Ruth had no answer. She had always supposed that David's English Rose had no reason to keep Hilde any more; and that Thomas, away at school, had simply detached himself. If what Thomas said was true, there probably was nowhere else for Hilde to take her crippled memories, if not to Mimi's bereaved husband and motherless Ruth. It was also true that she had never been made welcome, for Ruth had never found it any easier than her cousin and his family to love this bearer of harboured wrongs. Only Chris, she thought, with an unexpected pang, could find time for Hilde: but there was to be no more Chris. And here Ruth was, with the only relative who might be expected to do his part, sitting opposite her stone-faced, arms folded.

"I don't know what to say," she stumbled. "Is it even true that she got out of Berlin just in time? Can I believe that? What was she by then — fifteen? She might just have qualified to be on the *Kindertransport*, I suppose, and no more. Was it true what she said — that she got a warning the very day before she was to travel, telling her to go immediately? She said the next day's train was cancelled. But was it really as late as '39? After what you've told me, I wouldn't be surprised if she made that up. Was it really the last train out of Berlin?"

"As a matter of fact, I think that bit was true," said Thomas. "That's the trick with a good lie: always have a grain of truth in there somewhere."

"And the visit from her teacher? By then a Nazi? Was that true? I knew the bit about how she had been a favourite, but she said he insisted she — and only she — take the earlier train. None of the friends who were to go next day got the chance, though he must have taught them all. Why just Hilde?"

"Maybe he had a reason," he said, looking at his watch. "The passer-by who stopped her from pulling my father under the wheels of the train? My father told me that the passer-by *was* the teacher. If so, then ..."

"If so," said Ruth, thoughtfully, "then, yes, I can see, he might have felt some responsibility for her. It could explain his helping her, even if he was a Nazi: but would it? I don't know. I don't know what to think."

"Think what you like," said Thomas, reaching for his bags. "I have to go."

"No, wait a moment," said Ruth. "There's something else I need to tell you. That conference I organised in the summer. Something happened there that affected Hilde very much, more than I realised, certainly in the light of what you have told me. I had to bring her with me to hear Clara Anderson reading from *Heimkehr*. Wasn't there a film once called *Heimkehr*? Something the Nazis made? I think there was. I have a feeling it may be one of those loaded terms."

"It is," said Thomas, drily, straightening up. He looked again at his watch.

"Yes, well, I knew the book was about, or based upon the war experience of her mother — you know, Anna Liebermann — but the book is set in Prague, not Berlin. I suppose that's why I do wish I had listened more. I hadn't picked it up that until *Kristallnacht* Anna Liebermann had lived in Berlin, though I did see later that it was in Clara's book. It's just that when Anna got up to speak, Hilde seemed to recognise her, though I don't know that she recognised Hilde. But Hilde started. It would have been a disaster, if Chris hadn't appeared."

Again, that pang: what was that about?

"Ah yes, Chris. The on-again, off-again husband." He paused. "What's going on there?"

"I ..." she began, then saw that he was looking over her head.

"What *is* going on there?" he said again.

Ruth looked where his eyes were fixed, and saw a man and a woman turn on the point of entering the room and swiftly make their exit. The man was her husband, Chris Applewood; and the woman beside him, nimbly disappearing through the doorway, was Cory Latimer.

The Memory Book

❧

Ulm

Kitty was gone when I got back to the hotel. I found it hard to believe that she had done that, even though she had said she was going to, even though I repeated her intention to Paul. Now, he was gone too. I had never felt so much alone. Yes, the Schmidts were still there, but in my mind I was alone and, overgrown schoolgirl that I was, forgot my good fortune at being young, and in Rome. As it was, the Schmidt family took me under their wing, and invited me in their generosity to travel on with them. So, I didn't stay long in the Eternal City. I could have, and I didn't. Once Paul wrote, I was ready to leave.

For he did write to me at the hotel, as he said he would. It was only a postcard, little more on it than an address in Berlin. There was nothing very romantic about it; yet, it was enough. Enough for what? For the building of dreams, I suppose, or of hopes. I thought he might have written to the address I sent him from Ulm, in Germany, where I soon found myself with the Schmidts. They all but adopted me

85

once they realised Kitty had gone off for good. There was much shaking of heads, much clucking, much sympathy. I did not need sympathy. I needed a letter.

I sometimes think about the journey to Ulm that summer of 1938. I remember travelling through the region of Verona, at Gardasee; then we passed through a startlingly beautiful alpine area along the German/Italian border. Early in the morning we arrived at the station at Brennero, then after the border control on into Innsbruck. After Innsbruck, the railway brought us through the Tyrol, and we passed by the Bodensee after leaving Konstanz. Finally, we arrived at Ulm. The Schmidts were kind to me; I stayed with the uncle Ernst and his wife Ursula, and Kurt, who turned out to be their nephew, taken in after the death of his parents, and Gerda, their shy, stammering daughter, whom I swear I had never set eyes upon all the time we were in Rome, though she must have been in there among the swarm. Yes, they were kind to me.

Kurt, despairing of Kitty, transferred his affections to me, and Gerda shared with me her dreams of becoming a nurse — though I wondered how she would manage with her stammer — and both of them urged me to stay for the whole summer. I might have done, had Uncle Ernst's embraces at close of day not lasted rather too long, had I not heard his tread pause one time too many outside my bedroom door. I might have done, had Paul written to me in Ulm from his parents' house in Berlin. Yet, though I looked every day for post, none came, and I grew anxious. I made my plans to leave, giving them to understand that I was going to meet Kitty in Berlin. I am ashamed to say it now: then, I was not. When Uncle Ernst, seeing I had made up my mind, offered to drive me to the station, his quiet wife looked thoughtfully at me for a long moment: but, though Kurt looked stricken and Gerda's lip trembled,

Ursula did not press me to stay. Her husband drove me to the station, kind, attentive Herr Schmidt; and I daresay his hand slipped off the gearstick and landed quite by accident on my knee as we arrived. Naïve I certainly was, but not entirely ignorant: my thanks at the station were brief, and my exit swift.

"I shall be meeting my friend in Berlin." That is what I told the Schmidts. That is what I told myself. Perhaps I half-believed it. After all, there was a room in Berlin which Kitty and I had booked, and I had not cancelled it: for all I knew, she would be there when I arrived. She might be there already. None of that explains why I wrote to Paul at the Berlin address he had given me on his postcard. I did. I wrote to Paul, and told him where I would be.

I never saw or heard from the Schmidts again, though in the usual way of goodbyes promises were made on both sides. I think I may have seen one of them, however, in a photograph. That book, *Heimkehr*. There was a photograph of camp inmates, including the author's mother, Anna Liebermann, who had survived Auschwitz. Beside Anna Liebermann stood a guard, fair, sharp-featured. I felt an instant shock of recognition. I am sure that it was quiet, mousy Gerda Schmidt, who wanted to be a nurse. I even went to hear the author, Clara Anderson, speak in June. And, of course, that is where I saw Ruth Deacon, if it was indeed she whom I saw: Ruth Deacon and, I think, my neighbour Hilde. I remember considering asking Anna Liebermann whether she knew the name of the guard. In the end, I did not. It was a muddled, confused day; people coming and going, people talking, talking, noise and confusion. I left early. In any case, did I really want to know? Perhaps not.

I do still wonder about Kitty, though, about her leaving me like that, but I can't write any more about it. It would just tire me. It would upset me; and I don't want to be upset. Apart from the fact of Kitty's sudden exit, I am happy to remember Rome, the heat of the sun that day outside the Pope's summer palace. What I would not give to be in Rome now, and able to walk!

I read later that when Hitler had paid a state visit to Mussolini, just months before our visit, the old Pope ordered that the galleries of the Vatican be closed, forbade Catholic students to take any part in demonstrations of welcome, and removed himself to Castel Gandolfo, refusing to have any part in his visit. "A crooked cross," he is reported to have said, "which is not the cross of Christ, is fluttering in the breeze above the Holy City of Rome." A year later, old and frail as he was, he would be dead. A year later, I would still be wondering where Kitty had got to, because I never did see her again. Unless, unless maybe just once: but I doubt that was she.

Ruth

❧

Back Through the Wardrobe

"Hello? Hello? Yes, could you put me through to Sandra Harvey, please? She's where? Oh. I see. What sort of training? I beg your ...? Re-what? I'm sorry, this is a very bad line. I'm in Italy. *Italy!* Look, forget that, just tell me when she's expected back in the office. Sorry, you have what? Oh. No idea. Yes, I see. Well, thank you. I'm sorry? Yes, of course: it's Ruth Deacon. Yes — Dr Deacon. No, no message. Thank you, yes, goodbye."

Ruth, icy-calm, was no wiser. All she now knew was that Sandra was not available, and that she was training. Or else she was retraining: certainly one of the words swallowed in the long-distance crackle began with "re". Was she receiving training, or training others? For what? Or did the "re" signify the lost beginning of "restructuring", that same obfuscatory term which, despite Thomas's warning, meant less and less to Ruth each time she uttered it.

What did it matter to someone in the state of detachment she had achieved, on seeing her husband and her nemesis?

89

In that moment of existential freedom, she had ceased to care about any of her cares, and had indeed spent the next morning drifting about the golden town as if she had no worries of any kind. She had not looked for Chris and Cory because she did not care. She had not asked Thomas to intervene or investigate their presence, or try to do it herself, because she did not care and, as Thomas had already made clear, neither did he. She had telephoned the College to speak to Sandra only to tell her, as a matter of courtesy, that she thought she might extend her holiday.

Now, however, after the frustration of that phone call, despite the seductive gentleness of the Italian evening, of the waves below the sea wall lazily lapping, of the lure of waiters all around the square deftly placing gleaming silver and shining glass on starched and spotless tablecloths, Ruth finally understood that her brief idyll was over. It was time to go back through the wardrobe, back through the looking-glass, back to everything she did not want. She turned away from the only place she wanted to be and, in her mind, with the dullness of an incipient headache, she was already feeling the chill of home.

The Memory Book

❧

Berlin

I scarcely know what exactly I expected, but I never realised Berlin would be so beautiful. The Brandenburg Gate, alone: I don't know any more whether my idea of it comes from images seen since, but it stays in mind as a shining magnificence. It was as if I had slipped through a door in time, as if Bismarck and his mighty Prussians might at any moment appear in glory round one of the splendid squares. For it was splendid. We have little splendour, and very little magnificence here in this part of our island; they used to say that once there was beauty in our buildings, an understated elegance now swept away by grasping vulgarity. Berlin, stately, assured, did not appear vulgar and, if it was commercial, it hid that from my dazzled eyes. What it did not hide, and doubtless had no desire to hide was a certain feeling of waiting, of excitement, of something about to happen. I cannot describe it any other way. It was like the anticipation of a great event — Natasha Rostova waiting for her first ball, Becky Sharp the night before Waterloo. In 1938, I believe we thought we were waiting for the great event of peace.

In the meantime, what I had to do was more mundane. I had to get myself to the little pension where, before she left, Kitty and I had planned to stay, and she had booked. By myself, I would also have to try to make myself understood. It is one thing to write a letter in halting German — I found a draft of my letter to Paul, and what a childish attempt that was. The one I sent was much better. I told him when I was coming and where I would arrive. My goodness, but it was quite another thing to make myself understood by people who use the language with fluency in everyday speech. And then, there were colloquial expressions. All I had with me, apart from my guidebook, was an ancient pamphlet I had picked up in the market at Smithfield. Even its title looks odd now: *What You Want to Say and How to Say It in German*. I used to have one called *Le Français Tel Qu'on le Parle*, which was rather good, but this German one was really a comedian's dream; not that I knew that when I arrived in Berlin in the summer of 1938. I learned quite quickly, however, not to trust it, if only through embarrassment. The author, as I had not realised when I bought it, turned out to be an arrogant bully, throwing his weight about and making loud demands of the stupid foreigner. As soon as he arrives in his hotel he cries: "Bring me soap and towels!" Then, "Bring me the newspaper, writing materials, tea, coffee, chocolate and hot drinking-water!" That's not even enough. "I want another blanket," he says, "and a mosquito curtain." They don't help matters. Next, he tells them "My bed is hard. Turn the mattress every day," but before they have time to do that, he announces: "I want to speak to the manager. Are you the manager?" It continues in much the same vein. After requiring a manicure and, interestingly, a permanent wave, he demands a doctor, the fire brigade and the highest official at the embassy. Along the way, he requires a ladder, screwdriver, a glass-cutter and an axe: I remember thinking he might be a dangerous as well as an uncomfortable companion.

Paul did arrive, though not until much later that evening. He seemed tired, and a little preoccupied.

"You got my letter," I said.

"I did, but you —" he started, then stopped. He continued to stand outside the door; as if, now that I was there, he was suddenly shy.

I asked him to come in, and he came, looking almost nervously about him.

"Are you quite comfortable here?" he asked. "I could try to find you somewhere else, if you —"

"I'm perfectly comfortable," I said. "Kitty may have run off, but she was clever enough to book this place beforehand."

He did not speak. His eyes glanced swiftly about the room.

"My only worry," I said, to fill the silence, "was that she might have thought to cancel it; but really, it would have been unlike her to think that far ahead."

"Would you like to go out?" he said, suddenly.

"Out?" I said. "Now?"

"Yes," he said. "Now. We can have something to eat, and we can talk." He paused. "Since you are here, I'll show you something of Berlin."

I was surprised that he seemed surprised to see me. Yet, I was delighted. "I've something to show you, too," I said, and pushed my absurd German phrase book into his hand. "You see, I know what to do if our food should be overcooked, or the bill turn out to be incorrect. And I can demand to see the manager if need be, and require him to bring an axe and a mosquito curtain."

He relaxed, and even smiled a little. By the time we got to the restaurant, which was small, unassuming, pleasant, if rather more out of the way than I would have wished, I was beginning to see the Paul I remembered.

Then it all changed again. We had just stepped inside the door. The owner was coming towards us, with smiles of welcome, menus in his hand, when Paul stiffened, took my arm, quite hard, and waved the proprietor away.

"Do you know," he said, and his voice to me sounded hurried, "there is somewhere else I'd prefer to bring you, somewhere uniquely of Berlin, that I think you will enjoy."

And that is how we came to be in Clärchen's Ballhaus on the most extraordinary night of my life. I don't need a memory book to remember that. I couldn't write about it then, and I don't know if I can now but, oh, I do remember it. I do remember that.

Clärchen's

I can't imagine what Clärchen's is like now, or if it's even still there. It might not be. How many conflicts can a place survive? Tables, I remember, and candlelight, soft music, and that delightful soft whisper of people dancing, a shared intimacy in which we all, as soon as we entered, were included. I knew how to dance, but I never thought of myself as a good dancer; not until Paul, his hand in the small of my back, my hand on the sinews of his shoulder, seemed to set me afloat. I thought then of Fred and his sister, skimming the earth like two sprites; and in that moment I seemed to be one with them. Something else happened, too. Perhaps it was a firmer pressure on my back; or his scent, musky, between soap and a darker, sweeter something that I had never smelt before; maybe it was the presence of his face, so close that I could see the fine hairs on the back of his neck. Whatever it was, I know we moved about the floor as one, his limbs my limbs, his breath my breath. Heaven, I was in Heaven; and Fred Astaire was singing; I think I sang too, softly, in the delicacy

95

of the neck and the ear and the fine scented hair of the man in whose arms I reposed. It seemed that time expanded or imploded: Paul's lips close to my cheek singing, softly, echoing another melody, a new one all around us; and I heard the words he sang as we drifted about the floor, the candles flickering about us, the world a spinning, dizzying dream. The seventh heaven of love, he sang, and he danced with me into a heaven I had never known, lifting us up, beyond ourselves, dancing away on our own cloud, and I think something in me has never come back. So precious was it, so ineffable the experience, that I cannot share it even with this paper and my pen. Yet, I can feel it, like a mist, like a silken sheet, like the morning that dawned, to my amazement, too soon, the sun breaking in through curtains that had never been drawn, like the music that swam in my head like champagne all that day and the next, and in my dream all I knew was that he was my own, and I was his, then and forever. It is too painful to write more. I may tear out this page if I read it again. I'll stop now. It hurts to remember.

All Change

I had such a vivid dream. I was on a train, and I was going home. Why was I going home? Something had happened. What? What had happened that I had to get on a train so hurriedly? I'm on a train, and I'm going away. Someone is handing me fruit and flowers and a magazine through the window. He's kissing my hand. There are tears. Are they mine? I think they are his, shining, unshed. I recognise this man. He is Fred Astaire. He says they can't take this away; he is singing those words as the train begins to pull out with a slow, inexorable hiss, a deadly cranking, moving slowly, slowly, slowly, further and further away from the song and from him; and he is walking, that dancer's walk, light and quick, and then he is running lightly alongside, but he cannot catch the train; and he gets ever smaller and further away and we pull into the countryside and I want to get out and I can't.

I woke, or they woke me, and they said: "Edith, you're crying. What's the matter?" It was Louisa, kind Louisa. I couldn't tell her I was dreaming of Fred Astaire. In any case, I know what it was about, and it wasn't seven fat years and seven lean years. It was Paul who put me on the train, after the night we danced in Clärchen's, and he wouldn't tell me why I had to leave, but I was afraid, and I didn't want to go, and he wouldn't let me stay.

"Everything's changed," he said, and I felt it, the way you feel a change coming in the seasons. I can even remember the date; I remember the exact date. It was the 12th of August, 1938. No more. I'm not writing any more today.

Ruth

❧

New Broom

"Sky," said Ruth, in disbelief. "What is this?"

"Why, my chapter, Dr Deacon," said Sky McDougall with a bright smile. "Didn't you say I was to bring a chapter?"

Ruth looked again at the jumble of papers, haphazardly gathered in a large plastic bag.

"Sky," said Ruth, "this is not a chapter. This may one day be," she riffled through its bulk, "three, if not more chapters, but that happy day is not yet upon us."

"But, Dr Deacon," said Sky, a troubled cloud across her fair brow. "Professor Latimer thought ..."

Ruth held up her hand.

"Professor *Latimer*?"

"Yes," said Sky, sunny once more. "Professor Latimer — at the library?"

"What library?"

"The Benner Centre. But Professor Latimer calls it her library."

Does she, thought Ruth.

"She runs it," said Sky. "Do you know her? She's so cool. Don't you think so?"

No, thought Ruth, can't say I do: and I don't know what she's doing in the Benner Centre either. She handed back the amorphous mass of paper, with the terse suggestion that Sky put it in order and bring it back when she had.

Indignant, and angry, Ruth returned to the post she had picked up just before Sky drifted in; and there she saw, among the familiar pile of exhortations, invitations, memos and minutes two letters marked "*Personal*". The first was a handwritten note, beneath the formally headed address of **Professor C. B. Latimer, Acting Curator of the Benner Archival Repository for Original MSS** or, as it was usually known, the Benner Centre. Acting, was Ruth's first thought: she is only acting curator. What does she want, was her second; then, beneath the usual platitudes, found an answer. Cory Latimer wanted to meet Ruth for coffee and, she said, to "catch up". Nerve, thought Ruth, dropping the letter, with its great, curling signature, into the bin. Then she picked up the other and saw that it was from Hilde's nursing home; and memory stirred. Had she not seen it before?

This, too, was handwritten, but the hand was not Hilde's. Ruth, frowning, opened it with a mixture of curiosity and trepidation, letting her eyes slide to the end to read the signature. For the second time that morning, she was taken by surprise. The letter was from Edith Barratt. Memory clicked into place. Oh, dear God, she thought, this is the thing Sandra wanted to give me at the start of the summer. Guilty and unreasonably annoyed, she read it through. If, the letter said, Dr Deacon was indeed the Ruth Deacon who had been her pupil between the years 1961-1968, perhaps she would be so kind as to visit Miss Barratt, to discuss the matter of some personal papers and manuscripts, presently housed in the Benner Archival Repository.

One fact leapt out, overriding everything except the instant reaction of the jobbing academic: there were papers. Papers could mean an article, maybe two, if not a book. The only difficulty, of course, was that these papers appeared to be in the Benner Centre, and Latimer was there. All the same, something like this might keep the President quiet; it might mean a lessening of teaching; it might even mean someone else would take on at least some of the responsibility for the wandering scholar who was Sky McDougall. But, but, but and but again, it meant meeting Latimer. Oh God, she thought, why did I not open this in July?

It was bad enough to be back, bad enough to read that the IRA hadn't gone away, that the various Loyalist factions wouldn't decommission unless the Republicans did, and that the Republicans wouldn't. It was bad enough to realise that Thomas was right, that she needed to look to her job, that she could take only a fraction of the leave to which she knew herself to be entitled. It was intolerable to be obliged to add a new ingredient to the cocktail of problems already swirling in her head. And then to go home, to what? To Chris, of course; for Chris, like the poor, was always with her. Yet, even turning the key in her own front door, she could not have said why he was still there.

As if on cue, there came a loud thump from upstairs, and something in Ruth gave way. Oh, drop the other one, she said, through her teeth and, sliding towards her the keys she had just placed on the hall table, repositioned the bag over her shoulder, hefted the other one from the tiles, stepped outside and straightaway pulled the door behind her. Almost immediately, she heard a window open, and looked up. He said nothing, but raised his head in the opposite of a nod, and reached out his arm — skinny, the hairs, prominent in the cold, strangely grey — to pull the window to, closing himself into the stale musty place that had once been their shared bedroom.

Ruth stood looking up at the space where he had been. This time, he had been in the house pretty much since she found him, or found him out, in Italy; after which, he had assured her, the affair was truly, finally over. It did not matter. However much her feelings might have wavered before the conference and the business of Latimer, there was no going back after it: when the decree absolute came through, that would be the end of it. If, for the moment — for old times' sake, one might say — she let him stay there from time to time in another room, well, that was her business. No wifely duties, her solicitor said; she performed none. Talking to him from time to time about work problems, or Hilde problems, was companionable, but hardly wifely. Of one thing, however, she was sure. She would say nothing to him about the return of Cory Latimer. She raised a pointless hand to the blank window, and turned away.

And in the bright haven of an off-campus café, Ruth took a decision, lifted out her mobile, and called Sandra Harvey. "Put me up tonight, could you?" she said, and Sandra, asking no questions, agreed.

It was not until later, after they had eaten, poured a glass, and settled themselves by the fire that Ruth began to articulate her difficulty.

Sandra shook her head. "But," she said, her face in a puzzled frown, "why would you even think of meeting her? She wrecked your conference, she wrecked your marriage —"

"Don't," Ruth said. "I don't want to think about all that. What's really on my mind are these letters. This one's from Edith Barratt. Writer? Mid-century?"

Sandra shook her head. "Your department, not mine. Is she important?"

"She had a reputation, at a time. Not prolific but, you know, well-thought of, well-reviewed. Went silent and then got more or less forgotten. But, she has papers."

"Ah," said Sandra. "Papers. Okay."

"The other one's from Latimer. And now I find out Latimer's in charge of the Benner Centre."

"So she is," said Sandra, thoughtfully, reaching for the letter. "You're right. I hadn't got round to telling you. Sorry, Ruth."

So Sandra already knew. How long had she known?

"But if you want my first reaction, I'd say: see the one who has the papers, but don't see Latimer. Why would you?"

"Because, the papers are in the Benner Centre and, as everybody seems at pains to point out, I have to publish to get the President off my case. I've had another thing in today, wanting to know what I propose to submit for the Research Assessment. The President wants to know. And now a new round of financial cuts is mentioned. Were you aware of that?"

"Well, yes, I was," said Sandra slowly, then adding, after a brief hesitation: "Actually, I typed that. You know I'm in the President's office now?"

"Of course," said Ruth, who had not known that. A little cold realisation began to take shape in her head. "Then you know, as well, that I've to have a proposal in by the New Year."

"At the very latest," said Sandra, and in her voice, just perceptibly, Ruth heard something new, and the coldness in her grew.

Of course. Sandra had seen all this coming in July.

Sandra's job, too, would depend on her carrying out the
bidding of the new men; and sympathies and old alliances
might not count for much when it came to it. Cards on the
table, then.

"This is what it comes down to. Edith Barratt's papers
could, possibly, give me a publication," Ruth said, "but
that's what I'm telling you: she's put them in the Benner
Centre."

"Oh," said Sandra, slowly. "Yes. I see." She reached
forward and poked the fire, sending up a shower of sparks.
"And she's not taking up the Fellowship."

"Who's not ...?" said Ruth. "What, you mean Latimer?
Not taking up the Fellowship? But she was shoehorned in.
By Mr President!" She put down her glass. Why would he
do that? Why would she? "Who *is* taking it up, then?"

Sandra gave the fire another vigorous poke, and the heat
from it flamed her face.

"No-one, I gather."

Ruth fell still, her mind cold. "No-one?"

"No-one. It's too late for this year."

The cold deepened.

"And the money allocated to us for it?"

"Will be re-allocated."

Ruth did not need to ask any more. The precious hard-
worn Fellowship was gone, not just for that year, but for all
years, simply because Cory Latimer did not feel like taking
it up. Or, because it suited the President to take it back for
redistribution and give Latimer something else: and the
something else was the Benner Centre. Ruth was so angry
that she became calm.

"Slope," she said, almost to herself. "I keep thinking of
Slope."

"Slope?" said Sandra.

"You know, Obadiah Slope. Trollope. The new broom,

sweeping away the old and most of the good in the parish of Barchester."

Sandra shrugged. "Never read Trollope. Good word for Latimer, though. All the same, now you put it all together, perhaps you do need to go and see her. Sorry, Ruth."

"Oh, God," said Ruth. "For a publication."

"Yes," said Sandra. "Exactly. Go and see the one with the papers, too. And lose no time about it." She stretched, yawned, and stood up. "I'm going to bed. Yours is all made up. Everything you need in the bathroom."

"Sandra," said Ruth, just as she was about to pull the door to. "Who's in the firing line?"

Sandra looked blank.

"Come on," said Ruth. "Who's the scapegoat? Somebody has to be, if there's a change of plan."

Sandra said nothing.

"Is it me?" said Ruth. "So I took a bit of sick leave. Can't hold that against me."

Sandra shrugged, then nodded her head. "No, but ..."

"But? But what?"

"You weren't around all summer. You're right. He does need somebody to blame — and all that with Chris and Latimer and now the Fellowship: well, your face fits the frame. I did try to tell you something was in the air."

"He is one bastard," said Ruth, and instantly checked herself. She raised the bottle she had brought. "Look," she said, "come back and sit down. We'll have another glass. I don't feel like going up yet."

"Not me," said Sandra. "I've a breakfast meeting with him, but you go ahead if you like."

Ruth, watching Sandra close the door behind her, did not go ahead. Pushing the cork back in, she felt the beginning of a loss: there might not be many, if any more shared evenings. She knew that, whatever about seeing Edith

Barratt, she would have to see Cory Latimer, trollop or no trollop, and try to ignore the fact that, too careless to take up her Fellowship, she was brazenly back scarcely two months after Ruth had found her out.

And so it was that, early the very next day, the newly appointed Acting Curator of the town's venerable and justly famous Benner Centre, sat boldly opposite Ruth in yet another café, just as if nothing had happened, nor any time passed: and, except for an inexplicable blue streak in the already improbable blonde hair, she appeared substantially the same. Cool before, cool now, Cory Latimer made no reference to anything that had occurred: not the affair, nor even, which would have interested Ruth much more, how she came to take over the Benner Centre. Ready for either, Ruth did not anticipate her opening line.

"What are you writing at the moment?" Cory said, her smiling mouth, like the nails extended round the cup she raised to it, boldly carmine.

"I've been very busy with work," was all Ruth, in the end, was able to say.

There was another, longer silence.

"Well, I hear," said Cory Latimer, finally, brazenly, "that you need a new book or, at any rate, a publication."

And I wonder who told you that, said Ruth to herself as, suddenly too angry to stay, she got to her feet, picked up her things, and left.

Night of Broken Glass

Every year, every term takes on its own character. That year, like any other, the mellow weeks of September shortened into a cool and crisp October, passing all too soon to short days of branchy trees and a bitter eastern wind. The College lost the camaraderie of the early days of term; students slipped quickly from initial enthusiasm to the dull quotidian requirements of study and assessment; and no-one on the staff talked about anything but shortages and cuts. What happened, Ruth wondered, leaving the library late one November day, to scholarship for its own sake, to the training of the mind? Surrounded by books, cursed like Tantalus, she was no nearer a publication. How could she be, with an unrelenting timetable in work and out of it?

She was on her way, this day as every day, to visit Hilde; not that Hilde seemed to want her. Still angry at Ruth's apparent desertion of her in the summer, she frequently ignored her; yet, if Ruth did not come, the nursing home rang to see why, and to remind her that it was unkind to set up expectations and then fail to live up to them. Natalia did anyway. Natalia was good at that.

Today, however, one of those cold clear days, when the trees are bare and branchy and the sky reaches into beyond, Ruth was not as despondent as she might have been. Resolved, since her meeting with Thomas, to be kinder to Hilde, and to try to distract her from her destructive fantasies, she planned to tell her about a radio interview she had just given to the BBC. It might lift her spirits: it had lifted Ruth's, if only by taking her away from her usual surroundings. She paused outside the door, gathering her strength, then took a deep breath, and went in.

"Hi, Aunt Hilde!" she said, as cheerfully as she could. "Guess what? I'm going to be on the radio."

"Are you?" Hilde said, without interest. "We had Princess Anne."

"Oh?" said Ruth, a little taken aback. Princess Anne certainly trumped local radio. "In here?"

"No, of course not. We were outside there, Edith and I, just beside the piano. Lovely. She was lovely."

Edith? Was she talking about Edith Barratt?

"She's the same age as you," Hilde said, and Ruth realised they were still on Princess Anne.

"Yes," said Ruth, distracted. "I suppose she asked you if you had come far."

"What?" asked Hilde, with irritation. "Why would she do that? I've been here all the time. I'll never be anywhere else."

Ruth, despite her resolution, weary already of Hilde, rose and went over to the window.

"You want to be away, I suppose," said her aunt, and her resignation irritated Ruth more. "Don't let me keep you."

Ruth did not rise to it: she had another nettle to grasp.

"Who is Edith, Aunt Hilde?" she began and, as if in answer, there came a knock upon the door.

A voice said: "It is I. May I come in, Hildegarde?"

It was the voice she recognised: deeper, a little querulous, yet still, the voice, and Hilde's in reply sounded miraculously, if momentarily, welcoming. Ruth saw the door slowly opening, and the gradual, almost menacing advance of a wheelchair, of gnarled hands pushing large wheels, with what looked like considerable difficulty; and then she saw a bent white head, the sparse hair exposing the delicacy of pink skin, painfully laid bare. Yes, it was the face she thought she had glimpsed at the conference. This, though hard to believe, must indeed be Edith Barratt, her teacher of thirty years before. The voice belonged to that Brunhilde she had been; not tall, yet commanding, visible in any crowd by the snow-white hair which, even all those years ago, marked her out; dark eyes, almost navy blue, deep set, watchful and, turned on the unwary, ready to strike. Ruth found herself uncomfortably conscious that she had not yet replied to that letter.

Before she could speak, even attempt to rectify the mistake, the dark hooded eyes were turned on her.

"Ah, Ruth; it was indeed you. I thought it must be."

The conference she meant, of course: when Ruth had made no attempt to acknowledge or greet her. Deeply embarrassed, Ruth felt all her years and her suddenly slight achievements fall away: she was twelve, and she had not done her homework.

Hilde — suddenly, splendidly Hildegarde — made no attempt to introduce her, but that was Hilde. Ruth remembered a crowded train to Dublin, mid-July, the annual exodus for those wishing to escape Northern Ireland's noisily vulgar celebration of itself, battling to get a seat for Hilde, standing two hours herself in a miasma of

109

beer and re-fried food; trailing round shop after shop until Hilde got something she did not hate. She remembered the assistant. "No-one will be looking at the bride, will they?" she said, glancing coyly, a co-conspirator, at Ruth, while Hilde, gazing discontentedly at herself, declined to inform her that Ruth was the bride at whom no-one would be looking.

Well, that was then; and here they both were, with Miss Barratt, and everyone was looking at her.

"I'm so sorry, Miss Barratt," she said. "I should have —"

An imperious hand: stop. Ruth remembered the dismissive gesture and, as years before, was silenced by it.

"I have followed your career," Edith Barratt said. "I've read your articles and your critical studies, and that book of yours on unreliable narrators."

Yes, Ruth thought: that book of mine — *The Heroine's Secret: Unreliable Narrators in Nineteenth-Century Fiction* — initially well-received, quickly remaindered, practically a runaway success in academic terms; and no book since.

"You have a good mind," she said, as if she had read Ruth's thoughts. "You always did, but," and she sighed, as she so often had in the past, "you lack courage. You must strike out into wider waters: I told you so years ago, but you didn't listen." She paused, looked up at Ruth, her head slightly turned away as though she could see her only from an angle. "You think I was hard on you, I suppose."

Ruth, still twelve, could not reply.

"I was. I was always hard on the good ones, and I make no apology for it. I wanted the best for you. You could easily have gone to Oxford or Cambridge." She sighed. "Still. You've done well enough. Hasn't she, Hildegarde?"

Hilde shrugged, a gesture speaking not only of indifference but also of confusion. Ruth's heart sank: Hilde might be about to take off on the time train, always pulling out of Berlin, always leaving Hilde abandoned and alone.

"Miss Barratt —" Ruth began again.

"Edith," came the reply. "There are no titles here, in God's waiting-room."

Hilde made a small noise of distress: Ruth stiffened.

"Now, look," Edith Barratt continued, eying Hilde quickly, "since you're here, let me get to the point. It's quite simple: as I told you, I have papers. I take it you did receive my letter?"

Ruth opened her mouth to speak, but stopped. The hand was raised. There would be no interruptions.

"I've placed them for the moment in the Benner Centre. I believe that in addition I may have need of a literary executor."

She reached with slow fingers into the handbag suspended from her chair, and took out a long, narrow brown envelope: she extended a hand quite bent with arthritis, brown spots marking painfully prominent bones; still, she reached with surprising firmness.

Ruth, humbled, took the envelope. "Am I to —"

"Yes, yes," said the older woman with impatience, "or read it later." She glanced across at Hilde, now beginning to rock back and forth. "It's a copy of my will," she said, briskly. "I've named you as my literary executor. You may refuse, but I hope you won't. I still have faith in you, and you're young enough and able enough to do something good."

She wheeled away from her, turning back to Hilde. Ruth, holding the envelope, sat, faintly stunned.

"Well, Hildegarde," Edith said, loudly, though Hilde's hearing was still fairly good. "We had a pleasant morning, didn't we?"

"We had Princess Anne," said Hilde, with some animation.

"No, Hildegarde," said Edith Barratt, gently. "She was on television. You remember. She was visiting the Chelsea Pensioners."

"Were they here, Edith?"

"No, Hildegarde. They were in London, and we watched them on television, but we shall soon have a distinguished visitor here in the town. Perhaps President Clinton will come and see us? Or Mrs Clinton?"

"On television?" said Hilde, shaking her head in puzzlement. She evidently did not want to leave Princess Anne, so lately taken to her heart, but the American President proved an acceptable substitute.

"There's a man, now, with charm, wouldn't you say?" said Edith Barratt, including Ruth in the question. "Charm to spare."

"Well, yes," said Ruth, "they say that; but I wonder how he'll get on with this lot in Stormont. I don't know that charm cuts much ice there."

"It was cold," said Hilde, almost to herself, "but I don't remember ice."

Ruth glanced at Hilde: was she about to take off? Edith Barratt seemed to feel a similar concern.

"Not like Kennedy, of course," she continued more loudly, addressing her remarks only to Hilde. "He had charm; but it didn't save him. Poor young man, butchered in broad daylight. Do you remember that day, Ruth?" she said, turning round to face her. "I'm sure you do."

"The assassination?" said Ruth. "I do."

Ruth remembered. She was momentarily back in the study hall, back in the days when all was well, her parents alive, Hilde safely far away in England with Thomas and his family: the choir singing songs for the feast of St Cecilia, a ragged, windswept November rain outside, a cold walk home, and that night, to their disbelief, the news that the glorious young President who had walked among them that summer was dead, shot down in broad daylight. How would she not remember, given that the following day her own mother, barely thirty-five years old, had dropped dead at the sink of a heart defect no-one knew she had, and that, for Ruth and her father, nothing was ever the same again.

Hilde sat suddenly upright.

"*Kristallnacht*," she said.

"What, Aunt Hilde?" said Ruth, lost in another time. "What did you say?"

"*Kristallnacht*," she repeated. "They smashed everything. Took away our neighbours. November. Long before Kennedy. Long before. Smashed everything."

Outside, the day, which had been clear and bright, clouded over in the damp and saddening way of late November, and the darkness of too early evening began to creep into the room. Silence fell: no-one spoke, and Hilde fell into an unhappy doze.

"Now, Ruth," said Edith Barratt, leaning forward. "About my papers. I think you are the right person, not simply because I taught you and have long known your potential. It was clever of you to have Clara Anderson to speak about her book at your conference."

"Ah yes," said Ruth. "You were there." What more could be said?

"I was there," said Edith Barratt, her eyes disconcertingly opaque. "You did well, in the circumstances."

In the circumstances, thought Ruth. Yes, she was there.

"Thank you," she said, not knowing what else to say. "Perhaps we'd better not ..." Silently she indicated Hilde's presence. "Another time, though, I'd like to tell you of something Anna Liebermann said to me, if you —"

"Yes," said Edith Barratt shortly, her face evidence that she had no wish to know what Anna Liebermann had said.

"Another time."

She slid her hand down by her side, and removed from the recesses of the wheelchair a large notebook, which she placed on her knee.

"I'm ..." she paused, seeming to weigh her words. "I am interested in that time, in what happened to people then: my papers will tell you more about that. And during the summer I kept a ... what would you call it, a *memoir*, a record anyway, in this book. My *Memory Book*. I would like you to read it."

"You haven't talked to my aunt about all that, have you?" said Ruth, quite ignoring the book which Edith was now holding out. "I mean about that time? You can see she gets very distressed. I didn't realise how much, until Clara's talk at that conference. I shouldn't have brought her: it was a mistake. I didn't have a choice, but it was still a mistake. It opened up floodgates. The ..." she lowered her voice, though Hilde, slumped sideways on the chair, seemed to be fast asleep, "the memory of the *Kindertransport* upsets her very much. She was on one of the last trains, you see — I think the very last, but I don't know if that is what happened, or whether she has decided it did. You may have noticed," and even to herself her tone was bitter, "that she has a keen sense of drama where her own story is concerned. I mean, she seemed to think she recognised Clara's mother. All in her head, of course."

Over in the corner Hilde, head shaking from side to side in her uncomfortable doze, was beginning to talk to herself in German: never a good sign. Then she cried out. "*Nein, Herr Herrold!*"

Ruth, in the instant of hearing this, heard also a sharp intake of breath and saw Edith Barratt suddenly, as if involuntarily, jerk back in her wheelchair.

Ruth stood up.

"Are you in pain, Miss B— Edith?" she asked.

There was no reply. Ruth, watching both of them with increasing alarm, realised she had a very short time to make Edith understand that the war was strictly off-limits for Hilde.

"It's like this, you see," she said, in the same low tones. "She's back there. That's what the muttering is about: it was her teacher who came to tell her she had to leave on the earlier train, a favourite teacher: but he was in Nazi uniform. That seems to have been one of the worst things about it. She didn't know he'd joined the Party; she didn't even know he'd gone into the army."

As she spoke, it happened again: the involuntarily jerk backwards, the sharp intake of breath.

"Shall I get someone?" she said.

The room grew darker. Edith sat like a stone, unnaturally still.

"I'm getting someone." Where was the panic button? Where had Hilde put it? She reached beneath the blanket round Hilde's knees.

Startled, Hilde sat bolt upright: "*Oh, nein, nein, Mama!*" she cried, and began to weep piteous tears.

"No, Aunt Hilde!" said Ruth. "No, it's all right, everything is all right," and she pressed the button, stroking the small bony shoulder, and experienced a momentary glimpse of compassion for the little lost person Hilde had been.

Yet, there was no calming her. "*Nein, nein,*" she kept repeating, wringing her hands, Ruth reassuring her, Edith, eerily unmoving, a shadow in the background.

Ruth pressed the button again. "Oh, come, come, can't you?" she said, to no-one.

No-one came.

"Miss Barratt," she tried. "Edith! Are you all right?"

There was no reply, no movement: Edith Barratt sat like

a statue, her face pale as wax. Ruth, helplessly stroking Hilde's shaking bones, soothing her moaning distress, did not know what to do, or which of them needed attention more. Why did no-one come?

"Aunt Hilde," she said, "I want you to try to be calm. I'm going to get someone. Can you do that?"

She tried to ease herself away, as gently as she could; but Hilde, clutching her, tried to stand. Ruth, tangled in the blanket, in the flex of the emergency button, bleeping and flashing unheeded, caught her as best she could. Too late: she, and Hilde, and Hilde's wheelchair all toppled over and, as they tumbled in their ungainly embrace, they knocked over one of Hilde's salvaged possessions, a glass vase holding flowers Ruth had brought just a few days before. It fell, heavily, in a long slow arc, splintering with a crash into many pieces, splashing them all with water.

With a shriek, Hilde clutched at her, the bony hands like little claws: "*Nein,*" she cried. "*Nein, Herr Herrold! Lassen Sie mich sein, lass' mich sein, Herr Herrold, bitte, bitte!*"

Ruth, pinioned beneath the surprising weight of her weeping, struggling aunt, looked up in desperation at the door, but still no-one came. In the gathering gloom, Edith sat motionless, a film suddenly frozen; and then her arm flopped down, and Ruth saw to her horror that her face had fallen on one side.

"Edith!" she cried. "Edith!"

There was no reply. The old lady sat in her freeze frame for a second, two seconds, three.

The light flicked on. A nurse came in: an agency nurse, whom Ruth had never seen. She asked no questions, walked past Edith, came straight over to Hilde and quickly, wordlessly, helped Ruth extricate herself; then managed, with surprising ease, to lift Hilde, quiet now, worn out, into her chair. She tucked the blanket round her, then stepped calmly over to Edith.

"Edith," she said, and she shook her arm. "Edith, speak to me."

Ruth, legs and arms aching, moved cautiously to her side.

"Are you all right, Miss Barratt?" said Ruth. "Your arm! What happened?"

Edith, slowly, majestically turning, eyes like dark stone, looked straight at the nurse, then Ruth, then, still in slow motion, at her arm.

"What do you mean?" she said very slowly, not quite distinctly. "I'm perfectly all right. Turn that light off, will you?"

Ruth, now standing uncertainly by the door, watching the agency nurse render them both quite normal, found her own heart was racing like an engine. She was clearly superfluous: despite her attempts at explanation, the agency nurse virtually ignored her. After a few indecisive minutes, she began to make what she knew was a confused and unsatisfactory exit, stepping with shameful relief into the comparative calm of the corridor.

"I'll let them know," she said, from the door, though quite what she meant was a mystery to herself. There was no-one to let know, and the agency nurse was clearly competent if uncommunicative: it would be better, much better, if one of the staff dealt with it now. The agency nurse would be obliged to make a report to Natalia and Natalia, though she might be difficult to like, was an efficient nurse. The fact that her manner spoke disapproval of a people and a system disinclined to look after its own elderly was simply part of Natalia's character. Today, however, Ruth did not need Natalia's disapproval as well as everything else. Bruised, confused, and anxious to escape, she did not slow her pace until she was safely out in the welcome damp of dusk.

The exchange with Edith Barratt, however, stayed with her. She lay long awake that night, listening through the wall to Chris, restless and remorseful even in sleep. So long as he did not wake, it would be all right. Still, she could not get over the memory of the envelope and the short conversation returned and returned, wrapping itself round Cory Latimer's parting remark, lodging itself, like an irritating grain of sand — yet, as she told herself with a glimmer of tired hope, with the possibility of turning into a pearl. It was true, as Latimer said, that she needed a new book: had she not already identified that herself? As to how Latimer knew ... well, how she knew did not matter. Chris, the College President, even Sandra — it was not important. Hiding behind the necessary tasks of her profession, she was not getting on with any work of her own; and that mattered. A literary executor: new papers that no-one had looked at! At one o'clock, it was a scholar's dream; at two, the papers were not worth the bother, almost certainly receipts and rejected essays; at three they contained a hidden gem of a novel which would astonish the literary world; at four there might just be something useful; and with that, her eyes gritty as sand, she finally fell asleep, and her last thought, confusedly, was that the cuckoo was the herald of spring.

The Benner Centre

The phone rang early, too early, next morning. Ringing and ringing through her exhausted sleep, it rocked itself right off the table, and lay ringing, demented, under the bed until it gave up. Ruth, exhausted, ignored it. The house phone, however, could not ring itself off the table, and did not give up. Ruth swam confusedly out of the depths. Hilde, she thought, scrabbling for the receiver, something has happened to her; but the voice at the other end, though familiar, did not come from the nursing home.

"Professor Deacon?" it said, and the misnomer, followed by the rising intonation, told her instantly who it was. Indignation replaced confusion.

"Sky," she said, "is that you?"

"Yes, Professor, I —"

"Stop there, Sky. I'm Doctor, not Professor, and you have no business calling me at home. I don't know who gave you this number, but you have no business ringing it."

"Yes, but Prof— I mean, Doctor Deacon, I need to —"

"An appointment, Sky. You need to make an appointment,

119

through the office. And never, never ring anybody's home number without permission. Goodbye, Sky. I'll see you in the office."

Fully awake, she threw back the covers, showered, dressed, and walked purposefully out of the house without breakfast and, perhaps even more importantly, without the mobile phone, still lying under the bed. It rang again, many times that day, until it flattened its battery and simply lay there, helpless and silent. Ruth, unaware, marched straight past the College, straight into town, ignoring even the lure of the College Bookshop, and passed through the quiet portals of the Benner Centre. "My library," Cory Latimer had called it; but it was not her library. It was not, in fact, a library: it was an archival resource. Like the rather older and even more venerable Linen Hall Library, the Benner Centre was a small oasis in an increasingly soulless town: it, too, had survived more than one attempt to destroy it by starvation of funds or, most recently, by firebomb. Where they burn books, one day they will burn people: where had she read that? It was true: in history, recent and ancient; in Germany and in Poland; and here, in the ugly war euphemistically described as the Troubles, much had perished in the fires of wilful destruction.

Now, in a time of tentative ceasefire, when every shop, every building grew daily more and more like every other shop and building in any other town anywhere, the best hope for scholars had to lie in such treasure-troves of books and thought. The Benner Centre, formerly the home of the same idealistic philanthropist who had established and given his name to the College where Ruth worked, existed to preserve the works and papers of struggling artists, philosophers and authors who might otherwise be erased from the public memory. Almost two hundred years old, established in that time when architecture was, in places, still serenely beautiful and thought was paramount, it soothed the senses in every way. The scent of old polished wood, the musty lingering sense of heavy linen, sewn and bound with leather; the discreet coughs of readers lost in thought beneath their green shades; all of these sent a delicious calm and a sense of purpose through Ruth. Not for the first time, she wondered at the irony of academic life, chosen that she might spend time with books and papers such as these, only to find her days eaten up instead with the filling of forms and the meeting of increasingly abstruse targets, while the books, silent, unopened, looked on in stillness from their shelves.

Not today, however. Riffling through the card index, its typed entries a tribute to someone's patience and devotion, filling out her request for the Barratt papers, politely declining to use the new computerised service, handing the completed slip to the assistant, she began to sense the beginning of contentment.

It could not last. Even as she stood, looking through the rack of journals and newspapers as she waited, she felt a touch on her shoulder, and turned with a jolt to see Latimer herself. Of course, was her first thought, there is always a serpent in Paradise. I should have kept out of sight, was her second.

"Hello, stranger," said Cory Latimer, breezily. "Thought any more about what I said? You know you've got to."

Ruth looked quickly at her face. Was she trying to provoke her?

"I have been thinking about our conversation, yes," she said. She would not rise to it. "Perhaps I should write a new book."

"As I told you," said Cory, evidently pleased. "What are you looking for?"

Ruth found herself, now it came to it, obstinately

reluctant to tell Latimer about Edith, and what she had said.

"I thought I'd see what you had by Edith Barratt," she said, as casually as she could.

"Barratt?" said Cory, and her face showed satisfaction. "Yes. That could work, putting you and Barratt together. You know she has left her papers with us?"

For the moment, thought Ruth.

"I do know that," she said. "All the same," she went on, carefully, "I'm not sure that I want to be *put together* with anyone." She paused. "I wouldn't mind having a glance at them, though."

Cory sighed, with a kind of exasperation, and shrugged.

"I'm only trying to help," she said. "Which of the boxes would you like to start with? There are thirteen."

Thirteen: there was bound to be something.

Cory motioned to the young assistant to hand her a large ring-binder from below the issue desk. She took it from him without a word or gesture of thanks, then flicked through it with a proprietary air. "Here," she said. 'This is a list of what's in them. Find yourself a seat, look at this, decide what you want, and Cormac will bring them over to you – won't you, Cormac?" and she smiled, pleasantly, almost flirtatiously, and yet, and yet. There was something of Bette Davis about Cory Latimer. Those bold, prominent eyes, the thin neck, age marks shrouded by a careless scarf; not that it hid the goitre. Catching Ruth's glance, she adjusted the scarf: silk, Hermès. There was little warmth in her returning gaze.

"Bring them one by one, Cormac," she said to the young man, eying his thin-wristed hands. "We don't want to overburden you — or Dr Deacon." Always that little stiletto, deftly aimed. "I'll be in my eyrie if anybody wants me." And, with an incongruously girlish wave of her fingers, she pushed open the door, and was gone.

When, thought Ruth, did she get so important in herself? Does she even know Edith Barratt has not yet donated her papers, but deposited them temporarily? And does she really want to help me find a new topic for a book, or does she want to offload the cataloguing? Or, does she think she can make it up to me — with papers? Still thinking, still wary, spying a table she liked, looking through the shade of trees across the busy town, she settled herself to examine the list that Cory Latimer had handed to her. It seemed promising. There appeared to be manuscripts aplenty: an entire novel, as well as a larger number than expected of short stories, typed, handwritten, some even in pencil; there were essays, radio scripts, diaries, travel journals, postcards — and letters. Letters! Something shifted in Ruth: letters, she well knew, tell more than they know or intend. She would start with the letters, and if they turned out to be to Edith's bank manager or the local council, there might still be something book-worthy in the other boxes.

Waiting for Cormac to bring the letters, she felt oddly excited. This part of research was always delightful: the time of discovery, of hopes almost certain to be dashed at a later date yet, at the beginning, so bright! The box arrived, brimming with promise, the heady scent of dust and cardboard filling mouth and nose as, fingers clumsy with anticipation, Ruth undid the archival tape.

Letters: letters to her mother; postcards from abroad; letters, yes, to the bank and the school and the Past Pupils' Association, and envelopes full of photographs. Half an hour passed, an hour and a half; and Ruth, suddenly tired and dispirited, was on the point of putting it all back and closing up the box when, right at the bottom of the box, almost hidden, she saw a plain brown envelope, marked "*Letters from P. 1938–9.*" Heart leaping, she drew them out; she saw immediately that they were worn, no doubt from frequent rereading. One had been unsuccessfully repaired already, with clear tape, yellowing and beginning to crack. What was worse, they were in German. Her German, she knew, was disgracefully rudimentary. It would have to be good enough, however; and whether it was or not, Ruth soon found herself believing she had found something, and that if what she had found was as she suspected, Edith Barratt's story might be worth the telling. That evening, Ruth did not leave the Benner Centre until a kindly security officer, with a respectful cough, asked her if she would be so good as to let him lock up. Only then did she see the young library assistant Cormac standing by the door, coat on, ungloved hands red with cold; only then did she realise that everyone had gone, and that darkness had fallen.

With a guilty start, she realised she had not been to the nursing home. She should have phoned, she would phone now, her hand automatically reaching into her bag for the phone: but where was it? Stricken with remorse, she made her apologies to kind Cormac and the patient security officer, practically ran out of the building and, by great good fortune finding a taxi, made her way as fast as she could to the nursing home. Everything will be all right, she said to herself; it has to be; in the next breath, where is my blessed phone; in the next, I need to ask Edith Barratt about those letters; then back to praying the two old ladies were all right. In spite of herself and an anxious nameless guilt, the excitement persisted. Those letters. She remained equally anxious and excited right until the moment when, hurrying into the nursing home, she was stopped by Natalia, just in front of the water fountain or, as Chris on one of his rare visits had renamed it, the incontinence trap — residents, on hearing it, would have to go hurrying back to the bathroom.

"Ah, Ruth," said Natalia. "You're here. At last."

At last? What did that mean?

"I take it you haven't received our messages."

"I meant to ring," Ruth said, conscious that she was not answering the question as asked and adding, uselessly, "I can't find my phone."

"Yes," said Natalia, thin-lipped. "No doubt. Well, now that you are here, you might wish to know Auntie is not too good today. You must avoid overexciting her, reminding her of things she wants to forget."

Ruth, bristling at the familiarity of a diminutive which she never used, restrained herself.

"And Miss Barratt?" Ruth said, drawing herself up. "Shall I try not to overexcite her too?"

Natalia looked straight at her, eyes narrowed. "I think you have done more than over-excite both of them," she said. "What did you start that — what was it, that *Kristallnacht* thing for? We had it all night. Hilde woke all the residents on the corridor. We've been trying to get you all day. If this goes on, we may have to ask you to take your aunt away."

Nothing like a veiled threat. Natalia's face, always pinched, was tight with anger. Hilde was not Auntie now.

"What are you talking about?" said Ruth, baffled. "I didn't start anything. They were fine when I left." It was not the time to mention Edith Barratt's strange turn. That was nothing to do with her. Nothing. "Are they not all right today?"

"I told you," said Natalia, which, Ruth told herself in pointless self-defence, she had not. "Your aunt is somewhat calmer today, but you caused her to have hysterics last night, exciting her about war and Nazis and breaking glass — and who did break that glass in there by the way? — and

125

trains and a teacher and soldiers and I don't know what else. What were you doing?"

"I —" began Ruth, an instinctive apology forming; then stopped, struck by the injustice of the attack. "As a matter of fact," she said, levelly, "it was my aunt who brought up the subject of her past. What's more, when she then tried to stand and I tried to catch her, we both fell and lay trapped for some considerable time under that very poor excuse for a wheelchair you have given her. And, just so you know, I rang the emergency button and no-one came."

"And as for Edith," Natalia continued, as if Ruth had not uttered a word, "you must have upset her badly too. Some book or other she wanted to give you; went on about it half the night. She made me promise to keep it for you."

Of course: the book, her memoir. Ruth had forgotten about it. How stupid.

"Well," she said. "That's all right. I can get it from her now."

"No, you can't," said Natalia, with a kind of tired triumph. "She's been admitted to hospital. She's had a stroke."

The water feature suddenly stopped, with a sigh. Natalia drew in her breath. Ruth pulled herself up. There was one thing she could do.

"Well, could you give it to me, please? If, as you say, it was meant for me?"

"I—" began Natalia, but the sentence was not finished. A light began to flash above her head; a loud urgency bleeped at her waist. She looked down, then quickly up at Ruth. "You'd better come with me," she said, and began to rush down the corridor towards the residents' rooms.

So it does work, was Ruth's incongruous thought, when they want to hear it; and she picked up her feet and followed Natalia, passing what seemed like the entire staff, working at windows and flexes, carrying cardboard boxes, coloured papers and baubles spilling out. Naturally: Hallowe'en over, Christmas must be next, with tinsel and enforced merriment from now until January. Still they rushed on, like Alice and the Red Queen, all down the corridors, past crudely jolly Santas and staring snowmen, coming to a sudden breathless halt at her aunt's room.

There, behind the garishly childish stocking hung upon her door, finding what they did, Natalia called the doctor and an ambulance.

It did not matter. It was already too late. While all the staff were harried with premature Christmas decoration, Hilde Bauer, her heart in the end as unpredictable as that of the sister she had lost, had passed quietly away in the gloom of the November evening.

Cuckoo

Dear Thomas, wrote Ruth, after the funeral. *Thank you for writing to me about poor Hilde. It was, as you say, quite a shock. Her heart, it seems, was weaker than they thought, and she just went. You were good to think of coming over to the funeral, but really, as I told you on the phone, it wasn't necessary, and you already have to travel so much it wouldn't have seemed right to bring you. And, yes, to answer your question, it was a standard Christian funeral. It's the same God, I suppose, if religion means anything; not that I think it meant that much to Hilde. It certainly didn't seem to bring her much comfort. Anyway, I did the readings, with appropriate references to her Jewish origins. I frankly hadn't the knowledge or energy to do it any other way.*

I hope in the brighter days you may get over. I'll take you to her grave. She's beside my parents: not alone any more. Do please keep in touch. It is comforting to hear from family.

Ruth

PS Chris came, you may be interested to hear.

Thomas did not reply. Why should he? Ruth had not even told him what had happened at the funeral. What he did not know was that at the last minute, that moment of almost breathless expectation, the service about to begin, the whole place silent, she had heard the breeze and the sigh of a door opening, the rush of cold air, the sigh of its closure; then the pressing and the rustle and the stage whisper of someone squeezing in at the end of a row already full of elderly, confused residents; and it had not needed the smell of alcohol to tell her that it was Chris, whom she had left dead to the world not an hour before. Chris, who could not get up to make his own breakfast and rarely dressed before four, had struggled into his suit, combed his hair, polished his good shoes and come down to see Hilde off. Ruth, composing herself to read the quiet words of comfort chosen with the chaplain, did not know whether to weep or scream in frustration; instead, she read the words, and sat down, as far from him as she could.

Yet, at the side of her vision, she saw someone else. Right at the back, silent, black-clad, a dark ghost, she saw Cory Latimer, her eyes sweeping round, taking in who was there, who not; and resting, finally, on Chris. Turning up, Ruth angrily thought, time and again, like an unwanted cuckoo in the nest.

And for whatever reason, or for no reason at all, Ruth suddenly remembered what it was that made Edith Barratt sit frozen the evening Hilde died: it was hearing the name *Herrold*. Something in Ruth clicked into place. She looked Cory Latimer in the eye, and she was no longer angry, weary, or afraid.

Our Mr Herrold

"What I don't understand," said Sandra when Ruth, desperate to talk to someone, told her about the funeral, "apart from why you're here at all, so soon after, is how you ever came to marry Chris Applewood in the first place. I don't deny he has — or had — charm, but ..."

"I'm here because I don't want to be at home," said Ruth. "And I don't think anybody ever really understands the charm one person exerts over another."

Sandra looked directly at Ruth.

"Has he any charm for you? Now?"

Ruth thought. Did he?

"No," she said, finally and a little sadly: for as she said it she knew that it was, simply, the truth. "It's just that he is not well, and things have gone so very badly for him lately that it seems cruel to abandon him." And, she added silently, maybe I'm not quite ready to be by myself.

Sandra raised one eyebrow. "Ah," she said, "abandon him — as he did you, for Latimer, right at the start of your conference. As to being not well, he's an alcoholic, isn't he;

131

and, as far as I can see, having thoroughly messed up his own career, he has done his best to wreck yours as well. I can see how that would be attractive."

"Leave it, Sandra," said Ruth, pushing back her chair to make a move to go. "What I really need to work out is how to mine those papers without Latimer getting wind of their potential."

"I'll leave it, Ruth," said Sandra, standing up, "the day you leave him, once and for all. For a start, you need to get him out of your house."

"Sandra," Ruth began. "It's not as —"

"Look, Ruth," said Sandra. "It comes to this. You were going places, if Latimer and he hadn't scuppered everything. You still could."

"I doubt it, Sandra," Ruth said, shaking her head. "Restructuring? Remember?"

Sandra, gathering her coat and her bag, sighed. "You're not listening," she said. "I said you still could." She swung the bag over her arm.

Opening her mouth to ask what she meant, Ruth saw that though much more could have been said, no more would.

"Is that new?" she said, instead, indicating the sleek, expensive-looking bag. "Rather nice."

Sandra looked at it, a little self-consciously. "Oh ... yes, I suppose. Bit of a pay rise. Look, I have to get back. And as to Latimer, if you didn't have Chris around, what power would she have over you? You're the executor of the papers: she isn't. Go down there and start on them, get rid of him, and get back to yourself. I mean it, Ruth. Start mining." And, with a brief, questioning shrug, she left the coffee shop.

Ruth, unasked question answered, chair pulled out to rise, did not rise, but sat on for a while. Then she, too, sighed, lifted her briefcase and left.

Following the funeral, in a rare acknowledgment of human feelings, Ruth had been granted some days of compassionate leave. She could not, as she had told Sandra, face the silence of the house; equally, she could not face being at work. Across the road, the College stood, broad-shouldered, weak sunlight glinting on windows inscrutably mullioned, holding upon the self-regarding town its implacable gaze. Yet, glimpsed for a second through a tracery of winter trees, it seemed, against the cold and brilliant sky, almost majestic. Ruth reached for her clip-on sunglasses. I should get my eyes lasered, she thought: then I wouldn't have to clip these blessed things onto my specs every time there's a blink of sun. Just one smart pair of sunnies; and I'd sashay out like a ... like a model, or ... Jackie Kennedy or somebody. Still, perhaps she would miss the routine and the rhythm of the spectacle-wearer. It was certainly possible to hide behind them, almost to see without being seen, to experience relief in taking them off, and feel the world return to a restful softness. Who wanted to see everything? Me, maybe, she answered herself; I seem to have missed what everybody else saw a mile off, starting with Chris Applewood.

Perhaps she had been wrong to marry him in the first place. She had managed perfectly well by herself until she was thirty, had seen off many prospective suitors, married to her career, as one of them said with some resentment, and preoccupied with a growing brood of publications. She found it easy, as she had once rather ruefully explained to Sandra, to focus on one thing to the exclusion of all else: after all, hadn't Hilde shown her by daily example how to drive people away?

What she had told Thomas was true. For Hilde it was second nature to harangue, with tales of the iniquities of

Nazi Germany, what her father had described as the long line of callow youths, one more callow than the one before. Poor lads: innocently, or not so innocently, calling at the house for Ruth, they could not have been prepared for Hilde and her woes. Thus, it had more or less continued, until Ruth's thirtieth year, when her father, finally defeated by his own stoic widowerhood, received in silence the cancer he acknowledged to no-one and, not yet sixty, slipped out of life. That was when Chris had appeared.

It was the merest chance. At thirty, Ruth still smoked and, slipping outside the post-funeral tea for a quick cigarette, she had bumped into a young man, looking a little lost. He introduced himself as a journalist, Chris Applewood, in the hotel to cover a society wedding. He was having difficulty finding the wedding party, he said. He knew no-one in Northern Ireland, and he was in need of help. Ruth's heart went out to him, with his crooked smile and his unruly lock of hair. It was not quite true, what he said: it became apparent, even in the course of their short conversation, that he knew quite a few people and needed little help. Yet, despite that, Ruth liked him: he showed a capacity for conversation beyond himself, and his face, with its ready and charmingly lopsided smile, responded with a self-deprecating humour to the ironic possibilities of finding himself at quite the wrong event; all of which, doubtless, were useful attributes for a young man seeking his way in the world. What had brought him to Ireland at all, Ruth asked. A woman, he told her, a woman in Dublin; but that was in the past. The North, he said, interested him; and now, he said, with his sideways smile, not just politically. There was a silence: Ruth did not know how to respond. There was more silence. Somebody, he remarked, looking about him, seemed to be enjoying herself: and, looking through the doors to the funeral gathering, Ruth saw that Hilde had an audience, and had managed to make herself the centre of attention at someone else's last big day. Then Ruth, despite the occasion, smiled too. "No show without Punch," she said. Chris laughed quietly in collusion, and a sort of guiltily friendly conspiracy was established. That was 1980. After that, for several months, she had heard nothing from him. It hardly mattered: it was the time that Ruth began to sort her father's possessions and papers, learned that she had inherited the house, and tried to face the fact that she had also inherited Hilde.

It was not that there was much forgetting the fact: at least once a week, Hilde would remind her that she hoped Ruth would look after her as she had done for all of them, the entire family, all her life. On one such day this recurring refrain sent Ruth to the attic, on the pretext of sorting out things of her mother's: Hilde, at least, could not manage the ladder to the attic. If I were Jo March, Ruth thought, or what was his name, Chatterton, the marvellous boy, I could either write a novel up here or starve to death; and either would be preferable to listening to Hilde.

It was a large attic, dark and dim, home to many spiders, and a great deal of dust. She took up the more portable of her father's personal possessions; they should be kept, but she was not yet able to deal with them. With a start, her eyes adjusting to the light, she found herself in front of Hilde's trunk, long undisturbed. Small, oblong, metal-cornered and, apart from the area beneath the cracked leather strap which had secured it, a long-faded navy blue, it had come with Hilde when she arrived that November of 1963, after Ruth's mother's death; and had been ordered straight up to the attic.

Ruth remembered that. Thirteen, grieving and stunned, she had heard Hilde begin the first of her complaints: "But, it's Mimi's — from our home, her home! From Berlin! I struggled on the train — I carried it all the way — so many little mementoes — Mimi's childhood — I struggled —"

"Please, Hilde," Ruth's father had said, his voice dropping to a coldness Ruth had never before heard. "No more. As to your struggles, I think we have all had our own; and my wife's home is here. Or was." He stopped, shook his head, set his mouth in the hard line it thereafter assumed; then, he asked the men to be so good as to take the little trunk up to the loft, and there was an end to it, except that it left Ruth afraid that he might make them move, if this was no longer home. It also marked the beginning of her resentment of Hilde.

Now, in the attic, when she opened the trunk, she could see the little mementoes: picture books, exercise books, and more. No. She closed the lid: the smell of another life had roused something, new and raw, rendering it impossible to look further. She was glad, actually glad, when Hilde called to her that there was someone at the door.

It was Chris Applewood. By then, Ruth had forgotten about him, forgotten even that she had given him her address. Dusty from the attic, fingers grubby, hair scraped back into a reprehensible elastic band, she was too surprised to do anything but invite him in. While she excused herself to tidy up, Hilde took over, and began on him. Returning, Ruth was amazed to see him listening to Hilde, not simply with attention and understanding, but conversing, engaging with her; and Hilde's voice, most unusually, was warm, even soft, and there were no complaints that day.

Thus it began, with Chris. Hilde not only made no objection, but in fact went out of her way to be pleasant, and to welcome him, at whatever hour he chose to appear. For Chris, it soon emerged, was unpredictable. His passion was music, he told Ruth; and now, posted by his paper to the North to cover its more interesting darknesses, he found he could also indulge this passion. Before long, they spent many surprising evenings at gigs and experimental exhibitions, in rooms redolent with a smokily scented enchantment and, in one of these, after Ruth had endured a particularly trying day with Hilde, and Chris had scooped an interview with a notorious if somewhat reticent paramilitary, he proposed, and she accepted. By the time she was thirty-one, they were engaged; and in the spring of 1982, on Ruth's thirty-second birthday, they were married.

For twelve years they had been what passes for happy: sliding, indeed, fairly quickly through the delirium of early attraction to mutual tolerance, each gradually accepting if not always liking the other's habits, friends and, inevitably, human failings. Chris was secretive, Ruth found: she was driven, he said. No children had come: he minded. Ruth, saddened at first, came to be glad that she would not distress another child as she had been distressed by her mother's too early death; and that she would not madden another child as Hilde had maddened her with laments for a distant and incomprehensible past. For always, in the bad days and the good, there was Hilde. Yet, for a long time, even on the bad days, Chris was good to Hilde; until he was not, until his career stalled, then floundered, and he found or decided he could no longer be good to anyone, including himself.

Then, Ruth was glad that no child would have to endure the misery of an alcoholic father, which she had to accept Chris would certainly have been. He always liked to drink, and drink deep, and the drinks grew deeper, and his liking greater as the troubled times he had come so eagerly to tackle in the early Eighties became the sour and murderous stalemate of the Nineties. When the paramilitary he had once so boldly, even recklessly, interviewed, became himself another victim of horrific revenge, and Chris became the new subject of the same threats, his drinks had deepened further and he was, for the first time, admitted to hospital. His contacts dwindled, then went altogether; he invested the only money they had in a music venture, the backing of a young band (Selsey Bill) who, he felt sure, could be as famous as he had once thought he might be himself. When Selsey Bill, unsurprisingly, sank, the money sank with them. After that Chris spent time in and out of rehabilitation, in and out of hospital, in and out of Ruth's house, in and out of her life.

That was what Ruth could not, beyond the essentials, explain to anyone: that for a long, long time, seeing to Chris, being irritated and exasperated by Chris was her buffer, her reason or excuse for inaction on every other front.

And now, step-quickening away those painful thoughts, she walked where her feet took her, all the way into town, until she found herself at the door of the Benner Centre. A quick look at the letters? Why not? It would be better than being at home.

And it was better. She felt more cheerful just walking up the stairs, seeing that the seat by the window she had used that first day was still vacant, inhaling the comfort of papers and books, and watching the dust-motes settle in slanting shafts from the high windows. She felt almost buoyant as she asked the unfamiliar assistant — Tracy, according to her shining name badge — for the letter file from the Barratt archive, and was not greatly concerned when the young woman explained that the new computer system was down. It didn't matter, Ruth told her, because all the papers were together; and she rather thought they might still be behind the issue desk. Tracy, smiling pleasantly at this unsought information, appeared not to be disposed to look. Instead, she spent a long and, to Ruth, frustrating time riffling through cards and puzzling through listings. Then she excused herself, promising to return directly. Ruth now felt not only frustration but also the beginning of irritation and more than a little anxiety. Why the papers had not been left aside for her, as had surely been agreed, she did not know. Minutes passed; the clock above the desk struck the hour. Someone outrageously took the seat by the window, slapping his papers on the desk with a thump and Ruth, increasingly put out, began to drum her fingers on the counter. She scanned without interest pamphlets on forthcoming exhibitions and instructions to new readers. The clock struck the quarter hour. There was still no Tracy. The maddening clock was ticking comfortably towards the half-hour by the time she returned, still brightly, perhaps too brightly smiling. She was sorry, she said, to be so long. There was no need to worry: she was just going to have one more look and, before Ruth could tell her not to, passed again through the silent baize to delve into the darkness beyond.

Many more minutes wandered by until, breathless, dusty, a cobweb clinging to her ear, Tracy reappeared. She shook her head: she was sorry, but the letters must have been wrongly filed. Wrongly filed? Ruth could not believe it. What did she mean? Tracy, her initial sunny willingness fairly exhausted, set her mouth in a firm line. Once more, she said she was sorry. The letter file was nowhere to be found, and no-one had seen it: therefore it must have been wrongly filed.

Ruth tried again. Was Cormac there? He was not: he was on leave. Perhaps Dr Deacon would like to speak to someone else? The Curator? Unfortunately, Professor Latimer was just out at a meeting, but if Dr Deacon would care to wait, she might be back that afternoon. Or perhaps

Dr Deacon would prefer to make an appointment for another day?

Dr Deacon would not: she would come back, she said, with a confidence she did not feel. What was the point, if the letters were gone? Defeated, she left the Benner Centre. The bright morning dulled into grey afternoon as she walked back up the road past the College. She did not go into the office, trailing instead back to the home she did not want to be in and, for no reason that she could give herself, then or afterwards, climbed straight up to the attic and opened Hilde's trunk.

Now, at last, she examined the little things of that lost childhood: a tin horse and a staring ballerina; a little musical box, topped by a shell-made mother, a baby in her arms. When she turned the key, it seemed to work, jerkily revolving to Brahms' Lullaby until, faltering, it slowed to a dying halt. Poor box; poor shell people: she tucked them back into the trunk. There was an exercise book with childish drawings, names printed beneath them — *Mama, Papa, David, Hilde* and *Mimi*, stick people with stick dogs and cats. And, besides the stick family, there were photographs, tenuously held at the corners with fragile paper mounts, of the real family — Mama, Papa, and the three children at the Tiergarten, proudly standing at the Brandenburg Gate, walking by the river in spring, skating on the river in winter. Yellowing, curling with the damp and the mould of long neglect, they were the fragments of a life lived before *Kristallnacht* and the *Kinderstransport*, before Papa was taken away in the night, before Mama was left behind when first David and Mimi and, finally, Hilde were sent away to the unknown West.

Last of all, she saw two photographs, both dated February 1933. The first was of the young Hilde, nine years old, just before the other two got away, a serious, big-eyed child, plaited hair, a woollen cap, innocence and hope in her eyes, one mittened hand trustfully in that of the big brother, the other holding the little sister, all about to go skating on the frozen river. The second a school photograph, the same child Hilde close beside a little friend, all around them solemn flaxen-haired boys and girls, and behind them the protective presence of a kind-faced man, their teacher. On the back only three names were written: *Hilde, Anna, unser Herr Herrold.* Our Mr Herrold. It was those two final images which brought Ruth, at last, to tears of regret and grief, not only for the lonely traveller whom no-one, after that, had ever had time to love or heed, but also, inexplicably, for herself, for a loss she could scarcely name.

The Book

Despite the apparently endless tasks of post-death administration, Ruth did go back to the Benner Centre. Really, how would she not? She made it her business, letters or no letters, to spend the next two days going through the Barratt papers, working out how they might be best grouped, noting what she could use and what she could not; and, though constantly returning in her mind to the question of the whereabouts of the letters, began piecing together what she could of Edith Barratt's life. Without the benefit of the missing correspondence, her impression was of a bright young woman with a certain facility, even a gift, as a writer, and a greater gift as a teacher. The knowledge of the existence of the letters, however, changed her perspective just enough to require a careful rereading of the manuscripts. The children's stories, complete and published, were cleverly written, sharply whimsical without being sentimental; there was an edge there, a poignancy, an awareness of the inevitable incongruities and disappointments of the world, rather in the spirit of James Stephens, or Lewis

143

Carroll. Something might be made of them. They might be reprinted, or there could be a new edition. There were photographs, too: mainly school events, in some of which Edith was present. There were others: photographs of Edith as a bobbed and serious child with her parents, and one of her as a strong-featured, yet touchingly innocent-looking young graduate, in gown and ermine hood. She glanced at them quickly, and replaced them in the box. They could be looked at later.

The novel and the play, both in manuscript, first intrigued, then dismayed her. Their themes were war and lost love: yet, the conflicts were distant, the love chastely diffident. The manuscripts were complete; but there was nothing to suggest they had ever been published. Ruth searched through box after box for evidence of anything more; and in the end, tucked away in an envelope of neatly paid bills, found the clutch of rejections: the kind and constructive, praising the quality of the writing, while regretting the lack of heart in the story; and, inevitably, the curt and dismissive. Ruth, remembering articles sent back for more and more work before they might even be considered for peer review, felt for Edith. She went back to the manuscripts; began to look for clues, hoping to find them in what was not said, if they could not be discovered in what was. It was no good: stilted farewell scenes at the border; large and fatally heroic gestures. Yes, the events of the wars described — the Franco-Prussian, the second Boer war — had been well-researched. What was missing was any trace of passion. The woman she remembered, who could bring all of literature and its time to vibrant life for restive and sceptical adolescents, had not lacked passion, nor had she in her stories for children, and her newspaper articles showed that clever lively mind. How could her undoubted sense of the vivid, of the sheer joy of being alive in the world, be so singularly absent from these two works, so long and so carefully kept? Into her mind came a picture of the last day she had seen Edith in the nursing home. There was a notebook she wanted her to have — a memoir?

The memory was painful. She had not been back to the nursing home since the funeral. She had allowed herself to avoid even an inquiry about Edith Barratt; there had been so much to do — the aftermath of the death, her work; and Chris. Perhaps, she thought, she need not read the memoir: perhaps it would even cloud her judgment. It would be, of necessity, a revised version, a reworking of events. Until, through the papers in the boxes, she had a clear sense of Edith as she was when a young woman, it would surely be best to stay away from her subject's reworking of her own story. Besides, she would have to go back to the nursing home to collect it, and from Natalia, and she did not relish that prospect. Moreover, as her function as literary executor was to see to the proper disposal of the papers, it was hardly to be expected that she should also act as if she were a family member. No: the letters, if they could be found, and the papers would be her priority. All else would have to wait.

Such was Ruth's state of mind at closing time in the Benner Centre on Tuesday evening. By seven o'clock on Wednesday evening, however, she was walking into the nursing home; by ten past, at once relieved and ashamed to learn that Edith Barratt was again in hospital, and was not to be visited, she was on her way home with the *Memory Book*; and by one in the morning, having just seen Edith leave Berlin by train she fell, book in hand, into a sleep that lasted almost until dawn.

145

The Train

Ruth woke with a start. Her heart racing, breath in quick gasps, she sat bolt upright. There was a train; she had to catch a train. She was late; why was she late? Her fingers, tingling and sharp, were caught in a book. She looked about her, confused, the room of her childhood suddenly unfamiliar; then memory seeped slowly back in. Night, yes; darkness and silence, except for the steady tick of the clock. Slipping out from beneath the too-hot quilt, splashing cold water on damp head and wrists, she padded downstairs, past the stale, open darkness of Chris's room, and, suddenly and perversely cold, made tea and a hot-water bottle.

Then, settling herself in the nest of quilt and pillows, she picked up the *Memory Book*. Come on, Edith, she thought, give me something — anything.

"*A few bad days,*" she read, "*dreadful headaches ...*"

The Memory Book

❧

My Greatest Love

A bad few days, dreadful headaches; but I feel better now, and I had better keep writing or they will think of something else to torture me.

Paul put me on the train, and he had to go in one direction, I in another; and then the letters started. He wrote first in September, which was how I learned he had been called up in the general mobilisation of the 12th August. Of course; and if I had not been drifting round in a dream — what did my mother say, head in the clouds? — I would have realised that that was part of the waiting, part of the excitement I sensed all about me. All the young men must have been waiting for that call. It was in the air. It was everywhere, that waiting, and all the time, foolish girl that I was, I thought we were waiting for some grand resolution, for a considered peace. I thought he was, too: no, I know he was, certainly in the first letter. And he was going to make a painting for me, for me, because I was his great love — his words: "*Meine grosse Liebe.*" *My true love hath my heart and I have his.*

I treasured those letters: yet, I once tried to tear them up. I could not; even pieced one together, like that frightening wife of Charlotte Brontë's teacher. I used Sellotape, not needle and thread, though Mme Heger may have been wiser: now Sellotape, crackling and yellowing over Paul's writing, his drawings, is almost all of his that I have, or had. Stitching would have endured; how clever, how pathologically patient of Mme Heger to collate her evidence. I could not destroy my letters, the only evidence of the only time in my too long life when I knew without a doubt that I was fully alive; every sense, every nerve, alive.

Before I came in here, I gathered up the letters without reading them; there is no need to reread. I remember perfectly what they said. I put them in an envelope, with the papers I wanted to keep, and placed them in the archival depository. I hope, I do hope, that Ruth Deacon may be the one to read them, to understand them and, perhaps, tell my story. She has a good enough mind to do that. I helped her, I believe, though she may not realise it: I did not let her waste herself in easy smartness. I like to think I burned that out of her, as out of all the good ones. One sometimes has to be hard on them, to temper them for the struggle ahead. It is a difficult task, a difficult balance to maintain. They rarely understand that. I trust in time that she will; and indeed, that my papers may help her to do so. I believe I have some understanding of Ruth Deacon, and I should like her to enable me to be understood. We may not all find love in our lives, but we may perhaps hope for understanding.

As to myself, after that strange day when Paul put me on the train, I picked up, or tried to pick up the threads of my life, and waited for more letters. There was so much going on: every day, uncertainty in the newspapers, on the wireless, in the very air we breathed. Kitty was on my mind, a permanent, background niggling anxiety. I did not know what had happened to Kitty, or where she had gone because, even after the holidays, she did not come home. I had somehow expected that she would, but she did not. Had she gone to meet her father? Was that just a story? Perhaps something had happened to her; perhaps she was ill, or in hospital somewhere; at the back of my mind I felt responsible, and at the same time angry at her for putting me in the position of feeling responsible. I thought of ringing up her parents, but what could I have told them? That Kitty went off one day to meet the father from whom, if the old rumours were true, they had been long estranged? How could I do that? I told my parents she had decided to keep travelling, and hoped it was so; and they did not ask too many more questions, since I was home, and apparently safe and sound.

Their main concern was that I open a letter which had arrived during my absence. My heart turned over: what if it was from Paul? Would there be an inquisition? It was not, and there was no inquisition, because it was from the principal of the school where I had been a pupil, offering me, with immediate effect, the post of junior English teacher. I had made no application, had had to undergo no interview: I was a past pupil with an excellent record and a good reputation. I was chosen: such was the custom in those far-off days, and I was openly delighted.

My parents' raptures were more muted: they were calmly pleased, and seemed unsurprised, even a little preoccupied. Consequently, they wasted little time on questions about my travels, beyond establishing that I'd had a pleasant holiday. I might have wished for a little more display; but my parents, all in all to one another, and increasingly so as they grew older, treated me then as ever

151

with a benign and distant kindness, which suited them, and which, especially then, suited me almost equally well.

I was Donne's compass, the point of me now rooted in the man I loved, the free arm radiating out to here, to there, to everywhere, but coming home always to him, and the night we danced in Clärchen's: our love, *gold to aery thinnesse beat*. I was there and not there and, however curious they may or may not have been, all my parents said to me about it was that I had grown very quiet. It was true: I intercepted Paul's first letter from the postman, and took the decision that I would not give my parents occasion to ask me about any more correspondence. Gradually, perhaps because at the outset I had not felt able to tell them about Paul, we settled into silence. I cannot explain it any more than that. I had no Jane Bennet to confide in, no sister or friend; until, that is, I met William.

William Hamilton started at the school that same autumn, as a peripatetic music teacher. I saw him on the first day of term, and I felt a little sorry for him. My job was a delight, discussing the pleasures of poetry and drama and fiction with girls who wanted to learn; his, which was fairly thankless, was to take the choir and, outside school hours, teach piano to those whose parents wished or could afford special tuition. William replaced a fierce and ancient dame who whacked their knuckles and sent them weeping through the mottled glass door of her room, her attic lair: sent them with their humiliation down ninety-nine stone steps to their friends or their families. Not so, William Hamilton. He came quite quickly to be well-liked, indeed possibly well-loved though, at the outset, because of the legacy and reputation of Miss Delagard, he had few pupils, and could be found most lunchtimes going over scores in the staff room.

He was thus occupied, one of those golden days of

September 1938, sitting quite close to me at the big table in the middle of the room; so close, I could almost hear his heart. I could also hear his watch ticking, and I had forgotten mine that day. The clock on the staff-room wall was broken. I tried to see the time on his watch without his noticing, but he noticed, and he looked over his glasses at me, and his eyes surprised me, warm and brown.

"Quarter to," he said. "You're all right for another while." He tapped his watch. "My grandfather's clock," he said. "More reliable than Big Ben."

I remember that I was embarrassed at having been caught and, managing some thanks, tried to go back to my reading. It was that first letter of Paul's. He did not take his eyes away: I felt them through my still hot embarrassment. I felt compelled to look up.

"You speak German?" he said, with a tentative smile, nodding towards my necessary dictionary. He had a kind smile, like his eyes, like him. Dear William. I told him my German was still in a state of prolonged infancy, but that I was trying. I think I managed to give the impression that my letter was from a German penfriend.

"Well, if it's work," he said, with a look that now I remember as both wry and considered, "and, of course, learning a language can be, then get her — or him — to write to you here at the school. That is, if you'd rather not have your … friend discussed at home."

Such a simple solution; it was as if he understood, without needing explanation. I had never had that in my life. So I took his advice, did as he suggested and, gradually, found that I was able to confide more — not all, but more — to William than to anyone. He spoke German, almost fluently; he had studied in Heidelberg, and he knew Berlin. He had shared rooms there with a good friend, his best friend, whose name was Robert. He wore a signet ring:

close up, if his hand was on the page, or sitting by mine as we spoke, I could see its pattern, an R and a W, intricately entwined. I believe that, though no words of explanation or expiation were ever spoken, we shared secrets, William and I. He would lean trustfully close to me, in his tweed jacket, heathery smelling, a little waft of pipe tobacco when he moved; he would help me with difficult phrases in the letters, and I recall that his eyes crinkled behind his glasses when I got it right. More and more, we went about together, and everyone, our parents included, said they thought we made a lovely couple. There was talk of wedding bells, amusing us both. Yet, now, thinking back, I see we were. We were a lovely couple, in our own way.

Paul wrote again quite quickly, congratulating me on my improved German. Not wanting to have any secrets between us, I told him in my next about William, that he was a colleague who was helping me. I still do not quite understand his reaction to that. "*It was a beautiful dream we dreamed together in Berlin,*" he wrote. That I could translate: but I did not show it to William. What did he mean? "*It seems to me today, a dream that came too soon to its end.*" Did he mean what that seemed to say? Did he mean that, a dream that ended? What was going on? I sat down and wrote to him straight away. It was no dream, I told him: this is reality, and William, I begged him to believe, was no threat. I heard nothing then, for weeks; and the bright days began to shorten; the leaves tumbled about my feet; the high summer skies grew low and clouded; and my misery was very great.

Throughout September, everywhere, the talk was of the meeting due to take place in Munich, between the Prime Minister and the German Chancellor. Everything, for all of us, not just the Czechs, depended on this meeting, but there was no cause for concern. Mr Chamberlain, William said, my parents said, would know what to say and do. No-one wanted war, my father said, least of all the Germans. How could they? They had suffered so much in the last one. My Uncle Patrick said they did want war, and there would be a war, and it would be the end of us, but no-one listened much to poor Patrick, because by then he was spending more time in his terrible past than the always tenuous present, and more time in hospital than out of it. Sorry though I should probably be to say it, this came as a great relief, almost greater than the general relief over the peace achieved in Munich. Yet, all that time, through all that was happening, I was somewhere else, and my only true concern was for Paul — where he was, what he was doing and, most of all, why he had not written.

Finally, at the end of October, a letter came to the school. I fell upon it; I devoured it, every word. Those I remember are imprinted on my mind, just as if I were reading them on the page. He was sorry not to have written. He had been away; he had been in Czechoslovakia. My eyes raced to the next line: "... now in the lovely old Reichstown of Ulm." He was in Ulm. Ulm — where I had been with the Schmidts! I was torn between wishing we had been there at the same time and imagining him there, in places I knew, and could see in my mind; after a little, I felt I *was* there with him. His letters, he told me, had been forwarded and he had received mine. "*Your dear letter,*" he called it. He found it wonderful to think that two people — the other, he said, was his mother in Berlin — were praying for his safety. This letter was full of his relief at what he described as the disaster that had been averted by the *"magnificent and successful efforts of the Four Statesmen"*. Now, when I consider the phrase, I think more of the Four Horsemen of the Apocalypse — but then! Then, my spirit, my whole being was in Czechoslovakia, with Paul, who wanted peace as much as we did at home; sharing his pity for the terrible misery of the poor people of the Sudetenland, their homes and their towns destroyed by the fleeing Czech army; I felt his satisfaction at their joyful *Heimkehr*, their homecoming, their return to the safety of Greater Germany. I rejoiced to read that on the 29th of September he had seen the Prime Minister. "*Champerlain*", he called him for, endearingly, he sometimes wrote as he spoke. I could hear him. Mr Chamberlain, he said, had endeared himself to the German people as "*a great peacemaker*". And then he wrote that because of our Prime Minister's efforts and those of the "*Führer*" — his Leader — there would not now be another war between England and Germany.

That was all I needed to hear about politics. Whatever anyone said, whatever anybody believed, I knew there would be no war, because Paul had said it: and he was there, and clearly Germany did not want war, and all would yet be well. And, even more importantly, at the end of his letter he asked me if I would be able to translate his letter; and if I thought I might not, he said: "*Should I just come over with it to Ireland?*" Oh, my imagination took flight that day, that night, and for many days and nights afterwards; and it needed to, for I did not hear then from him until nearly Christmas. In all those weeks, I had no idea where he was or what was happening.

I remember that Christmas letter: "*Christmas stands at the very door,*" he wrote. How lovely a phrase. Christmas stands at the door. I remember he rejoiced that Austria had been reunited with Greater Germany, that we had been brought back from the brink of war by what he again described as the heroic efforts of the four statesmen. Who knows, he wrote — and it chilled me to read it — if he would otherwise be alive for the glorious feast of love and joy that was Christmas, when, he said, "*joy would sweep once more into our hearts*". I was glad to have persevered enough to be able to translate such loveliness of language. "*Your letters are very dear to this lonely soldier,*" he wrote, "*and with the passage of time, I find they grow dearer still.*" How I treasured those words.

He wrote again the following week, thanking me for my Christmas card, with its little image of a bird. It was a robin, I recall, but it reminded him of our little friend, our Amico. Yet, there was sadness in his tone: he was thinking back to Italy, to the day the little bird, Amico, brought us together. "*Ah, the brief time we shared together!*" he wrote. "*Only he, free in the world, carries it unburdened through his little life.*" For him, he said, "*Life means the soldier's march, one foot after another, until we arrive at our appointed destination.*" I did not care for this tone; I did not want an elegy for the past, and I did not want to be relegated to the past. I wrote at once. I sent him a calendar, looking forward, to the future, our future. His reply was short. He promised me a painting, yet it was so short. And yet it was a precious letter, all the more so as it was the last I would receive for several months.

He wrote again in March. All those long winter months, the news from Europe worsening with every day, and I heard nothing. If it had not been for William, for his kindness, his unfailing good humour, I do not know what I would have done. There was talk of the introduction of conscription, not just in England, but here too: William's friend Robert, himself trying with some unexplained difficulty to get out of Germany, wanted him to go over our border, where there existed, in a victory of semantics, no war, but "an emergency". William said he would not do it, that he intended to join up straightaway if war came.

I asked him why: I had not thought him eager for war.

"But you wouldn't think me an Orangeman, either," he

said, with that wry smile of his.

"You're not!" I said. "I don't believe you!"

"I'm not," he said. "I'm teasing. But my grandfather was a member of the Orange Order — though not my father. Don't tell the nuns."

I thought he was still teasing.

"No," he said, "he really was, my grandfather. My father didn't believe in it — all the marching, and the drums and the open triumphalism of the whole thing. I gather he told him so, and it caused friction between them — that is, until he joined up. It's my mother who was, and is, Catholic, though not what you might call Nationalist. She's probably the reason I'm teaching in this school. And my father's the reason I'd have to join up."

"But why?" I said. "I don't understand."

We were walking round the Botanic Gardens, I recall, and the sun was shining on the great jungle plants of the Palm House. I didn't want William — my friend, my companion, almost my brother — to go away and be a soldier. He shrugged, and smiled, this time a little sadly.

"He was in the Ulster Division," he said. "He was at the Somme. I think he wanted to do something that would make his own father proud."

"Well, I don't believe he'd want you to join up, William," I said, and I meant it. "The ones who were there don't want it for the next generation. I know that. I know from my father and even my batty uncle. I think you should ask your father."

"I can't," he said, and I remember the sun seemed to go behind a cloud as he spoke. "He never came back."

When Paul's next letter came, on the 12th of March 1939, I could hardly open it, my hands were trembling so; and what I read filled me with a nameless fear. "*I write only a few words, Edith, my little friend,*" he said, "*so that you do not worry unnecessarily about me. I know I have been absent for quite a while. You will, I trust, hear more from me in the next few days. It may be that I shall soon be stationed in Berlin."*

I did not hear from him in the next few days. I did not hear from him in the next few months, indeed, not until the summer; and my dread grew, and still I could not say why.

I did, however, receive another letter from Europe early that March of 1939. It came from Prague. I remember every word of it, from the cool cheek of its greeting, *"Dear Edie"* to the breezy tone, as if its writer had been away for a long weekend. It was from, of all people, Kitty. Kitty, whom I had not seen since she left me that day in Castel Gandolfo.

৩৯৫৩

This, thought Ruth, is more like it. I wondered where Kitty had got to. Come on, Edith: wake up, do something. As if in answer, she read: "I haven't been too well ..."

Kitty

I haven't been too well. I didn't think I could write any
more. It's hard to go back there, hard to bring them back
from the past, my parents and William; and Kitty, that
blade. The cheek of Kitty was beyond anything. "*I imagine
you'll be a little surprised,*" she wrote, "*to hear from me
after all this time.*" There was no trace of irony: Kitty and
irony were unacquainted. She said she felt a little badly
about the way we had parted the previous summer, and
perhaps I might like to pick up where we left off, maybe see
a bit more of Europe? "*You know,*" she said, and these
were her exact words, "*as it turned out, there was no war
— you were worried for nothing.*" I had to laugh: *I* was
worried? I was not remotely worried. That was Kitty,
forever imputing her own behaviour to someone else. So
then, Kitty thought, I might like to come to Prague where
she was teaching — "*Nothing to it: they love me!*" — or, it
might, as she put it, "*suit my trains better to meet, say, in
Munich and go on from there. Prague is a little
overcrowded these days.*" Suit *her* trains: I was to suit her.

And then she said, "*We always did plan to see Germany together, didn't we?*"

I was taken aback. I had forgotten that; I remembered at the outset we had thought of travelling on to Germany, but even when we were in Italy, I had almost completely ceased to think of Kitty as any kind of companion. One thing I knew: I did not want to travel to Berlin with Kitty. How could I, after all that had happened, bad and good? Berlin was Clärchen's, and Paul.

I told my parents, however, that I had heard from Kitty, and that she was all right. To my surprise, my mother said she knew. They had met Kitty's grandparents one evening in the Opera House. She was safely in Prague, they heard, and in no danger.

"You never thought to say to me," I said, and I am sure I sounded petulant. I felt petulant.

"Well, you know, Edith," my mother said, as I recall rather sharply, "beyond saying that she was travelling on in Europe, you've scarcely mentioned her since you came home last summer. In fact, you've hardly said a word to either of us for months. Whatever interests you these days, it doesn't seem to be anything to do with your father or me."

It was true: shaming, but true; and now it was something that needed to be addressed because, shortly after Kitty wrote to me, a new plan began to form in my head.

It would not have been any easier for me, in my parents' view, to travel alone to Europe in 1939 than it had been the year before; unless I had a good reason. And whatever Kitty thought, they did not think Prague, full as it was of the German army, the best place for me to go. Did I have a good reason? Of course I did, but I had no intention of telling them. After all, I was over twenty-one. I did not have to tell them everything: did they tell me everything? I made a meeting with Kitty my ostensible goal, said we were meeting not in Prague but Munich where, as they well knew, the Peace had been signed. Perhaps I could bring her news of her grandparents; perhaps they might like to send Kitty something if she was planning to be abroad much longer. That pleased them. They agreed to my plan: they were glad that, though Kitty was not my mother's favourite of the young people who had once come to the house, I had not quite forgotten all my old friends. That note of recrimination was always, by then, in my mother's comments. All in all, they approved. I did not feel it necessary to say that then, with or without her — for I did not owe Kitty anything after the previous summer — I would go on to Berlin and meet Paul.

It was almost too easy; especially when I told them that William and his mother were also travelling in the summer, at the same period. I knew they would not have approved of my travelling with William alone. They liked him very well, and still nurtured hopes for a marriage which I knew to be out of the question. Yet, to travel alone with a young man would have been not simply unsuitable but also quite improper, while to have as chaperone an older lady — whose son, my colleague, would naturally offer me protection until I met my female friend — that was, in their eyes, an entirely different matter and quite in order. In any case, I found them particularly abstracted at that time, forever in conversations that ended as I came into the room. I suppose, as my mother said, I was too absorbed in myself to query it: still, they had always, after my childhood was over, been happier in company with each other than with me. Kitty's assurance that travel round Greater Germany was not only allowed, but actively encouraged by the government, allayed any residual fears.

So I set out. There were two more things I did not tell my

parents: one was that I had written to Paul, telling him to expect me in Berlin; the other that William's mother was travelling only as far as England, to her sister, so that when we changed at Crewe, she would no longer be with us. All in all, given how little they communicated to me, I thought it unnecessary to burden them with unnecessary information.

Shadow

What do I remember about my second visit to Germany? I remember, or think I remember, that an air of expectation hung still over Europe in the early summer of 1939; it seemed to me, though, that by the dog days of August a wary tension had entered, a sense of waiting for something, like the kind of dread there must be when animals head for shelter, or birds leave the sky, before a thunderstorm or an earthquake. That is how I remember it; yet, knowing the way memory imposes, superimposes, later impressions upon the first, I may simply think that now.

My impressions of the journey, I know, exist: they are now housed in that archival repository; safely, I hope and must trust. Travel accounts of the young do not differ so very much from one another: enthusiasm and naïveté, touching or irritating, seem to me their most usual characteristics. One thing, however, stood out, and my journal, I know, captured it: I saw Hitler himself. Face to face, I saw him, and it was after we left Zurich, and had arrived in Munich, where I was to meet Kitty. The Chief

City of the Movement: that was how Germany described it at the time and, as luck or fate or perhaps Providence had it, we were to be there for the very weekend in July designated for what was described as "The Day of German Art" — *Der Tag der Deutschen Kunst* — the great pageant of German culture.

William and I made our way to the hotel, glad of our reservation: but there were no hotels, and the written confirmation of our booking made no difference. All available rooms, we were informed, had been officially requisitioned for officials attending the celebration. No private parties were to be accommodated. All hotels in Munich, it seemed, were similarly full. If it had not been for the last-minute kindness, or afterthought, of the hotel receptionist, we would have been obliged, as William said, to sit on our suitcases or go. Perhaps it would have been better if we had. I don't know. The receptionist, an elderly man, must have taken pity on our youth, for he wrote down the name of a pension we might try. Perhaps, I said to William as we left, he thought we were a young couple in love for, by that stage, we had given up trying to ask for separate rooms. William said he thought not and, though he admitted it was an ungallant remark, added that he believed it might have been his allure rather than mine which had produced so unexpectedly helpful a result. Who knows? He may have been right; and it did make us laugh. In any case, we got our two rooms — the last, as the pension's concierge most dramatically informed us in all of Munich — and, finding ourselves safely billeted for the next two nights, set out to look about us.

It was a most beautiful city. I am no longer sure how much of it survived all that would shortly and, it seems with hindsight, inevitably happen. For all I know, it is all gone, for I never returned: yet, even now, I can see the

Frauenkirche, its near-Byzantine towers, its coppery onion domes; the tombstones in the outer wall; those cleverly hidden windows, so delighting the devil, they say, that in glee at the foolishness of the architect who had blocked out the light of heaven, he stamped his foot, leaving his print in the entrance hall; and the painting of the Virgin Mary, gathering beneath her sheltering cloak all the tiny figures of mankind, from the peasants to the Pope himself. I remember the Alte Pinakothek, room upon room of paintings by Van Dyck, and a self-portrait by Rubens, world-weary, one hand held beneath the light touch of Isabella Brant, his first wife, watching the world with her knowing eyes and her impossible hat. I remember the Town Hall, the mannered, elevated theatre of the Glockenspiel; I remember the Residenz.

Ah, the Residenz, palace of the Bavarian kings! It was indeed a palace, a child's Box of Delight, each room leading to greater, grander rooms, mirrored like Versailles, ceilinged like the Vatican, chandeliered and gilt-ornamented; and all of it still, miraculously, left just as if the kings and queens of Bavaria, in the blindness of their opulence, still lived and ruled.

I remember that when we came out into the sunshine, reduced to a kind of sated, over-indulged silence, we both instinctively stopped. Opposite us stood the Feldherrnhalle: this building boasted a plaque, a memorial, guarded by armed soldiers, to the memory of those who fell in the failed Putsch of 1923. We watched, fascinated, at the different reactions of those who passed. The loyal members of the party were not hard to identify: as they passed, they raised their arms in the straight-armed Nazi salute. Our entertainment lay in the observation of the different salutes: the SS officer with his swift, rigid arm; the absent-minded wave of the harassed office-worker or preoccupied businessman; the contortions required of women juggling prams or shopping baskets; the risky salute of the cyclist speeding towards a junction; and now and again — and I must say, this was where we watched most intently, but without laughter— the few who would walk past, grim-faced, with no salute. These few were watched, carefully, followed by the eyes, only the eyes, of the soldiers on duty; but behind them in the shade of a doorway, I could see another figure, a uniformed officer and, as one young man walked past, his thin, sallow face a sardonic mask, I saw the officer move out of the shadows, swiftly, silently, graceful as a dancer, and turn to follow him. I caught my breath: in those few elegant steps from stillness to movement, I could have sworn, for a second, just a second, that it was Paul.

Then, before I could do or say anything, we heard cries of *Heil, Heil*. A crowd seemed to be gathering, further down the street, moving, propelled like tumbleweed towards us, and as it approached some people turned and stood; others ran to the edge of the pavement; and the cries grew louder and mingled with the overriding sound of noisy engines, as three great open cars swept past us: and there, in the first, I saw Hitler himself.

I saw Hitler, a slight, hunched figure, declining to acknowledge in any way the increasingly hysterical greetings which must have been as deafening to him as to us; a pale, pale man, his hair darker, blacker than I imagined; and in that brief moment he seemed to me little more than a cowering misanthrope on the edge of his nerves.

The second car held Goering; and when he came into sight, the crowd laughed: whether with him, or at him, I do not know. To me, he appeared ridiculous, self-important in his over-decorated uniform, beaming like a fat, incongruously dangerous baby, bestowing upon all his great pleasure in himself. Yet, he was by no means the main attraction. That was Hitler, only Hitler, silent, white-faced. I remember his eyes, a startling blue; and, I remember that when a curious cyclist drew too close, it was a matter of seconds before the Black Guard on the running board blocked his view. No threat, no violence, and yet, watching it, I felt a momentary shiver, as though a shadow had fallen across the summer day.

Was it because of Hitler that I felt that? I do not know. I had a strange feeling, that feeling of someone walking over my grave; as if I were being watched; and as I write this, I feel it again, cold upon my skin. And then, a sudden shaft of sunlight blinded me: my eyes were drawn up to a window opposite, some floors above the shadowed doorway where the officer had slid out. I saw a hand on a hasp; I heard the soft sound of closure. No doubt, someone watching the parade had leaned back in, and shut the window. No doubt: yet in that moment, the sensation of cold fingers crawling on my skin, I imagined that in the glare of light I glimpsed Kitty's face. I knew it to be impossible, for Kitty's train was not due to arrive for another day. And yet, and yet.

William, surprised I suppose at the intensity of my grip, asked me what was wrong: I said I was feeling the heat. We went back to the pension, and I lay down. It was hot: I may even have had a touch of sunstroke, for walking back, hot and cold by turns, I looked at a man in a passing tram, his face intent on mine, and for a nonsensical second I could have sworn it was my father. I was sure I must be ill; but in the cool of the pension, I slept for a time, and when I woke I was a little better.

Later, William, gently knocking on my door, persuaded me to go out in the cool of the evening. We had a drink, and watched the guests arriving at the Chancellery, for the reception to be given in honour of the Führer. In the street, made suddenly darker by the chandeliered brilliance of the windows, taxi upon taxi gliding up, spilling out into the shadows the uniformed and the medalled, the glamorous and the glittering, I thought of the old Bavarian monarchs, their glory lost, like Ozymandias, King of Kings. We did not see Hitler again: perhaps he was among the shadows passing across the pale blinds, drawn in discretion against the prying of vulgar eyes; yet, having seen his tense and pallid littleness in that car, I could not see him drifting about a ballroom with a cocktail in his hand. In any case, I had no real wish to see him again. Those eyes ... The evening advanced, it grew cold, and we left.

The next day, the day of the pageant, it rained, pouring down in torrents. Did the great dictator mind that he, commander of a whole nation, could not control the weather for his pet project? Who knows? The fact remains, however, that despite the downpour all seventy of the tableaux — the history of over two thousand years of German art and culture — continued as planned. They were drenched, they were almost washed away, yet they continued, and no-one withdrew and — though they may have been miserable, and certainly looked it — no-one complained.

No, I did not see Hitler again. In fact, for the rest of my stay there, excepting William, I hardly saw anyone, apart from the guards on the train that took me out of Munich. For I did not meet Kitty, then or ever again, because a telegram, at least one day old, redirected through the same kindly receptionist from the hotel whose address I had given my parents, told me that my father was dead, and that I should make immediate arrangements to return home.

Waiting

He had been ill for quite some time, said my mother, with that weary patience reserved by the long-suffering for the thoughtless. She did not point out that I had failed to notice, but it was unnecessary: I knew I had failed to notice. I had been too self-absorbed to notice, and I knew, with a kind of despairing resignation, that there was probably nothing I could do or say, now or ever, to make that right. I could see a future for us, locked together, perhaps for years, in a bitter symbiosis, a tangle of unspoken recrimination; and I did not look forward to it.

We did not, however, settle into that unhappy state or not, at least, straight away. There are so many details and distractions surrounding a death that it took some time for us to realise that my father was gone, was not coming back, and that we were all there was of our family. In addition, there was all around us a gradually encroaching war. After the first shock of the declaration in September 1939, it took time to sink in, for us to understand that this could not be reversed any more than my father's death. In a way, the creeping annexation of most of Europe that began in 1939 and, especially, that strange time of limbo between my return in August 1939 and the devastation of April 1941 reminds me now, if not then, of the ruthless disease that had so inexorably claimed my father while I chose to look away. Clothes and books, books and clothes: all had to be burned, all up in flames. Tuberculosis, our doctor said, demanded it; and we did what was required. Yet, even as we did, we looked away.

It is also true that I chose to look away from the war. How could I do otherwise? Nobody I knew was taking it at all seriously. Nobody thought we would be attacked, or were worth attacking. England's war, I heard time and again, not ours: London would be the target, not us. It was strangely comforting, since the man I loved, not seen now for over a year, was in this war that could not, surely, be seen as our war. The man I loved was in the uniform of a nation which I must, if I thought about it, see as the enemy. How could I see Paul as the enemy?

I looked every day for letters, but no letters came. I did not worry unduly. Everyone's letters were delayed at the beginning of the war; it was a major grumbling point and, indeed, so advanced was my ability to ignore the unpalatable that I persuaded myself that silence brought hope. He was busy, I told myself, never thinking what he might be busy doing; or, he was a prisoner and, again, I decided not to think about whose prisoner he might be; or else, he had detached himself entirely from the war which, as he would then be a deserter and likely to be shot as a traitor by either side, could not be contemplated. It could not, any more than the other question, deeply and unpleasantly lodged in my mind: could I love a man involved in any of the darker manifestations of these behaviours? Questions which cannot be answered are best left aside, until such time as an answer presents itself. I have always believed that. I believe it still.

What I could do, apart from earning my living as a teacher, was to read and to try to write. Encouraging children to read, seeing the moment when they begin to fly by themselves, makes one think about the great gift that reading is, the very key to independent happiness; and teaching them to write makes one long to write. I was reading poetry with them, hoping to give them even a glimpse of what we had just lost through the death of Yeats, some sense that they must be the makers of beauty in the unknown world to come. Then it came to me: though I loved poetry, though I had grieved at the death of Yeats, I was myself no poet; but since I was telling them stories, why not write some for them myself? It was a wonderful time for Irish short stories and novels, and specially, it seemed to me, for the Irish novel. I remember reading *At Swim Two Birds*, delighting in its joyous anarchy, losing myself with Shorty and his unexpected band of cattle rustlers from Ringsend; and, closer to home, I felt in my bones the heartbreak and tortured beauty of Michael McLaverty's first novel, *Call My Brother Back*. I already knew his short stories; we took the *Irish Monthly* and the *Irish Rosary* and the *Capuchin Annual*, and they kept *Modern Reading* in the municipal library — and one story, "Pigeons", which I had read first there when I was, I suppose, about twenty or twenty-one, touched me deeply. I could see the delicacy with which, melded with another early story, "Leavetaking", it grew into his first novel, *Call My Brother Back*.

I so admired his skill. Because I was trying to write, I knew how different a discipline the short story was from the novel; and I knew that it was almost impossible to let a short story become a novel. Yet, he had done it. I wanted to know him, to learn from him. I could say I knew him a little at that time, by which I mean I saw him, on occasion. He, too, was a teacher, in a school near one where I had my longest temporary post; and sometimes I would see him on the bus, a quiet, contained man, not tall, quite spare and always, glimpsed from afar, seeming to inhabit his own world far away from this one. His stories examined, with compassion and a lyrical tenderness the days and the ways of the dispossessed, of children and the old, men or women, uprooted from their homes on an island, or the fields they loved, almost inevitably condemned to exile somewhere they did not want to be, often this very city where I lived. I saw it all through his eyes, through his restrained and exquisite prose; and more than anyone alive at that time, he made me want to work at writing, to make writing work.

Yet, what was I to write about? My father's death? I could not. The war? Again, for all the reasons I have listed, I could not. Paul. Why did I not write about Paul? I do not know. I tried. I did try. I tried and failed, and the more I tried to reach him in words, the further away he went, drifting into a mist that was like a nightmare. Would his letters not help? They did not. Already, they belonged to a different time, when his homeland, his *Heimat*, could have been, indeed I thought was going to be, my homeland too. No more of that; I could not take those thoughts any further.

I thought instead of all my reading, of Wordsworth and Jane Austen and our own Maria Edgeworth who lived through wars and revolutions, who knew exactly what wars did to families and friends, waiting for news at home; yet, they managed to write about the things they knew, and find in them, what Coleridge — was it Coleridge? — termed an objective correlative. What did I know? I knew my town. I knew some of the countryside about me.

So, I sketched out short articles about forgotten and ancient places, monuments and villages, once belonging to our surrounding hills and lakes, and now subsumed into the city, just as Michael McLaverty's people and places were gradually subsumed. When I was satisfied with them, I sent them to two of our best-known newspapers: and they published them, and they paid me.

I cannot describe what that was like, to see my work in print, and to receive payment for it, unless to say it was joy. It was true joy, deep as love; and I found that as long as I was writing of subjects I considered safe, in which I felt safe, then I was not thinking painfully. Pain, like a dangerous wild animal, had to be kept at bay; and those articles kept it all well at bay.

Now, at this distance, I can hardly say whether my writing was good or bad: it was certainly of its time for, whatever I thought or did not think, I had the basic good sense to appear cheerfully optimistic and self-deprecatingly patriotic. This was not easy. All about me, among my friends, out shopping, at the cinema or the theatre, life at first went on as if there were no war. There was little of the jingoistic fervour, the frenzy of self-deprivation celebrated in newsreels and newspapers from across the water. Here, there was rather an apathy bordering on resentment at shortages, then rationing of food, the introduction of clothing coupons and, especially, the tiresome blackout requirements. They were indeed tiresome: it took at least ten minutes every night to fix the blackout curtains to the windows, without the benefit of any light to see what I was doing; and to remember to switch off the hall light before opening the door for any reason; and to remember not to carry any lights anywhere near a window, even in the event of an air-raid or, indeed, especially in an air-raid. I cannot describe the depressive effect of the ban on opening the blinds in the early morning, except to say that there was not the chance to enjoy even the faintest rays of dawn. And always, I had my mother at my elbow, querying the necessity for such elaborate precautions for, as she rightly put it, it had not worked too well in England, and if they could find a blacked-out English town, what difficulty would they have finding us, when three quarters of the island was lit up like a Christmas tree?

My mother had become something of a trial. There was no more singing in the house. She never went out. She would not have anyone in. My father gone, she withdrew. Was I any help? Probably not: I daresay a psychiatrist would say I was angry; yet, after all, as I believe I may have pointed out, I had something to be angry about. My parents had chosen, both of them, to exclude me from the knowledge that my father was dying, from the chance to spend with my parents our last months together as a family. Yet, knowing those were indeed his last months, my mother thought it perfectly acceptable to blame me for that exclusion. Yes, I daresay I was angry.

What better dissipation for this suppressed fury than fantasy tales where everything could be overcome by magic, or by the intervention of a deus ex machina conveniently distant in an unnamed past; or in an anthropomorphic animal kingdom? I was thinking of the kind explored by Carroll or Grahame – both troubled men in their own ways — where order might be achieved through a fairly draconian regime, thinly disguised beneath a veil of gentle humour, and the spoken or unspoken promise of better days to come. I wrote for children, those unredeemed little savages who know the meaning of impotent rage so much more closely than we who, calling ourselves rational adults, claim to understand and rule their world.

In this way, despite the business of the war, life appeared to go on much as before: except that, my father gone, my mother withdrawn, and no letters from Paul, I had little hope of anything getting better. Yet, I must say, like most people, I never thought it would get worse, until May 1940 and the fall of France. Even then, it took William to explain to me the very real danger of what was happening or about to happen.

Though William's anxiety seemed lessened by the fact that Robert had made it safely as far as Coventry, he still felt strongly that he had to, as he put it, do his bit; even more now that Robert was, so to speak, directly in the firing line. He was, as it turned out, directly in it. Coventry was bombed in November 1940, and Robert was killed, after which a change came over William. Pronounced unfit to join up — his sight, damaged by measles in childhood, let him down — he insisted on volunteering as an Air Raid Protection Warden. In that thankless position he saw, and gradually told me, not only the resentment and bitter hostility he frequently encountered, but also the frightening inadequacy of our preparations in case of attack. There were rumours, he said, of an overheard wireless broadcast in which the Germans had threatened to reduce Belfast to a ploughed field, because the North had not joined with the Irish government in declaring neutrality. He had heard — though, again, it might have been rumour — that fire-fighting equipment, recommended as essential by the Home Office, had been returned to London, since our government chose to maintain the position that we were unlikely to be a target. William said, from what he could see of what we had, we were far from ready if something were really to happen.

In April 1941, of course, it did, and everything changed. Not at first: few people, my mother and myself included, took the first air-raid warning of September 1940 all that seriously: after all, we were doing what they had told us to do. The noise was terrific, an ominous wail, building to a screech and only after a long, long, ear-splitting time, gradually subsiding to a moan, before dying away on the wind.

It was the fact of its dying away, I do still think, that led us to feel more secure than we should have: I would see it again forty years later, when we had bombs and bomb scares all over the town. By the early 1970s, it was almost a matter of pride or bravado to stay put, not to fuss, to laugh to scorn those who dived for cover. We were veterans, we thought. And before the Blitz, we were every bit as insouciant, as hubristic: I can remember sitting quite unmoved through one air raid warning, because I was enjoying my book, and thinking I would move when I heard it land which I felt, of course, it never would. Air raids were something that happened over there, in England. Those poor people, we said, and on we went. Yet, even here, in this city, I read and heard of evacuees in the summer — women and children — returning, voluntarily, to their homes. Some people even refused to carry gas masks. We were like sleepwalkers. There were probably twenty false alarms and at least four red alerts between October 1940 and the spring of 1941, but that was all. Why would we get excited when, really, nothing was happening?

And then, on the night of the 7th of April 1941, it came: on London, Glasgow, Bristol, Liverpool, Great Yarmouth — and the Belfast Docks, our Docks. I heard it begin, in my bed, just as I was drifting into sleep — bumps, thuds, and a loud, loud, bang.

It went on till well after three, the sky so eerily lit up. Then at half past three, when it seemed it had almost ended, one last act before leaving: a bomber swinging over the lough, swept in and sent down a parachute bomb. Hovering dreamlike, elegant, almost tantalizing, drifting here and there, as if making up its mind, it found its landing on the roof of our massive shipyard, Harland and Wolff itself, famous or notorious for having built thirty years before the great and doomed *Titanic*. Acres of shipyard, all destroyed by the explosion and the fire that followed.

It was four in the morning before the all-clear was sounded. I heard it all, lying in my bed, unable to believe, or frozen by fear: I will never know which. My mother did not wake at all. I can see the headline from the evening paper next day: "**Ulster at Close Quarters with War: North's First Blitz: Night of Thrills.**"

For us, who lived through it, the only thrills we felt were of fear. And then to read that we were now on the front line, just like the rest of the United Kingdom, and that we would not have it otherwise? I could have named quite a number, myself and my mother and William included, who would gladly have had it otherwise. All that such reports did, with their assurances that there was a great plan and that all would yet be well, was to prolong our false and foolish sense of security.

I know there were heroes. William was one, staying at his post in order to evacuate people, even when the windows were blown out, the ceiling was coming down and he knew there was in the building a great and potentially lethal petrol tank. Would he have done that if Robert had not died? He might have: I think he would have. William was like that, and he was not alone. Two men he knew, voluntary fire-fighters, died that night trying to deal with the blaze. Another was badly hit by shrapnel, but kept on with his work. Yet, the next morning, when I was passing through town on my way to school, my main impression was that, though everyone was talking about what had happened, everyone trying to out-do someone else in experience of the terror, it seemed, apart from unusually long lines at bus-stops and the railway stations, that everything was oddly normal.

Most people, myself included, changed nothing in our habits. We called it stoicism, I suppose; the newspapers boldly blazoning **"We Can Take It"** must have affected us all more than we knew; and our united indignation at Lord Haw-Haw, taunting us on the wireless with his promise of *"Easter Eggs for Belfast"*, seemed to stiffen our resolve. Those who predicted grimly that we were bound to be attacked again were simply dismissed. We acted as though we had been somehow immunised, blooded, as if we had proved ourselves beyond hope of any further attack. It is a fact that when, scarcely a week later, another alert sounded, neither I nor anyone I knew paid it much attention. And even though, on that Good Friday, my mother and I, on our way home from the ceremonies, actually saw and heard an aeroplane fly so low that we had to duck our heads, we thought little of it; and even though, walking to the cemetery in the early afternoon of Easter Monday, we heard the sirens go, and saw aeroplanes in the sky, we just waited for the all-clear. We did not ask ourselves what the aeroplanes were doing. The next day, Easter Tuesday, the 15th of April, we found out.

Easter Tuesday

It has struck me from time to time how often extraordinary events happen on days that begin as ordinary. Today, for example, is a glorious day: I have just heard, to my joy, that Seamus Heaney, that gifted, thoughtful young poet I first saw thirty years ago, has won the Nobel Prize. Hope and history, as he has taught us to believe, may yet rhyme.

Easter Tuesday 1941, however, was far from glorious, quite the reverse. Yet it, too, started out as a pleasantly ordinary day: not that Easter Tuesday is ever really ordinary. After the long fast and ritual sadness of Lent, it almost never fails, even when it is unseasonably wet or cold, to lift my spirits. Easter Sunday, Monday, Tuesday — I think of primroses, and violets, the birds busily building and calling to their mates, I smell damp earth, and in the mornings am wakened by the dawning light of spring, and I know the winter is at an end.

So, despite the blackout, despite the anxiety, it seemed on Easter Tuesday that better times were coming. The day was fine, fine enough for a trip to Bellevue Zoo, up on the slopes of the mountain, overlooking the lough. We shared that idea with everybody else, it seemed, but I did not mind. I thought we had seen the worst of winter and the worst of the enemy onslaught for, by then, like most people, I had come to think of Germany (though never Paul) as the enemy. I thought an outing would lift my mother's spirits, and to make sure it did, to make sure she would sleep that night, I even arranged that we would go out that evening, to hear the popular singer Delia Murphy in the Ulster Hall. I don't say my mother entered into these plans with any enthusiasm, especially after she became convinced she heard the drone of aeroplanes when we were at the zoo. She might have done: it did happen, but it meant so little by then. We had had our go: they would not be back. She agreed in the end, but only because I told her that William, who was not on duty that day or night, was to accompany us.

It is quite remarkable what one strategic telephone call from a public box can do. "That nice young man," she said, watching him arrive to collect us at the entrance to the zoo, and following it, not exactly to my surprise, with: "I should like to see you settled in your own home." She did not add, and did not need to, that she might also like to see herself settled in my own home, and have no more worries about rates and pipes and meters and shortages and ration books. My mother wanted me — with a nice young man — to take over where my father had left off. William she saw as that man, and it never occurred to her that marriage to me was the last thing on his mind.

She was simply taken by him, by his quiet voice, his interest in music — popular as well as classical, for William was no snob, she said; just like Daddy in so many ways, she said; and she loved the way he squired her round, handed her in and out of his car, pulled out her chair for her when we went for tea. His idea, his Easter treat, he said, as he led us into one of the teashops she liked. Was it the Bonne Bouche, or the Abercorn? I can hardly remember. She was devoted to both, as much, I think, for the memories they evoked of her life with my father as for the sense, especially when William came with us, of attentive company so lacking since his death. I knew I was no substitute. William listened to her with his usual quiet patience, commenting when required on her opinions. He was, in every way, she said, the perfect man. It was not untrue. He just was not the man I loved; or loved in the way she wanted to see. I wonder what would have happened if I had said to her, across that snowy tablecloth, across the plate of scones, and the large, hot pot of tea, and the Indian Tree cup and saucer she was holding to her lips: "How would it be, Mother if, instead of this perfect young man, you were sitting here with an enemy soldier? How would that be?" I did not say it. I am perfectly sure I did not even think it at the time. I would never have said it, certainly not after the one instance when I had brought up Paul's name, tentatively, not long after I had come back from Europe the first time. I should not have done it. I hardly know why I did, unless it was that longing, that sometimes overwhelming need, to speak the name of the loved one. "I wonder," I said, "if you remember Paul Herrold? He was in the hospital and we were sent to visit him, Kitty and I." She looked blank. I prompted her: "A teacher on holiday here?" She shook her head, a puzzled frown on her face: really, her memory had gone shockingly after my father died. Then her face cleared, but not pleasantly. "Oh, yes," she said, with distaste. "You mean the German." Even then, I did not give up: not yet. "But you and Daddy liked him," I said, "didn't you?" She shrugged. "*He* did," she said, "but he was forever picking up strays. And I don't like the Germans. Look what they did to my brother." Well, yes, there was Patrick, by now so far gone in his own nightmare that he did not know any of us, sitting ghostly in his hospital chair, prisoner of his unremitting past. It was not Paul's fault, but there was clearly no point. I didn't pursue it any further, then or ever again. So, if she wanted to think I was on the point of saving my coupons, booking the organist or ordering the orange-blossom, she could. And, though we never discussed it, I am inclined to think William did the same with his mother. All in all, it suited everyone.

The concert, which was more of a *ceilidh*, was well under way when we heard the sound. That sound. The unmistakable sound of an aeroplane low, low, as if it was just above the roof; then the *ploof* and the whine and the shriek and a sickening, dizzying thud as the building shifted and shuddered about us. A gasp, like a wave, like air sucked out of a bag, swept through the hall. Seats were scraped back, people exclaimed; but Delia Murphy was nothing if not a trouper. She remained calm, calm with all the polish of the seasoned performer. "Stay in your seats," she said. "You'll be safer here." She was right. She was later commended for her courage and command of the situation and even when, eventually, we managed to leave, she was still settling everyone into some kind of anxious calm. I wish we could have stayed all night, like the rest of them; but my mother simply would not settle, and William, realising it, somehow managed to get us out, unchecked. Was it madness to do it? Probably, for the first thing we saw was that the town, like a film set, was bathed in light, a pitiless white light, like those horrid strip-lighting things they used to put in kitchens. They still have them in here. I can hear, as I write this, the noise, the drone, a moment of terrible silence; then the shrieking and the dreadful thud and the boom that filled the air, reverberating all about us. I longed to go back in, but I knew we could not. The door behind us was fast shut.

"Take us home, William," my mother was begging, through tears. "Please take us home."

William's face was white as he led us round the corner to his car which, thank God, was still there, mercifully left intact. I thought of that, too, thirty years later, when a parked car in a lonely street was an immediate signal to run, as fast as your legs would take you.

William put my mother in the front seat, and we began to drive through that eerily lurid light. Sitting in a tin box, a target — what were we doing? Years later, not that long ago, I read that one of the fighter pilots, charged with the task of exploding his bomb over the Falls Road that night, looked down and saw the life-size *Pietà* outside St Paul's Parish Church, minutes from the Monastery. He was Catholic, and his heart failed him; he swung away, discharging his bomb into Belfast Lough.

And out of nowhere, I remembered my mother's unkind remark about strays, and I thought of Paul. He wrote to me once that he could imagine flying over the city, seeing St Paul's and the *Pietà*. What if he was in one of those aeroplanes, now, looking down at us? No, he was not a pilot: a moment's relief. Then, what if he was one of the people who planned this? What if he had gone one day, in a patriotic spirit, having wrestled with his conscience, having overcome a sentimental attachment to a place and people he had known for, really, such a short time; and what if he had said to his superiors: "I've been to that town. I know it; I know where you should hit." What if this was the reason I had heard nothing, nothing since July. What if Paul truly was the enemy?

I could not allow the thought: quiet, deadly, like the

parachutes the enemy sent, drifting like daydreams through the air, hovering gently, mesmerising us all below, softly floating to land, then blowing our lives apart. I could not allow that thought. I did not.

"Edith, did you hear what I said?"

I had not heard what William was saying.

"Sorry," I said. "What?"

"I need you to listen now," he said, and his voice was urgent, peremptory, as I had never heard it. "I can't take you home. I can't take the chance. I'm going to go up here towards the Falls Road. There doesn't seem to be as much happening on that side: it's mainly over in the east as far as I can see."

"But our house is not so far," I said. "Surely you can get us there?"

"I don't know what's happening there," he said. "Let's think. Where is there nearby that might be safe? Would the school be open? The convent?"

"Try the Monastery," I said, thinking as fast as I could. "It has a crypt."

"The Monastery, yes, good," said William. "We'll go there."

We drove through nervous streets, the horrible quiet punctuated by explosions, the blessed protective darkness of night shattered by that pitiless searching light. Then, at last, we saw the welcome spires of the Monastery, stretching calmly into that jagged sky.

To our astonishment, as we drove in, we could hear voices in the priests' garden. William pounded with his fists on the door, and an elderly priest opened to him, in mild surprise.

'Father, what are you doing?" demanded William, loudly, much more loudly than I had ever heard him speak. "Why are you not indoors?"

"We were watching it," said the priest. He spoke quietly,

with the calm assurance that only faith, pure, enviable faith, can bring.

"Stop watching it," said William, curtly. "I'm a warden, and I'm telling you to get indoors now."

The old priest — I could see now that he was quite old, though quick of foot — bowed his head in agreement, and brought us swiftly through the garden, where we could see five or six other men standing in equal stillness, as though in prayer. William, so uncharacteristically brusque, gave them the same terse message, and then we were swiftly ushered into the cold darkness of the crypt, where the dead of the Monastery's community lay in readiness for their maker. As we were possibly on the point of meeting Him too, it seemed suddenly not only restful, but appropriate to be there.

Settling my mother on a bench, I turned to say this to William, and saw that he was not there.

"Father," I said to the priest who had let us in, "where is our friend?"

"Did you not see?" he said. "He has gone out to do his work. He said goodbye. Did you not hear?"

"No," I said, and I was overcome with a sudden and terrible misery. William, my dear William, had gone out into the firestorm and I had neither seen nor heard him go. I had not so much as wished him God speed.

"We'll pray now," said the old priest, "for those who may die tonight."

It was said so simply, and with such sincerity, that I felt I heard the words for the first time. I knelt, and my mother bowed her head, and we prayed the prayers for the dying, for the dead, that the angels might receive their souls and present them to God the Most High. Then the Rosary, and the "Memorare". Never was it known, we reminded the Mother of God, that anyone who fled to her protection, implored her help or sought her intercession, was left unaided. And, in that quiet place, that sanctuary, we were kept safe all through the long and terrible night of bombs and fires and mass murder, all through the hours of darkness when places we knew tumbled into rubble, and people we knew and people we did not gasped and died in flames and scorching smoke.

When at last dawn broke, the sky, dully laden, was no sky of spring. The grey dust of destruction catching in our nostrils and our throats, we made our way slowly, very slowly down the long street from the Monastery. I remember the incongruity of the April morning. Where we should have rejoiced in the sound of the birds, the sight of the buds on the trees lining the street, we walked instead through a pall, of silence, of smoke, of suspense.

Crowds of people trailed up the hill towards us: I thought they must be in search of the sanctuary we had found. My mother shook her head: they were going to early Mass, she said. It was just before six. Yet, among them, there were those who must have sought refuge. They carried belongings, suitcases some, some bundles terrifyingly small, which could have been clothes, or could have been a child too still too move: and beside them trailed dusty, bewildered children. I saw one small boy carrying a cage, with a little bird peeping out through its bars inside it. As we passed, I saw that one of its wings was stripped to the bone, all its feathers blown away in the blast: still, it hopped from one foot to the other, its bright eyes merry and, as I passed, it cheeped, because it was alive.

We trailed on, through a landscape of nightmare, through a town we hardly recognised, torn buildings and shattered people, aghast at what had happened. When we reached our home, we found it miraculously spared, except that by some freak of the wind, its east-facing windows —

our bedrooms — had been blown out, or in. Looking at the eyeless wall, it came to me with detachment, as in a dream, that if we had indeed persuaded William to bring us home, we would certainly have been killed by that force. My mother fainted at the sight. I could hardly get her inside, hardly knew how to see to her, how to deal with this, where to begin. Our bedrooms were covered in grey sticky dirt and dust, and our bedclothes slashed and torn with shattered glass. I could not think. I did not know how to think, did not know where to turn; and then I thought again of William, who must surely by now be home, even if he had been working all night. But William did not appear that day, that night, or next morning.

Yet, we hardly remarked his absence. The shock and confusion of all that had happened seemed to numb us, so that all rational thought stopped. We did not know if we had been invaded, whether it was safe to go out on the street, or what would happen next. What was clear was that the town, the whole place, was completely taken by surprise.

How could we all have been so blind to the danger? I think back to that Easter Tuesday, and I see us, foolishly standing gazing at the zoo animals, my mother admiring the proud lionesses with their little cubs, even as the aeroplanes gathered above us, ready to strike. Later, I heard that they had to shoot many of the animals in the zoo, including the glorious lionesses, and their enchanting cubs, because the people who lived nearby were afraid they might get loose. I never told my mother that.

Among the people who lived near the zoo, of course, were Kitty's grandparents, in their handsome house above the lough. They had to accept, after the first raid on the 7th of April, that their house was vulnerable and agreed, after much exasperated persuasion from their ARP warden, that they would go to a shelter if there should be another attack — persuasion would have been necessary, for no-one wanted to go to the shelters. They were poorly constructed, and all too likely to be used for purposes for which they had not been designed, with the consequence that they contained and smelled of all manner of waste, and were avoided by anyone who could find an alternative. In those days of confusion and false hope, however, it had begun to dawn on those who were near the coast, the port, the airfields, the big factories — anywhere that could in any way be seen as an enemy target — that they were at serious risk. Kitty's grandparents, it emerged, were among those who were finally persuaded, when the sirens went that Easter Tuesday of the second raid, to take refuge in a nearby shelter. By an irony of fate, it was the one air-raid shelter to receive a direct hit that night, killing all those inside; by another, their lovely house was hardly touched. One window, the stained glass Kitty's grandfather had himself so lovingly designed, was destroyed, but the empty house, where they might have survived, remained almost intact.

The way we found out about this I will not forget. When we got home the morning after the raid, there was so much to do: so much clearing, not just the house but the debris in the garden. So, I was out there, unslept, in a daze, trying to make sense of it all, trying to keep my mother calm and keep her inside the house out of danger. I had just straightened up — where all the stuff that had landed in our garden came from I will never know — when I saw an ARP Warden on his rounds. For a second, one joyful second, I thought it was William. Then the man turned round, and I saw it was not; but I recognised him as one of William's colleagues. So, I stopped him and asked him about William.

"Haven't seen him," he said. He sounded exhausted.

"You weren't on duty with him last night?"

He shook his head. His face was grimy with dust and sweat.

"I was over near the Lough," he said. "All those houses overlooking it. I had to get the people out, and they didn't want to go. An old couple, they were the worst: great big house with a huge stained-glass window. Talk about a target." He shook his head. "Well, I got them all to go to the shelter in the end. But the shelter was hit. No survivors."

I knew who lived in that house, and it's not that I wasn't sorry, but I was beginning to be afraid, and not for Kitty's family.

"And William?"

He shook his head again.

"You've no idea?" I said. "Can you not tell me where he might be?"

That is when he said it.

"Go to one of the places they're laying them out," he said.

"What?" I said, not quite comprehending.

"For identification," he added, then, slowly. "The dead."

This time I know I stared.

"Go to the Markets," he said, not unkindly. "Or the Swimming Baths. Start there."

I could scarcely take it in. It was impossible. I asked if he would come with me, He shook his head again. "I have enough to do," he said. He did not quite say 'Let the dead bury their dead'. I could not be angry, watching the weariness of him as he trudged about the broken streets, trying to convey to people who could not hear him that the danger was not over, indeed might not yet really have begun.

I did not know whether to start at the Markets or the Baths, but the Baths being nearer to where we had been that night, I started there. I told myself, and I told my mother, I was looking for Kitty's grandparents, but I wasn't. I didn't really believe the ARP Warden: I still thought William might appear. After all, if his colleague had been busy, was still busy, too busy to go and look for him among the dead, might not William be just as busy? So, I asked our neighbour to look after my mother for a few hours, set out and made my way across the town, refusing to think that William could be dead and refusing to think at all of Paul, or the fact that it was his countrymen who had devastated our city.

I arrived at about noon, and I saw the hearses. They were still unloading: coffin after coffin after coffin, laid out at the side of the Baths, the lids removed for identification. I see it still. There were two children brought in together: she in a little Communion dress, worn in proud celebration of Easter, her pinched little face as white as the ragged dress: he, the young boy, in what must once have been a grey suit with short trousers. A blue silk ribbon lay askew in his lapel, and his dark hair had tumbled over his forehead; yet his small, dusty face seemed unmarked, almost serene; and entirely dead. I saw faces frozen in an agony of surprise; a mother and baby, locked together in death; I saw, as in a butcher's shop, or an abattoir, disembodied limbs — arms, legs, even trunks — delivered in grim parcels, then piled on planks beneath a sheet.

Still, I did not find William; still, I could not leave. I was sure he must come here; he could surely not have got far enough away that night to be brought anywhere else. I waited a while longer as more and more bodies were unloaded; listened for the sounds of the ambulances, stood outside while more and more vehicles came — coal lorries, bin lorries, every kind of conveyance — piled high with bodies. They drained the pool. They began to load them up:

the stench now compounded with the smell of the pool's chemicals in the eyes and the nostrils of all of us standing helpless, disbelieving the terrible sight of the pit that was the empty pool, filling up with these poor unclaimed dead. All these years ago, but it stays with me still: the look and the odour of death. In the night, sometimes, I see those green-grey faces, shocked unto death.

Eventually, I do not know after how long, I made myself leave. I could not in conscience leave my mother much longer to my neighbour, who was every bit as busy as we were with debris, so I made my way down towards the horrible hush and dust of the town. I was nearly there when I saw and heard a loud commotion; in the remains of a house at one of the corners, clearly hit in the night, they were trying to dig while keeping the crowds at bay. What is it about a scene of disaster that attracts the human in spite of himself? I was no gawper or gawker; yet, here I was, elbowing my way to get to the front, knowing it was not even safe to be there, yet drawn by some irresistible desire, a need, to know what was going on.

They were digging, someone said, because they could hear faint cries; someone must still be in there. My heart leapt: it was still near enough to the Monastery; it could be William. It could have been anybody, but it could be William. In a matter of seconds my mind and my heart and my whole hope had decided it must be William, that it was William, and I stood rooted as they dug, even as they tried to move us back, for the upper storeys, they said, were not safe, and ominous gratings and creakings threatened a fall of some kind. No-one moved: we stood, a solid wall of curiosity and hope; and then one of the men called out, the digging got faster. Then the men threw aside their spades, and began to scrabble with their hands, raising clouds of dust that choked the air, and still we did not move. When one cried that there was somebody, maybe two people, and the rubble and a huge beam was shifted, I became utterly immobile; and when they shouted that someone was alive, my heart turned over; when I saw, as clear as day, an arm lift as if in greeting, I thought my heart would leap from my chest. I gripped the arm of the person next to me, and she did not flinch. "God send," she said, "God send they're alive, whoever they are!" I could not reply. All my energy, all my spirit poured into one silent prayer: that it be William, alive.

A stretcher was brought; and the person buried was lifted from the debris and eased gently, with tender painstaking care, onto the canvas; and as he was carried past us, I saw that he was alive, though badly injured; and I saw that he was not William. Head hanging, stunned by the shock of this realisation I did not, at first, notice the shifting interest of the crowd around me, or see the second stretcher until it went past me. This, covered with a blanket, was clearly a corpse; but as it passed the poor dead arm dropped over the side of the stretcher, like a hand flung out for help.

Then I knew. I knew the signet ring, and its intertwined initials; I knew, though its face was smashed and broken, the watch that had never lost a second, more reliable than Big Ben; I knew the tweed jacket as well as I knew the coat I was wearing myself; and though I do not know how I did it, or when I moved from my frozen position, I found myself beside the stretcher, holding the broken hand, and telling the exhausted men who carried that stretcher that they need not take this corpse for identification. There was no need, I said: I knew who it was.

A House in County Down

My mother grew increasingly nervous, especially after William's death, and the trauma of the funeral. With the confusion, the uncertainty and the anxiety about her, I scarcely knew where to turn. If it had not been for William's mother, his poor mother, I do not know what we would have done. I had met Mrs Hamilton, of course, with William; but it was through our common grief at his death that we became thoroughly acquainted.

There was the house, she told us, in County Down, where she had always taken William for the holidays when he was a child. Poor Mrs Hamilton, her only child dead; of course she had to think about something else; and the something else was the house. He loved it, she said. I had never known that: there was so much, it seemed, I did not know about William. Yet, what was she to do about the house, she asked, over and over, wringing her hands. He had planned to take her there, to get her out of the town. How could she now go alone, knowing he would never come, knowing she could not manage on her own?

195

I took a decision. "We will go with you," I said. "We will go with you, and settle you."

She breathed out a sigh. "And you'll stay with me," she said. It was a statement, not a request. "You and your dear mother will stay with me."

My mother then, to my surprise, answered firmly and at once. "We will," she said, "for our children's sakes."

"Yes," said William's mother. "After all ..."

She did not finish, but I guessed what she was about to say. The two mothers, still believing like everyone else that William and I were on the brink of engagement, had decided that it was the war, the cruel war, which had held everything up. Any slight difference in religious background they had set aside: hadn't William's parents made a good marriage in spite of it? And after all, they said, had we not all gone through the Blitz together, and made common cause? Surely there could never again be any question of sectarian bitterness between Catholic and Protestant. Ah, the wisdom — or the innocence — of the elders. Let me set down here, now, where no more subterfuge is necessary or desirable, that their delusion suited me admirably. I do not mean that I did not grieve for William, for I did, and I do. He was the best man, after my father, I ever knew. I would have loved to be in love with him, to be able to marry him, and my life would have been quite different: that I knew, and know still. I know also that it could never have been. Unlike the two mothers, I had no illusions about the depth of sectarian distrust in our society. That alone, I was certain, would have made it impossible for us to live here as man and wife; and I also knew he was, in his heart, no more free than I. For I was not, and never would be free. Was I glad? Not especially. Love, I already knew, is no respecter of persons: it strikes, and it leaves one stricken; and it is more often cruel than kind. "*I've known a hundred kinds of love,"* Emily Brontë once wrote. *"All made the loved one rue."*

What was to be done? Getting on with living was all that could be done, so we packed up what we could, joined the exodus from the town and took ourselves to County Down. Crowded station, crowded trains, no room to move, confusion and chaos, the train itself apparently uncertain of its destination until the last moment. We piled on into a carriage, surrounded by screaming children and mothers fussing and livestock in cages and cats in baskets and bewildered dogs on leads; and bundles and cases and coats like obstacles everywhere we tried to find somewhere to lean. There was no question of finding somewhere to sit. We clambered on, and we spilled out at the other end, and it was not until we had found ourselves in the blessed quiet of the Hamiltons' little house near the shore that some sense of normality returned.

There, miraculously, even in the chaos of arrival, we found there was peace. Water lapped quietly on the shingle behind the hedge, birds sang in the delicate green of the trees. Here, still, there were quiet April mornings; and on our first night, damp sheets warmed with stone jars, and the tomb-like cold dispelled by a spitting, crackling fire. We slept through until morning in a peace we had forgotten could exist.

I had to travel the thirty-five miles back up to the town, next day, to get to school, which meant leaving my mother and Mrs Hamilton together. I really did not mind doing the journey in reverse, even with unexpected halts and unreliable timetables; this time, I had space to move in the carriage, and the blessed freedom of solitude. I don't remember any more how long it took, or how long it should have taken: for that little time I was liberated, freed of time and its constraints. It was not until we approached the city, and the pall of it, the stifling smell of death which hung still over the streets, enveloped me, that the weight of fear returned. I went to the school and, in class after class, only half were there. Their bleared, confused faces, their fatigued eyes and their lack of books or papers and, above all, their inability to think, called into question the wisdom of their being there at all. Some of our girls travelled in from the comfortable suburbs and beyond; some were children of the inner city; whatever their background, many could not come back, some because they were so stunned by the attacks, some because they were among the dead. There were children no-one could answer for, children no-one would ever be able to answer for, lying buried or unidentified or orphaned in the hospitals, or the Baths that had become the morgue. What was the point of reading with them or to them the tales of long ago, or gentle stories to reassure them that the world was a good and just place, or of trying to teach them about the morality of right behaviour, when all about them they saw nothing but destruction and the slaughter of the innocents, like themselves?

Some of these children had nowhere to sleep at night: even if their houses had survived, their families were too afraid to stay. For the Germans did come back a third time, on the 4th of May 1941, bringing another night of terror. Still, they would not go to the dirty, flimsy shelters. They preferred, it seemed, to take their chance outdoors. Each evening they would troop, as one of them told me, "up the road", to sleep in the fields, or the park, or even, God help them, under hedges in a ditch. Night after night. I saw them myself, in the evenings, lines and lines of them, like those I saw that morning trailing up the hill to the Monastery, where still some would go for sanctuary; their tired determination, their silent endurance, like waking ghosts.

Watching them trail past the cemetery, it seemed a vision of the resurrection of the dead, for indeed, some seemed the walking dead.

Slowly, however, as the days went on, the children's natural, life-saving resilience surfaced; they began to talk, to cease their silent watchful sitting. These children had seen bodies in the streets; one child, about eleven, told me how she had seen the trunk of a headless man, a neighbour, standing at his own window; another had found a horse, a dead horse, blown through the window and the wall, lying half-in and half-out of the bath. Children, acutely aware of the senses, remembered the smells, the taste, and the touch of the dead things they encountered every day. It became almost normal for them to recount the horrors; and that was almost worse than the silence of their shock and their trauma.

I was glad that, when it came to the summer holidays, Mrs Hamilton kindly asked my mother to stay on with her, and invited me to spend the summer. I welcomed the invitation. My mother and Mrs Hamilton had become, if not quite friends, at least tolerant companions; while they had not yet progressed to the stage of addressing one another by their Christian names, they had learned to live in the same space which, as my mother was not a naturally gregarious person, seemed to me quite remarkable in itself. Of course, Mrs Hamilton also reminded my mother of William, the second kind and attentive man in her life.

I did think of staying in town, of letting them get on with it together; but I remembered the relief of that first April morning, and so I accepted the kindness of Mrs Hamilton's invitation. When the summer holidays came, I packed up and made my way to Down. I began almost at once to feel the healing power of the sea, and the salt breeze that blew it all away, the horror and the memory of death in the streets. The very first morning I was there, a sweet-smelling summer day, the wind blowing slant from the sea, I went out to the line to hang laundry. Sitting here, I cannot think of anything nicer than to see white sheets blowing in the fresh air, to smell the heathery scent when they come in, cool, a little damp, ready for the ritual, the stretching and the pulling, to make them ready for the clotheshorse, and the hot and spitting iron, and the warm baking-day comfort that it brings to a house. I hung sheets out that morning, put the basket and the pegs back in the porch, and set off along the road, the lough to my left, small waves lapping on the shingle, the seabirds wheeling and calling above. Another scent drifted up to me; someone was smoking a pipe. With a pang that cut cleanly, I thought for a moment: William is here, it was a mistake; he is not dead. Just for a moment and then it passed, as it had to pass.

Down on the beach, then, I could see a man, head bare, walking slowly, reading a book like a priest at his breviary, and in his mouth there was a pipe. He must have felt my watching him for he looked up and, in that kindly way of the countryside, he raised his hand in greeting. And as I raised mine in return, I saw that it was Michael McLaverty himself.

After that, though I looked for him, I did not see Michael McLaverty again. I did, however, often see in the distance another walker, a long, spare man with the close-cropped hair of the soldier, or the ascetic. He, too, smoked a pipe; and that same sensation of longing and regret swept through me each time it drifted my way. One day, happening to step awkwardly on a treacherously unstable rock in the shingle, I stumbled, and had to sit down. He stopped, then, on his walk, and asked me if I was all right; which is how I came to meet F.X. Hadley, the reclusive but outspoken poet and sometime novelist whose recent public condemnation of war, of the fact of war, and specifically of the suggestion that conscription be introduced, had been rewarded not by praise but vilification in the press. Conscription had not in the end been extended to Northern Ireland, but F.X. Hadley was thanked by no-one for his part in an outcome which suited many.

Composing myself as best I could, I thanked him, and told him I was indeed all right but, as I tried to stand, I found to my embarrassment that I could not. Mr Hadley, without a word, without a smile, put out a hand to help me to my feet, and then offered me his arm, and said quite simply that I must go up with him to their house. I was embarrassed: he was firm. It was just across the road from the beach, he said. He lifted his pipe and indicated behind him. Sure enough, in the garden of a small bungalow, smoke curling comfortably from its chimney, I saw three youngsters chasing and jumping, two whooping boys and a long-legged girl, a ribbon in her hair. I felt a brief pang of envy. I think I knew in that second that this — home, family, children — was something I would never have: not for me *kinder, kuche, kirche*. I believe I knew it for certain, though I was still only twenty-five years old.

I let him help me to the house. I was introduced to his wife and, briefly, his children. Then, he excused himself and went to resume his walk. Mrs Hadley, almost as tall and as straight as himself, put a cushion beneath my foot and, with cool and expert hands, bound up my ankle, bade me rest, brought me tea, and insisted that I sit there until I could be conveyed home.

I have never forgotten my visit to that small, unfussy house. Nothing about it shouted writer; yet everything in it presented a spartan serenity. It was a place to think and reflect and work, mind calmed or stimulated by the sea and the ever-changing sky and, at night, the searchlight beam of

Sophia Hillan

the lighthouse. Sitting there, watching the changing blues of the water and the sky, the salt breeze riffling the curtains at the opened window, I felt my heart slow itself to the rhythm of the lough.

Mrs Hadley poured out tea, and handed me my cup. "And what do you do, Edith?" she asked me.

I told her why we were there, about my mother and Mrs Hamilton. She knew who the Hamiltons were, she said, but no more than that. How did I occupy my time, she wondered. I did not dare say I wrote anything for, so far, nothing had been published. How could it: I had sent it nowhere. She was interested to know I taught: she had, too, it seemed, until marriage. In that diocese, at that time, and for the best part of twenty years after it, no married woman could teach, however well qualified and experienced. I thought it an appalling rule, and said so; but she shrugged. She had enough to do, she said, indicating the children careering round the garden, the thwack of a ball or the call of someone's triumph the only sound against the summer stillness. "And of course ..." she added, with a nod and a slight, tired smile, indicating the door through which her husband had gone out.

I told her I thought I had seen Michael McLaverty out walking.

"You would," she said. "When he's down here, he beats a path up and down that beach in all weathers. Frank is almost as bad."

"Are they friends, then?"

"They're great enough," she said, "but they're both men who like to be by themselves." She refilled my cup, and looked at me, for a long, embarrassing moment.

I felt myself flush.

"Do you write?" she asked.

I flushed more deeply. I was not prepared.

"I try," I said.

"What do you write about?"

I told her about the stories for the children I taught, about the stories I told them.

She nodded. "What else?" she said.

I did not know what else. I searched for words.

"Tell me something," she said. "What is the most interesting or unusual thing that has ever happened to you?"

I thought. I had to be careful.

"Well, I did once see Fred Astaire," I said. "With his sister. They did this marvellous dance. I can hardly describe it."

She clapped her hands. "In London?" she said, and her laugh was merry as she spiralled her hands in the air. "1928. Or was it '29? *Funny Face*. They spun in circles, dizzying circles, like creatures of the air."

"Yes," I said, in surprise. "Yes! 1928. December. However did you know?"

"I saw them too," she said.

"The time of the explosion outside the Princes Theatre?" I said. "Did you see them the next morning? I saw them the next morning, sitting with their heads in their hands, and my mother said: 'Those poor young people: their careers will be ruined'."

Mrs Hadley shook her head. "No, I think I saw them after that. It was another theatre — whatever one they moved to. What was it? The Winter Garden, I think. But, there! You have a unique experience: start with that. Write about the things you know that no-one else does, even if they were there, even if they think they know. No-one else knows just what you do."

It was true. I had never thought of it, but it was true. No-one else could guess at my own experience. And after Mr

Hadley came back in, and kindly took out his car, and drove me back up the road to Mrs Hamilton's house, I heard those words in my head. That night, in an old, half-finished exercise book some child had left behind, I started to write down some tentative words and, as I watched them grow, I wondered: can I do this? Is it possible? Nonetheless, I filled that exercise book with things I remembered, and I sent them off to the newspaper, and over that summer, over the next while, I saw my name and my work in print.

What did I write about? I wrote about Knocknarea and Queen Maeve and the legend of her return, like Arthur, in triumph; I wrote about legends of the devil and his mischief; I wrote about seeing Hitler and Goering in Munich in 1939. What did I not write about? I did not write about my teenage fantasy of seeing Knocknarea with Paul; nor about the devil's foot in the cathedral in Munich, with William; I did not write that I was in Munich with one man, hoping to meet another; or that one man was dead and the other, an enemy, most likely dead too.

I wrote: and I wrote about nothing that mattered to me.

Could I do it? The answer to my question was probably no: if doing it meant being true to what I knew, writing of true and unique experiences that were mine and mine alone. I went back to writing stories for children, gentle stories, with a reassuring moral: animal tales, somewhere between the anthropomorphism of Beatrix Potter and Kenneth Grahame and the spare and unsparing animal tales of my elders and betters, Liam O'Flaherty, Michael McLaverty and, though he was best known as a poet, of F.X. Hadley himself. Ultimately published, my stories were generally well-reviewed. "*Enchanting,*" wrote one critic; "*Graceful and elegant,*" another.

That summer, however, though Mrs Hadley most kindly invited me to call again, I did not. I could not: I could not go into that house where truth mattered and present myself as a writer, when all I could write were the safe half-truths of my own life and experience; when all I was, was at best a kind of double agent, a spy for neither side.

I never saw the Hadleys again. They were not there the following year, or any year after that and, as far as I know, F.X. Hadley wrote no more poems or, if he did, they must not have been published. I never did take up Mrs Hadley's best suggestion: I never wrote about seeing Fred Astaire and his sister the morning after the fire. It was unique and precious, yet I could not write it. Unlike Mr Hadley, I was not true to my own experience, my own conviction of what was right; and when I finally came to tell of it, in here, all that duplicity came back to punish me; for of course, no-one believed me.

Ruth

❦

"*No-one believed me,*" Ruth read, and put down the book in exasperation. Of course they didn't. What did she expect, covering her tracks like that? Impatient, frustrated, she looked out the window. The reluctant winter day was gathering itself to begin, and she needed to do the same. She swung her legs out of bed, felt the cold, and swung them back in again. Not yet. There had to be more. There was bound to be more, and if there was not, it would not be for want of Ruth's searching. Why, she asked the *Memory Book* in furious silence, why did you want me to read this? Where is it? Where is *he*? Then, slowly, Edith's voice quiet upon the page, she began to be sorry at her impatience.

The Memory Book

❦

Breaking

There is one thing I have learned about the condition I hear described as denial: the first person to whom truth must be denied is oneself. Perhaps because of the meeting with the Hadleys, I think I rewrote my own history. It was a time in which it seemed only austerity and self-denial could be accorded virtues: consequently, to deny what I knew or felt remained the only truth possible. When I had convinced myself, I set about convincing others. My articles, after my first dismissive one concerning Hitler and Goering, assumed the current attitude necessary: we could take it, and the enemy would never prevail. I wrote light-hearted articles about how we were all managing during the blackouts, blundering heroically about in the dark and apologising to lampposts, enduring the removal of all the signposts in the hope that Hitler would be baffled if he did not know whether he was going to Killard or Killough, making do and mending, experimenting with dietary foodstuffs only to experience dire (but of course humorous) consequences. What a good little propagandist I was.

Not that they were any safer anywhere else in Ireland: I may have enjoyed relative bliss at weekends and during the summers in Mrs Hamilton's house in County Down, but Dublin received a hit. Was it because there was no blackout there, or because Dublin firemen came bravely to our rescue when our own resources proved inadequate? Who knows? If so, they suffered for it; and if it was an accident, which some thought, or a simple case of misdirection through weather and scrambled signals, it was apparent that neither Belfast nor Dublin could withstand any more such errors. Another such accident could wipe us all out. I fully expected to wake up one day and see German tanks come rumbling down the street, and thereafter to die, on the spot, or as a prisoner. It was scarcely sensible, of course, if I had stopped to think about it, for it was becoming increasingly clear that Hitler's new obsession was less to the west than to the east, in Russia. I should have paid a good deal more attention to that.

Instead, I played what I now think of as a self-indulgent game of denial. When I thought of Paul, his image and his memory softened at the edges, yet something of his being, his immediacy seemed to drift away from me. After all, what did I have? A memory; a handful of letters. Was he a Nazi? Yes, he was a Nazi. Did that matter? Not at the time. Did it matter once the war began to hit us, to kill the people we knew — William, Kitty's grandparents? Yes. Yes. Did it make me stop caring about him? No. I still woke remembering his arms about me in Clärchen's, dancing me into heaven; and then I would remember what else had come to all of us from the *Himmel*, the heavens above, and the whole thing would begin again, and I would have to get up and go and dig for victory in the garden, or rip out old jumpers to knit socks and balaclavas for our brave boys, until it was time to go to bed, and dream myself again in the Berlin of my mind and my heart.

Camus, I think it was, once wrote that man has the capacity to become accustomed to anything — *on s'habitue a n'importe quoi*. I like *n'importe quoi* — 'whatever' — the all-encompassing, careless insouciance of it. One becomes used, I found, even to being at war. We had almost forgotten that parliament buildings at Stormont had once been gleaming white, not painted black to fool the enemy; we forgot that we once had metal railings in front of our gardens, before we gave or had them taken for the war effort. We learned to do without bananas and white bread and proper coffee. Gradually, however, we all began to realise that the war was indeed being won, or at any rate coming to an end. My articles became more general, more gently optimistic about a future that seemed once more to be in prospect.

When, in 1945, VE Day finally came amid general rejoicing, we felt and said little, my mother and I. We were back by then in our own house, with the addition of Mrs Hamilton, so much my mother's companion that she had become an accepted member of the household. The two ladies argued from time to time, mostly gently, not always: on VE Day, they disagreed about whether or not we should fly the Union flag, as everyone else on the road was doing. Mrs Hamilton thought we should, because of William's death, my mother not. They appealed to me. "William wouldn't have cared," I heard myself say. I think it was true. Yet, it was not kind of me. Her son, my friend, was still dead. It would have been little enough to do, to please his mother — and still I did not do it.

I took some time off from teaching after the war. I had savings, and the nuns were understanding. They valued me. Not all of the staff had been able or indeed prepared to keep going throughout the war. They knew that I had been travelling up and down from the country, teaching during the week, trying to care for two older ladies and, at weekends, the resident evacuees, for there were many evacuees in County Down and they said more about the nature of poverty than I had ever guessed. Those children who came down from the city — and some of their parents — wore worn and dirty clothes for days or weeks on end, not just because of the Blitz, but because there were no other clothes for them, and no facilities; they struggled with fleas and lice and bedbugs and, indeed, more than once we who briefly took them in shared their experience. It was not one I should care to repeat. Had I been a better person, I might have decided to devote myself to reform of our social system, to making sure that no child ever had to live like that again. I did not. Princess of Denial that I was, I fled to the university, and the library. My job, I was told, would be there for me when I wished to return.

It was not a breakdown. I simply needed time, and a new start, and it was a new start. I went back to the university, and read with great enjoyment for a Master's degree. Needing no further qualification, wanting only to be there to read and to learn for the sake of reading and learning, I took my time, and was happy in a way that I had rarely been. My professor, not easily pleased, was pleased. There was talk of my proceeding to read for a doctorate. A life of pleasant scholarship seemed to beckon, and I believed myself content. I should have been content. I could have followed that path.

I might have done, except that one drifting summer day, Mrs Hamilton and my mother safely deposited in County Down for their now annual exodus, I decided it was time to put away childish things. I cleared my desk of papers and notes, and I packed up and gave away many books that, until then, I had greatly valued. Some of them I mourn still, but it needed to be done. I went systematically through my clothes: out went utility and, coupons or no coupons, in came the New Look, my waist waspier and my skirts fuller than those of anyone else I knew. I had a good figure, and I knew I would be the envy of my entire acquaintance. Ah, Kitty, I thought, even you could not outshine me now!

And at the thought, I stopped. I felt as if I had been running very fast along a road and had suddenly been halted. I had entirely forgotten, or decided to forget about Kitty for years. She had not come back, even for the funeral of her grandparents during the Blitz. There had been no letter, after that first, brazen missive. There had been nothing. Yet, the thought of Kitty, that day, brought me to a standstill. I realised I did not know where she was, or with whom, or whether she was even alive. It was dangerous to stop, and think. I should not have done it. Having successfully avoided it for so long, I should simply have kept going until every trace of that other life had faded by itself.

And, of course, it was the wrong moment. I had just reached into the back of the wardrobe for some hats I knew should be there — hideous wartime affairs — and pulled out, right at the back, a shoebox I had overlooked. I opened it. Pandora herself cannot have been as surprised as I was. Out wafted the essence of another time: the smell of the paper, the fading, intricate post-mark, the familiar, beloved handwriting. I had come on Paul's letters, so long buried away that I believe I had truly forgotten where they were. I sat down to read them all, one by one, right to the last one: and I wept then, for all that had been, for all that might have been, and for him, alive or dead.

I took a decision. I sat down and wrote to the War Office, or the remnant of the War Office, and asked them if they could help me trace a German citizen, lost during the war. They wrote back, not immediately, but after some weeks, with an address of the office of the United States High Commission for Germany, and I wrote to it. I waited again. More weeks passed: the summer ripened; the bright leaves of early June turned heavy in July, and dusty with their dense August green before I heard a word. Finally, I received a letter. That is how I found out what had happened to Paul and, then, there was a breakdown.

If I do not write about my breakdown, that summer and autumn of 1950, it is not because I choose to omit it. I find I remember very little about that time. They say it is often so with electric shock therapy. That was my treatment: electric shock therapy. The very name sounds like a contradiction in terms. All I can say is that in my mind it may be not dissimilar to the experience of counting back from ten under what is called a mild anaesthetic, and suddenly finding that all the surroundings are quite different and that time has inexplicably passed. As I write this, however, a memory — unwelcome, unbidden — comes back, which I shall write as I feel it, for I hope it may not be of long duration. My experience of anaesthetic was not at all mild. My mouth and nose covered by a rubber mask, I recall a smell like gas, the sensation of choking; I remember struggling to escape, like a swimmer drowning, and I remember restraint, heavy straps across my body, pinning me down; I remember trying to scream and hearing no sound. I remember thinking: now I shall die. And after that, I remember nothing, for which I think I may be grateful. I shall write no more today. I can write no more today, and I shall write no more about this.

Ruth

❧

"*But what happened to him?*" Ruth cried aloud, turning over the pages. "*Don't leave it there!*"

She stopped, and listened. I hope I really am alone in the house, she thought, or somebody's going to think I'm —

She jumped. The house phone beside her had sprung into noisy, imperious life. Unnerved, she looked at it. The last time that happened, she remembered, it had been about Hilde. Or no, it had been Sky McDougall. Either way, she reminded herself, I don't have to answer it; and in any case the clock still said only 8.15. I do have to get up, she told herself, but I don't have to answer that. She flung herself out of the bed and drowned out its shrill demands with a hot and very long shower.

The phone had stopped by the time she returned, but its message light was flashing. I hate you, thought Ruth but, unable to ignore the irritating light, she picked the thing up, heard the nasal, permanently questioning tone of Sky McDougall's voice and promptly placed it back on its rest. That girl, she said to herself, has some nerve, and, pulling on a dressing gown, she picked up Edith's book and went downstairs to make coffee.

"Come on, Edith," she said aloud, sitting down at the table. "I'm running out of time and patience. Come on."

The Memory Book

❧

Stormtrooper

The nuns were as good as their word. My job, once I had fully recovered, was still there for me. New people joined the staff and, instead of studying German, I discussed the events of the unfolding present and the safely long-past with Mary Parker, a young history graduate who had just arrived. She was good company, she had never known me before my hair turned white and, more importantly, she had no memory of my sitting head-to-head with William.

Mary and I used to attend plays and concerts during that time when, we were assured, we never had it so good. I can see us sitting mesmerised at the first night of Sam Thompson's startling, controversial *Over the Bridge*: such a brave thing, to show Protestant and Catholic together trying to confront the open sectarianism of the shipyards. We could hardly believe what we were seeing. And it had humour, just as this benighted place has humour, dark though it may be. Afterwards, lamenting the wilful intransigence of a government determined to deny the truth

217

of such work, our laughter was more rueful. More than one of the actors integral to that brave and doomed production left this place after *Over the Bridge*. Who could blame them? What was there here for them but the shackles of censorship? Yet, when, a very few years later, I saw one of those young actors, one of the best, starring in a popular television drama series, I could feel only sadness, and a profound sense of loss. Nothing, it seemed, would ever change here.

Teaching girls between eleven and eighteen, however, I found solace in the poetry of Shakespeare and read my pupils into Dickens's London. In time, I brought them to Stratford and after a longer time, I even took a group to Knocknarea, in search of Yeats and Queen Maeve. There, for the first time, though certain I should never again see him in this life, I found I could once again remember Paul without fear or guilt.

I did not stop writing. I stopped the children's tales: I found I had lost the feeling for them that was necessary, and I had no desire to write for adolescents. Truth to tell, by then there were many better writers in the field than I. How should I compete with, say, C.S. Lewis and his Narnian tales? Once, I saw Kate O'Brien herself. It was Mary Parker who pointed her out, one night as we were coming home from a talk at the university. I saw a woman, plainly dressed, standing alone in the university grounds, looking up at the library, soft light from its arched windows speaking of scholarship within. "Look," Mary said, "that's Kate O'Brien. She's probably researching something. I bet you there'll be a new Kate O'Brien soon. Don't you wonder how they do it?" And she began to speak of the new young poets, Philip Hobsbaum's group. It was she who first suggested that we go to hear them when they read. I am glad, of course, that she did, and that I came to know their work, but Mary never knew that I wrote: I never told her. Yet, the very fact of the existence of such writers as Kate O'Brien and Seamus Heaney and Michael Longley and Derek Mahon did somehow spur me to begin again myself.

I turned to a different kind of writing. Now that I was certain Paul had no hand or part in our purgatory of 1941, I began to write obliquely of him and of our love. I suppose I was still a kind of double agent: no-one could know when I wrote, for example, of Parnell and his lost love that I was thinking of Paul and myself. When I did finally complete a play, set in France and a much older Germany, and then a full-length novel, set in Ireland during the First World War, I knew that I was the only person who would ever guess at its inspiration. In this way, I remembered, and felt I celebrated all that was best of us. It made me happy. It honed my skills; and if publisher after publisher refused to see the merit of either piece, I came to the conclusion that they were at fault, not I. That is not to say rejection was not a blow: it was a blow, every time. I grieved over my poor manuscripts, my sad, dog-eared offerings in their torn paper wrappings, and it took me a long time to set them aside.

I read, not that long ago, that Michael McLaverty himself went through a similar experience with his third novel, set round the very roads and fields I came to know in County Down. Perhaps he was planning it as he walked that day on the beach. In his pages, it was possible to walk the lanes and smell the damp soil and feel the salt of the sea: yet his publishers, though they had championed him from the start, would not publish it. It was too bleak, they said, and they parted company; and his manuscript returned many times to him, as mine did, and he had a long period of heartache before a publisher finally accepted it as he had written it. He never forgot the experience, I read: and I understood why. I almost wrote to him. I almost did. I found out the name of his publishers and wrote a letter, but I never sent it. For me, without his delicacy and sureness of touch, without his extraordinary determination to see it through, there was only one route: I gave up, and stopped sending out my poor children for rejection. For a time, I put all my energies into being a teacher. And shortly after that, there came into my class one of the most promising pupils I ever taught, which is how I first encountered Ruth Deacon.

She was far from promising at the start. Braces on her teeth, unflattering spectacles; really, children then did not have a great deal of help to get through the awkward stage. I noticed, when I wrote her end-of-term reports that her overall progress was not so very good: and she seemed to struggle to keep up her place in class. Yet, to be there in the first place, she must have been among the small percentage who made it through our demanding Eleven-Plus examination. Every child knew from the age of eight that success in that was essential. Ruth Deacon had passed that hurdle, and passed it well; but what interested me about this dark, unforthcoming child was that she wrote so very well for her age. She wrote with flair and confidence and, once or twice, showed some talent for acting, unexpectedly revelling in the applause accorded her by her equally surprised classmates. They were not kind in those days to other children with anything out of the ordinary: braces and spectacles called forth their worst instincts. Children really are little savages: but then, so are adults. Did the revelations that emerged about the camps in Poland during the war not prove that? Every time I read about them, which I tried as a rule not to do, I became convinced of our closeness to brutality.

Yet, why go over the past when it cannot be undone?

Still, the topic came up in conversation — in the staff room, at teachers' conferences, even casually among acquaintances of my mother and Mrs Hamilton — and every time I shook my head in horror as everyone did, and hugged to myself the warmth of knowing that Paul had had no part in that. It must be said, however, that most of my acquaintance found the subject as distasteful as I did. I remember, not long after the end of the war, Mrs Hamilton trying to tell me of a lady she and my mother met at one of the church groups they attended together, I imagine for social as well as philanthropic purposes. They performed good works; I felt I had performed enough of those getting through the Blitz, and I let them get on with it. I drove them, and collected them, but that was all. I know they were not very pleased with me, my mother in particular. Why should I mind? I had been a third wheel all the time my father had been alive, and now here I was again, an outsider, beyond the unshakable alliance of my mother and her companion.

They had been sitting at their work — sorting out clothes for children, I think — beside a lady who confided that she had survived one of those camps. My mother removed herself at that point: she was always good at avoiding what she did not want to hear. What Mrs Hamilton heard, however, so upset her that she did not go back to her church group and, as a consequence, neither did my mother. I never discovered what it was Mrs Hamilton had learned, though she must have told my mother. I did not ask. I remember my mother telling her it showed her what William had died for; and I know I told her not to listen to stories, that it was in human nature to exaggerate. I said it was all over anyway, and could never happen again. They both shook their heads over me then but, since they did that so often, it hardly counted.

I don't quite know how I got on to that. I was thinking about Ruth Deacon. Her writing, I was saying, was good: and I wanted her to make it better. I encouraged her to write for the school magazine while I had her in the junior forms, and I corrected her prose, insisted she write carefully as well as with imagination. It was a matter of pruning back hard to encourage more growth. Was I hard on her? Probably, but she was worth it. I was not personally hard on her: quite the reverse. I remember her mother died sometime when she was in Form Three. Knowing what the loss of a parent was like, I did speak kindly to her, encouraged her to carry my books after class, and guided her reading. She said little to me, beyond the thanks of a well-brought-up child, but I like to think it helped. I lost her for a year or two after Junior Certificate, and I did hear that her work for my successors was not so good. I daresay the fault may have been theirs, for by the time she came back to me for A-Level, I could see the ability was still there.

I remember reading to the girls from the work of those new young poets Mary Parker and I had gone to hear, and watching Ruth Deacon listen, the spectacles now fashionable, the mandatory curtain of hair obscuring half her face. She listened, however, with attention; but though she still wrote well, she said very little in class, and her interest in performance seemed to have ceased entirely. Teachers want to bring out the best in their pupils; and knowing that David Marcus, who had edited *New Writing* after the war, had recently started a page in *The Irish Press*, naming it *New Irish Writing*, I had an idea.

Spurred on by the example of the young writers, I had gathered up my courage again, sketched out a story, polished it, and sent it to David Marcus. It was inspired by my reading a short article about a country house, what we used to call a Big House, outside the city, at Newtownards. I knew, for everyone knew, that the owners, Lord and Lady Londonderry, had notoriously gone to meet Hitler before the war, and had been visited by his Foreign Minister, Von Ribbentrop. Were they sympathisers, or did they simply have faith in a futile quest for peace, like Chamberlain and, I sincerely believe, Paul himself? No-one knew, but public opinion, at the time, condemned the Londonderrys as Nazi sympathisers. That was not news to me: but the article told me something else. A curious gift, brought to them at Mount Stewart by the notorious Von Ribbentrop was still in the house; and there was a photograph of it.

The gift was a little statue, barely eighteen inches high, in the most delicate white porcelain, of a helmeted Stormtrooper, brandishing a flag. Somehow, the bizarre oxymoron of that photograph, the beauty of the work and the horror it symbolised, woke something in me. That story wrote itself. More than anything I had ever tried to say, it came close to the tangle of feelings I had, and still have, about Paul, and about our finding ourselves on opposite sides. Mr Marcus, kindly remembering my earlier work, published it to my joy in his *New Irish Writing*. And he asked me for more. Nonetheless, I waited a while, in case anybody recognised something in that story, anything that would give me away. No-one did. The sense of relief outweighed my pleasure at its publication: but no more of that. There was no more of that. I did indeed have others, more stories that, briefly, tumbled out at the same time, ostensibly about that other life pre-war, our lives during the war, and the bleak time afterwards. In truth, every one was about us, all we had and did not have; all we might have had. They were written: I had an outstanding editor wanting to see them, and I did not send them.

Instead, I suggested to Ruth Deacon that she submit

some work. Somewhat to my surprise, she did, and Mr Marcus printed it; and that girl smiled, I do believe, for the first time in years. At that year's school prize-giving, I made sure she had a special mention, which is how I came to meet her family.

In those days, we did not have parent-teacher meetings, a much later invention. We wrote reports every Christmas, Easter and summer, after our school examinations; conduct and performance in weekly tests were monitored as we went along, so there really was no need to engage directly with parents, unless at an event like this, when one might easily disengage at will. I had once seen the mother, at a school performance of *Messiah* when Ruth was, I suppose, about twelve. There was something exotic, almost European about her; she had a look of Marlene Dietrich, fine-boned, almost haughty. I must say, I rather admired her, and the undemonstrative elegance of her simple wool suit, her well-polished court shoes.

When I noticed, therefore, the small person, far from elegant, who walked out of the school that evening between Ruth Deacon and her father, I was curious. It was not inconceivable that, five years after the death of his wife, Mr Deacon had remarried; yet instinct told me this was not the new Mrs Deacon. She had not been with them when I was introduced, perhaps for the simplest and most human of reasons. These ceremonies tend to be long, and the taking of tea does place a strain on sensitive systems. Whatever the reason, I did not meet the frail, anxious-looking woman, who was clearly of their party. A neighbour? A relative? I did not know. I would remember her, however, because as we stood to make our general farewells, I heard her ask one of the children about one of the stained-glass windows in the chapel, the Harry Clarke, circular, glorious in its detail, radiating colour. The child knew what to say, of course: we trained them well before these events. What I noticed about the lady who went home that night with Ruth and her father was her accent. Ruth sounded like any other well-spoken Northern girl; but though the accent of this lady was different, it was to me suddenly and painfully familiar. She spoke as Paul had done. I knew she was from Berlin.

That happened at the end of Ruth's final year, just before the examinations began. It was 1968. There were no more classes for the leavers, so there was no opportunity to speak to her, to ask her who that was, or how she came to know, to be with someone from Berlin. I had a hazy memory of a day some years earlier — certainly before her mother died — round about the end of term, just before the visit of President Kennedy, while he was still in Berlin. Of course we all admired him, enormously; but I remember asking the children if anyone had spotted the mistake he made in his wonderful speech at the Berlin wall — as fine an example of magnificently inflammatory oratory as I have ever heard — and she put up her hand.

"Well, Ruth?" I said.

"Miss Barratt," she said, in that quiet way of hers, "I think he may have said he was a German biscuit."

There was great laughter, and she smiled the enchanting smile I did not see again until five years later, when David Marcus accepted her work.

I held up my hand.

"Not quite, Ruth," I said. "It was more that he said he was a jam doughnut."

More laughter.

"But, girls," I remember adding for, end of term or not, teaching opportunities must not be missed, "this is important, and you'll find that speech was historic. He was standing at the very border between East and West! Yes, he made a small linguistic gaffe, for of course, "Berliner" does not mean "citizen of Berlin" as his speechwriters must have thought it did. It means "jam doughnut", or what we would call a jam doughnut. What he meant to say, standing at that wall where so many had died trying to escape to the West, what he most passionately wanted to say to those thousands — yes, four hundred thousand — of the citizens of West Berlin gathered there to hear him was 'I am a citizen of Berlin', after St Paul's *Civis Romanus sum* — meaning, girls, that we must all count ourselves citizens of Berlin, and hope as he did that that wall comes down. We know all too well that if there were to be nuclear war, which we pray there may not, the battleground would be Europe, with Berlin, and that wall, at its heart. The egalitarian spirit of Communism — and don't forget, girls, it was originally seen by many as a noble cause — has been overtaken by the power-hungry; and we must be conscious of those who are oppressed by the consequences of that. Which brings me to John Donne, 'No Man is an Island'. Open your books, please at page ..."

I think I made my point, but I remember wondering, idly, just how Ruth came to know that, for German was not then taught in the school. On that later night of the prize-giving in the summer of 1968, I wondered again.

We were into state examinations by then; and it was only a day or two afterwards that Robert Kennedy was killed in Los Angeles. Coming so soon after the assassination of Martin Luther King, it should have signalled to us that something dark, some new rough beast, was on its way. Yet, despite the shocks of those killings, we tended to have our eyes even more on Europe, on the Prague spring, and the students in Paris; those seemed to show where things were going, and we all shook our heads at how quickly everything was changing, the whole world shifting beneath our feet.

Primroses

Soon, it began to shift even more quickly. First, in that summer of 1968, my mother came back home to live with me. Mrs Hamilton slipped on a wet patch one day in the garden of the house in County Down, broke her hip, went into hospital, and never came out. The house in Down, it emerged, she left to my mother for her lifetime, after which it would go to a distant relative. It meant it was ours as long as my mother was fit to travel, but she was frail herself by then. I doubt if she and Mrs Hamilton could have gone on as long as they did in the little house if it had not been for the kindness of their neighbours. The kindness of strangers, however, could not be expected to extend indefinitely. My mother came home to me, and we settled into a respectful co-existence, and I expected that it would remain so.

That autumn, however, just as Ruth Deacon and her cohort went across the town to begin their university careers, we saw the whole town come under siege in a way not seen since the Blitz. Ulster, our Prime Minister told us, was at a crossroads. Civil Rights, an issue long debated by the moderate, became overnight a heated issue for the young. They protested, hundreds of them sitting down one October afternoon in Linenhall Street, just behind the City Hall. I was in town. I saw them. Some of them had been our girls. For all I know, Ruth Deacon may have been one of them. I looked at the faces of those brave, foolhardy children planted on the ground, their puzzled disbelief slowly working through indignation to outrage, as the guardians of law and order actively prevented them from making their peaceful protest. I knew then that the restless spirit of the youth of Europe, of turbulent America, had finally tumbled into the middle of our lives. They protested more; they marched and picketed the houses of politicians. And then it got worse, because on New Year's Day of 1969, they joined a Civil Rights March to Derry, and were attacked at Burntollet. By that time, that grim January, there was no getting away from it: we were once again at war. This time, however, we hardly knew who the enemy was, for the enemy could be anyone, it seemed, who held a different opinion.

I remember clearly the army's arrival in the summer of 1969. I was supposed to be at the school for a staff meeting, but it was impossible to get through the town. It was as if we were back in the Blitz. Fear and anger were everywhere: our neighbour, a courteous gentleman with four sons, quiet, clever boys, aged between twenty-two and ten, found his front door on fire one evening, his only crime to have refused to allow his boys to be commandeered as vigilantes. Slowly, the welcome which the army initially received dissipated, and the faces of the young soldiers I saw in the streets were wary and closed, sometimes hostile. Some of the girls would say they were abusive; they told tales of being thrown against Land Rovers, searched and insulted on their way to school, their uniforms identifying them as Catholic and therefore, it was decided, Republican. Times of arrival and departure had to be agreed between schools, then staggered, so that the almost daily clashes on the buses could be avoided or at least lessened. Naturally, all this had an effect on the school; the quiet manners and careful speech, for example, which had so distinguished girls like Ruth Deacon, began to disappear. Aggression crept in with their new, crude demotic. They had a language, and a culture that seemed alien: there was no question now of carrying the teacher's books, of standing back or holding open a door. On one occasion, carrying a pile of exam papers to the staffroom, I watched them fly in every direction as a girl came hurtling down the stairs behind me. I was fortunate not to be knocked to the ground. I heard a shouted "Sorry!" from the distance of a long corridor. She was not a bad girl, at all: she was simply in flight from something she did not want to do.

In the old days, even five years before, I would have pursued her, and made sure it did not happen again; by that time, however, the foundations of the school were rocked and shaken several times a day by explosions near and far. Classes in the top of the school were carried on to the accompaniment of helicopters above our heads, their pilots just outside the windows, occasionally giving an incongruous wave. Whether it was that time, those bizarre conditions, the sense that everything I had known and worked for was disintegrating before my eyes, I came to feel there was no point, no point any more in teaching or trying to make a difference to the lives of tomorrow's women. Standing before the girls, seeing the grim, battle-hardened exhaustion I had witnessed in the children of the Blitz, and on some, which was nearly worse, a fierce joy as yet another bomb exploded somewhere in the town, I realised I could not continue in the job I had so loved. After the Blitz, we all picked up together. Looking about me, I saw no spirit of the Blitz. Brother against brother, street against street; even in the classes before me, child against child.

Gradually, hope seemed to drain from our lives. Some of our children died, one shot outside the gates. They aimed for her father, but killed the child. My friend Mary Parker died because the Abercorn, my mother's second favourite tea-room, was blown up one Saturday in March of 1972. We should have been there, my mother and I. We had just come out of Woolworths, and I had decided I needed a cup of tea before the slow business of getting my mother home, when I remembered I had foolishly left my parcel sitting on Woolworths' counter.

"You go on, Mother," I said. "Go and get in the queue."

She would not: she would come with me.

I was exasperated. "There's Mary Parker," I said, catching Mary's eye. "You know Mary. Go and stand with her. Look at the size of the queue."

Mary waved to us. "Come on," she mouthed, indicating the queue forming behind her. Even as she turned back, I could see two girls slipping in at the head of the line: no manners, I thought.

Still, my mother would not co-operate. I shrugged my shoulders in Mary's direction by way of apology, and saw her shake her head in in that way of hers — okay, please yourself, she'd probably have said — just before she was admitted through the door. It is my last memory of her. I had just started the slow walk back to Woolworths with Mother when we heard the explosion.

Those two girls, it seems, who had pushed their way in, had gone into that busy, popular restaurant, knowing it was certain to be crowded with Saturday shoppers taking the weight off their weary feet, knowing full well the horrific damage their device would cause, and deliberately left a bomb under the very seat where Mary Parker sat down, where my mother would have been had she joined her. I understand, from the accounts of those who survived, that Mary saw the bag and even walked to the door to call the girls back. Afterwards, though horribly injured, she did not die immediately. Painfully lingering, sans everything but a terrible tenacity of life, eventually she too died of her injuries. Yes, it was an atrocity, greatly condemned by politicians; but nothing changed, and no-one could give back their lives to Mary Parker or any of the others.

After that, I lost the appetite for teaching. It seems to me now that Ruth Deacon's generation was the last I could begin to understand. With Mary Parker gone, I had little in common with the rest of the staff. Only Mary and I could remember another time, and none of the rest of them were interested. All through the darkness of the seventies, the days grey with the pall of smoke and acrid with the smell of burning, the nights riven with the sound of gunfire, I felt myself increasingly out of tune. Our teachers began to get younger. Some of them were the girls I had taught: some held views I had never heard in my life, and did not want to hear now. I was due to retire in the year following my sixty-fifth birthday; and when, on the day I handed in my resignation in May 1981, we heard that the first of the IRA hunger strikers, Bobby Sands, had died, I was glad to be leaving. I could not understand the world as it had become; there was nothing more I could teach young people who would have to inhabit it.

I had always told myself I would enjoy retirement, that I would travel, and join societies, and begin to write again. I suppose I did, a little. I had some friends, mostly young, mostly former pupils, though not Ruth Deacon. It disappointed me that she, the most promising of my pupils, was not among those who kept in touch at Christmas and Easter, or came to the carol service, or the poetry readings given by those young poets, now famous, to whose work I had introduced them. I was proud of many of these girls, grown into fine women, a credit to their education; but Ruth Deacon, the one I would most have liked to see, if only to tell her that though she was making something of herself, she could make more, was not among them. Well, it was the way of the world, and I did not regret leaving, except once.

My mother's care, of necessity, took up most of my time. The day of the Abercorn bomb had affected her deeply. The doctors thought the shock of seeing bodies mangled and torn in the street had brought back the experience of the Blitz. Nor did it stop. In that dark time in our Northern history, every day brought news of further atrocities, of bombings and shootings and kidnappings. I tried to distract her. I remember, for example, that in the mid-seventies, reading that the National Trust had purchased the Big House at Mount Stewart and opened it to the public, I brought her to see it. It lifted her spirits dramatically — the topiary wonderland in the garden, the exotic plants the family had encouraged, the whole vista sweeping down to clear waters on a pebbled shore. "It reminds me of County Down," she said and, I think, she was for once content. I longed to go inside, to see the house, to see if what I had read about it, the fact that had inspired my late burst of inspiration was still there, or if it had ever been there. I wanted quite desperately to know. She would not go in, however: even if it had been possible that day, and I can no longer remember if it was, she would not go in. "The garden," she said, "and the sea. That is all I want." I stood a long time, looking at the house, gripping the wheelchair with something like fury, and I remember thinking: the old are selfish as children. I still think it; especially now that, old as I undoubtedly am, I am well aware that I am as selfish as any child. But then! If I recall correctly, the reason for our outing — her treat — was that it was my birthday. I was sixty years of age. Sixty years of age, and still being told what I could and could not do; and I submitted, but I did not like it.

For my mother, however, immobile, incapable of any escape from the prison the house had become, it must all have been a great deal worse. The news did not help. Even if we did not listen, and I did try to avoid the news, then doctors and nurses and health visitors — my only relief, my only brief escape for a little shopping or a short outing — all came into the house bearing with them the daily despair. As attempt after political attempt at a solution failed, or was derailed, by this side, by that, by this splinter group, by that outraged faction, her anxiety became worse. By the middle of the eighties, when what I once heard mistakenly but most aptly described as the Anglo-Irish Discord collapsed, her anxiety had become depression. Tiny and bent, her bones would break at the slightest knock, and after tests it emerged that her bones were not the problem. Leukaemia, left too late, had taken hold; and though she had every care, at home, in the hospital, and eventually in the hospice, she died on the 9th of November 1989, the day the Berlin Wall came down. Only on that day, for no reason that I could discern, did I suddenly long for the noise and the comradeship and the blessed distraction of the school and the staff and the girls I had known. Longing for years for some relief, for the bliss of a little solitude, I learned instead the unremitting silence of loneliness.

I did manage, however, for the next few years. I volunteered in the local library, and tackled the garden myself until arthritis commandeered me, and slowed me down. I still did a little, however: the weeds feared me and the birds greeted me as much as ever. Indoors, I kept the place right, I read, and did crosswords. I listened to the radio and watched quiz shows on television to make sure my memory stayed in place. I swam to keep active even when I could no longer walk any great distance, though I walked as much as I could.

And one day, last spring, just by myself, I went once more to Mount Stewart. It amazes me to think I was mobile enough to do that, so comparatively recently. Yet, I was. It was certainly convenient that the tour of the house, advertised in the local paper, had a special bus leaving very close to my house; even so, it continues to astonish me to think that I was still so mobile and, more importantly perhaps, so independent. I was, however, very certain of what I wanted to see. This time, for a different reason, I stood again impatient in the gardens. This time, finally, I was able to go inside. I can hardly describe my excitement, bright as a child's, wondering and waiting to see if what I had read about was there. It was.

I saw for myself the extraordinary piece that had released and, however temporarily, revived me. There it was, the porcelain figure, of purest white: Von Ribbentrop's bizarre gift. I know nothing more about the rest of the tour; not looking at anything, I followed the rest of them round in my own daze, and as soon as I got home, late though it was, I took out pen and paper, and began once more to write, until I was compelled to stop. I had a cluster of floaters at the side of my eye. It was late at night: and I thought it was probably the start of a headache.

All the same I made sure the next day to get an appointment at the surgery. A young doctor, whom I had never seen before, mentioned the possibility of cataracts, and referred me to the hospital which, as we both knew, could mean a long wait. He then gave me tablets, and told me to remember my age, to slow down, not to tire myself with trying to see to the garden and the house. Bending was bad, he said, and so was too much reading and writing. He was firm on this point. I had to rest, and — perhaps — it would all come back.

"Enjoy life," he said. "Don't you think you've earned it?"

I looked at him. My regular doctor, who knew me, knew my mother, knew our lives, had just retired.

I thought, you are just a child, but I said, "Thank you, Doctor," and left.

Child or no, he was now my only recourse, and I tried to do as he suggested. One day, swimming, I forgot how to do the breast-stroke. I simply forgot; and, after I had struggled, breathless and gasping to the side, and been hauled out humiliated, I never went to the pool again. Without exercise, I stiffened: if I had wanted to get on a bus and go and look at somewhere like Mount Stewart, I doubt if I could have. Sitting at home by the window, day after day, I watched the birds go about their little, busy lives, calling to their mates in the morning, gathering twigs and feathers for their nests. I thought of Hopkins, lonely in Ireland, despairing that the birds could build, but not he. Sitting there, a prisoner as no doubt my mother had felt a prisoner, I watched the young birds hatch: I saw them make their first tentative flappings; and now and again I bade the young man I had at last engaged to tidy the garden to carry away the little fledglings who fell.

Like the garden, I muddled along, until this summer, until the waving lines started. It was that: the realisation that the straight lines of the window had taken to slanting and curving in a distracting fashion, and the floaters at the side of my eyes would not go away; that the writing I was attempting no longer read well, either in its content or it execution. Those things tipped the balance. I know now what it all meant: my sight, like the power of my hands, will go, sooner or later, and probably sooner.

Concerning my hands, my young doctor simply shook his head. "Arthritis," he said, and prescribed more painkillers. Yet, he speeded up the process of finding me an ocular specialist.

"You will never go blind," the new specialist said. "You will simply lose your central vision."

Simply said, it sounds almost hopeful. Yet, as I write these words, I struggle to read them, ever more obliquely, cocking my head like those busy birds in the garden, trying to catch them before they are obscured by those lethal floating darknesses.

I had carried out enough research during my mother's last, hard years to know what to do; and having put my name down for this place, began to dispose of my possessions. Some books went to the library, quite a few to the school, and most were received by charity. My mother's things, the furniture, precious glass and china, always kept, rarely used, had to go to an auction house. I would like to say it was sad but, by then, it was not; it all already belonged to another person and another life. I felt sad indeed at the loss of my garden: I would never see my young apple trees, nurtured from pips, come to blossom; I would not see the purple drift of my lavenders or the crimson glory of my rowan; and my little primroses would peep out shyly in the April sun, but not for me. In here, I could bring only a few possessions: some photographs and a shelf's worth of my books, and only some of my papers.

That was hardest of all, going through the papers to see what I must part with, and what I might keep. I had decided on the Benner Centre. Less revered than the Linen Hall, but a haven always for the neglected or, as I suppose I was, the less than successful writer, I felt it would be appropriate for my offerings; and the fact that they were duly accepted was a relief. I went through them, then: cutting, editing, burning, shredding. There was so much to do and, when the offer of this room was suddenly made, with a very short time given for acceptance and removal, I was obliged to work very quickly, more quickly than I had thought.

I had just gathered up a bundle to sort through — to be ruthless, I thought — when I opened a brown envelope and found the letters from Paul, that year before the war. I had not forgotten they were there. How could I? Yet, I had not looked at them or thought about them for a long, long time. Now, finding them, reading them, oh reading them, seeing his hand, his drawings, his little tendernesses, remembering, I was completely undone. The days of my youth, the memory of everything in this house, my father and mother young and glamorous, the theatre, London, the Astaires, and Rome, Berlin, Clärchen's, Paul spinning me in his arms to heaven, and the evening and the night and the morning of waking — all of that tumbled like a deluge into my heart, and I remembered all of it with more love and wrenching regret than I would have thought possible. I finally understood that that was the time of my life, and that all else was a dying fall.

So I came in here, but without the papers. The misery that followed the rediscovery, that night by the fire in my old home, of all I had loved and lost, made it impossible for me to look at them ever again: I must give them up, release them like a message in a bottle, and hope that someone would make sense of them and tell the story I could not. They have all gone to the Benner Centre, even the letters, tucked in their envelope under diaries and manuscripts; and, of course, my late children, my *White Stormtrooper*, and the stories I never sent to David Marcus. I suppose I hoped that maybe someone would find them someday, that someone would understand what had been, and what it meant; and then, like a visitant, a revenant, there came Ruth Deacon. Perhaps it will be she: perhaps.

Writing has become very painful. What I have written I cannot reread; and I can no longer tell if what I write is legible. This much I know: what I can remember, I have set down. I know, too, that having left my home and parted with my possessions, the task of understanding what has been is quite beyond me. I have given up everything; my only remembrance of that other life, some little wild primroses, dug up and placed in a pot at the last moment. So far, they have let me keep them. I hope they last until spring, that I may see them flower.

Ruth

⊙⥈⊙

By the time she reached the end, Ruth knew what to do. At last or at least, she had the beginnings of answers to her questions: except for one. Where were the late stories? Surely Edith would not have destroyed them, when she kept all the others? If all else failed, she would go to the Newspaper Library and find the one David Marcus had published in 1968.

By eleven o'clock, all of these thoughts held close like a secret, ignoring the telephone's last shrill attempt to arrest her attention, Ruth was on her way to the Benner Centre. Now that she had the *Memory Book*, she could begin to see what to do with the papers — even without the letters, if they had not yet turned up, though of course they were bound to, in time — and, then, she could go up to the hospital and tell Miss Barratt of her plans. For the first time since the summer, she believed she had a book, or the makings of a book.

Tired though she was, she ran up the stairs to the main reception area, and made her request for the boxes, all thirteen. She was momentarily taken aback to see that the seat by the window had been taken, and stopped short. Even as she did, the figure sitting at it began to rise and she found herself looking into the eyes of a reasonably tall, not unattractive man.

"Did you want to sit here?" he said. "I was about to leave."

A quiet voice, an oddly unplaceable accent: noting them, Ruth found herself looking at the envelope he held in his hands.

"You have the letters," she said, forgetting courtesy.

He followed her eyes.

"Ah," he said. "You must be the Dr Deacon who has been looking for them. Forgive me. I required them."

Ruth, though taken aback, was almost impressed by such brazen insouciance.

"*You* required them! I'm the executor."

"Forgive me," he said again. "The executor of what?"

"Of those," said Ruth, too indignant to be accurate. "Or rather of the papers of their owner, Miss Edith Barratt. She has appointed me her literary executor. You need my permission to look at them."

"Correct me if I am wrong, Dr Deacon," said the stranger, "but I believe copyright resides with the sender of a letter, not its recipient."

Ruth bristled, distracted. She felt the strange sensation that she had seen his face before.

"What do you mean?" she said.

"I mean that permission to read these letters should surely reside with the person, or the representative of the person, who wrote them."

Ruth felt silence gather round her.

"Who are you?" she said. "You're either a lawyer, or you are ..."

"I am Rainer Herrold," he said, extending his hand. "Paul Herrold was my father."

Clärchen's Child

"I don't understand," Ruth began, once she could speak.

He had suggested, perhaps upon seeing the expression on her face, that he go and bring them something restorative from the coffee shop next door, and now he had returned, with two disposable cups of something hot and steaming, and two flimsy plastic spoons.

"You are Paul Herrold's son," she said, "and you're only now looking for his letters? That doesn't make sense."

"Oh, I think you'll find it does," he said, pulling out a chair for her.

Arrogant man, thought Ruth.

"Sit down, won't you? Let's start at the beginning. What would you like to know about first?"

Her mind was spinning: but she sat. Who was this person — an impostor? According to the *Memory Book* Paul's only son — Rolf? Rudi? — had died as a small child in the early 1930s. And anyway, this man was not old enough: he could be no more than ten or so years older than she was, leaving him born — she stopped — leaving him born at the beginning of the war. Was it possible; could it be possible? Was this what Edith would not, or could not say? That he was the result of the night they danced at Clärchen's? If so, was the *Memory Book* almost totally fabrication? And if so, why?

"Your mother, for a start," she said, eventually. "I think you should tell me about your mother."

"My mother?" he said, with evident surprise, and a trace of what seemed like amusement. He pushed the plastic cup towards her, with a grimace. "Doesn't look too great, I know, but they did say it was coffee. You want to know about my mother. But was it not my father you were interested in? It was he who wrote the letters."

As he spoke, he lifted the envelope, lightly, tauntingly, smiling all the while. I could just grab it, thought Ruth: instead, she said: "You did have two parents, I suppose."

"Naturally," he said. "Most naturally, as far as I can ascertain."

Ruth waited. He turned over the envelope, as if seeing it for the first time. Ruth heard a door close, and instinct made her turn her head, in time to see the narrowing of a shaft of light from the door to the offices. Across her mind shot the swift thought: Latimer. Steeled, she turned back to Rainer.

"Well, then, tell me about your life, your growing up," she said. "When were you born? Round the beginning of the war?"

"Round then," he said, with a slight shrug, "though that is what I believe is called an impertinent question."

Ruth felt herself redden. "I think it pertinent," she said.

"Do you? Well, then, as to my early life, I lived it mostly with my grandparents." He paused, then added: "My father's parents, in case you wondered."

"Where?" said Ruth. "Where did they live?"

"In Berlin." He spread his hands. "And since you are so curious, let me assure you it wasn't luxury. They never had very much, my grandparents: their savings were lost following the war or, rather, following the peace. Like most, they started again, and eventually saved enough for an allotment, out in Berlin-Dahlem. It meant that, in a sense, they were prepared for what had to be endured when it all began again. I know we never starved." He laughed, without mirth. "We ate a lot of soup."

'What did he do, your grandfather?"

He shrugged again. "What he could, I suppose, as long as he could. He generally found work as a jobbing gardener, though as time went on his clientele became more and more restricted. So many of the best clients near the allotment were Jewish. My understanding is that they were required to leave; or that, if they were permitted to stay, my grandfather was forbidden to work for them."

"Forbidden?" asked Ruth. "Actually forbidden?"

"Why, yes," he said, with what seemed like surprise. "A party member could not be seen to work with Jews."

"So they were party members."

"Oh yes," he said. "Of necessity. It was almost impossible to be anything else. Everyone was watched: even those appointed to do the watching, like my grandfather, were themselves watched."

"Your grandfather did the watching," Ruth repeated. It was not a question.

"He was the Blockwart, the party's warden in charge of our block of houses: someone had to be. And it afforded his family some protection, or so we thought."

"Did it not? Afford you protection, I mean?"

He shrugged again. "It did, up to a point. At any rate, until the Russians came."

"Up to a point," repeated Ruth, carefully, a chill sensation

243

in her neck. "What happened when the Russians came?"

He turned the envelope over, as if it could answer the question, but he did not look at her.

"When the Russians came," he said, "my grandfather was hanged."

In spite of herself, Ruth felt a shocking thrill go through her.

"By the Russians?"

Again, he opened his hands, as if to show they were empty.

"Who knows? Russians, Germans — who could say, in a mob. They strung him up outside our front door, from a lamppost."

"Don't tell me you saw that," she said.

He nodded. "I did. I was in my bedroom, playing. I was not allowed to go out, with all the disturbances. My grandparents were packing to leave: they knew it could be dangerous once the Russians arrived. But they weren't quick enough. I was to pack my best toy and one book — that was my job, and though I did not have many toys or books, it was a difficult task and absorbed all my attention. I did not hear the commotion. I might have missed it altogether, except that the lamppost was outside my window. I used to find its light comforting at night, in the winter. Soft light."

He paused, seemed to swallow, then continued.

"That day, there was no light from the lamp. I heard a strange noise, a rasping, grating sound, and then I heard another noise, the unmistakable sound of a mob's growing excitement. In wartime Berlin, even children were familiar with that. I looked up at the window, and I froze."

He paused again, looking down at his hands.

"It was his face I saw. They were hoisting him up. He looked straight at me. I couldn't move, but I remember his face, an expression I knew, as if he were warning me to stay quiet — he used to do that when my grandmother was in a mood. I couldn't move, but somehow I knew I had to. Then his face swung away from me, and he began this terrible slow spinning."

As he spoke, his hands moved in slow, circling movements. He stopped, then seemed once more to swallow.

"All I remember next is scrambling up to the attic and hiding in the crawl space there. I don't know for how long. One of the neighbours must have found me, or else my grandmother did. Maybe it was a neighbour. I don't really remember."

"But you were safe?"

"For a time. The neighbours stood by us at first, anyway. It's ironic that my grandfather was probably hanged for being the party informant: everyone around knew he never informed on anyone. He was kind, a kind, simple-hearted man. He wanted to believe others were too, even Hitler. 'He is a good man at heart,' he used to tell me. 'He loves children, and he loves dogs. Whatever bad things are happening in Germany, you can be sure the Führer doesn't know about them, or he would stop them.' I don't know whether that was to make me feel safe, or whether he had taught himself to believe it. My grandmother told him he was a fool, but he believed, he said, what he believed. And he was hanged; but the neighbours remembered his kindness, and we were protected long enough for some kind of order to return."

"But your mother?" Ruth said. "You've still told me nothing about her. Where was your mother during all this?"

He looked at her in surprise.

"My mother?" he said. "She wasn't there. She had to …

how shall I describe it … stay in the background."

Ah, thought Ruth: now we will get to it. Either he was a fraud or, as she was beginning to think — if she could hear some dates — he was indeed Paul and Edith's child, the Clärchen's child. Edith must have had to give him up, which was why Rainer lived with the grandparents, and, either she was too ashamed to describe the fact of an illegitimate child in the *Memory Book,* or so grieved that she simply edited out the fact of his existence.

"Do you remember her?" she asked, heart beating.

"Of course I remember her," he said. "She stayed with us — with me — as long as she could. I must have been three or four when she had to get away."

Ruth's racing mind came to an abrupt halt. That's not right, she wanted to say, she was certainly not in Germany for four years in the war. Confusion descended. Then something else began to rise in Ruth's mind. Even if the *Memory Book*'s story of the year before the war was fabrication, the reason for that might yet be extracted; at the very worst, the fabrication was a story in itself. Let him finish, she told herself. Let him give his version. It would be time enough to correct him, or expose him for a liar, once she had the letters.

"It was my grandparents who looked after me," Rainer was saying, "and then my grandmother." His cheekbones were sharp against the light. "Gradually, my mother became little more than a name, a sort of dim memory. It's to find out more about her — about my parents — that I'm here. I have no memory of my father. And when I discovered, thanks to Cory — to Professor Latimer, that there are pre-war letters from him in this archive, I came to see them."

Ah yes, Professor Latimer. She had been too long absent from the mix, had she not.

"So, that's who told you," she said. "When? How long have you known?"

"Not long at all," he said. "About six weeks ago, I'd say. Professor Latimer and I have had a number of professional dealings lately in Dublin. It was at one of them that she mentioned them; and then at the next, about a month ago, she was kind enough to bring them. I've had to spend the last month in Berlin, or I'd certainly have come here sooner. But, as you'll see, I have translated them, which may be helpful. Is your German good?"

"Oh, no," said Ruth, absently. "Not very."

About a month ago; about the time Ruth came looking for them and found they were gone. Latimer had done that; but why? That she could not ask him. He called her Cory.

"So, just to be clear," she said at last, "it was you who had the letters all this time?"

"Yes," he replied. "And you have been looking for them. I'm truly sorry if you have been put out."

"But ... why was I told nobody knew where they were?"

"I gather," he said, "that that was the error of a young assistant. Naturally, Professor Latimer was not aware of the confusion.'

Naturally, Ruth thought, I don't think.

"May I see them now?" she said, standing up. It was time to show her hand. "I may be able to help you with your mother's history. I told you already: she made me her literary executor."

He looked blank. "She made you ...? What are you talking about?"

"The Barratt archive," she said, indicating the envelope. "Where those letters came from? I'm the literary executor."

He shook his head, clearly baffled.

"Is there a problem?" said Ruth.

"I don't know what it is you think," he said, slowly, "but

my mother's name was not Barratt."

"What?" said Ruth. "But ..."

"Brown," he said. "My mother's name was Kitty Brown."

Ruth, speechless, stared at him.

"And in answer to your earlier question," he continued smoothly, "I was born on the 24th of December 1939. A Christmas present, you might say."

Then he handed her the envelope and, without another word, turned away. Ruth did not need to hear the sigh and creak of the ancient door to know that Cory Latimer had come out of her den and was leaving with him.

And then, the letters — or, rather, the translations Rainer had made — finally in her hand, she shook herself into concentration; and if at first she was conscious of the empty seat opposite, the sense faded as she began to read.

Paul

⤜⥈⤛

21st July 1933

My dear little Edith,

I was glad to get your long and welcome letter. It moved me greatly; and I must express not only my gratitude but also my apologies that it has taken me so long a time to reply. You will understand that the last year has been difficult, in many ways.

Let me thank you, first, for the photographs of you and your family at Knocknarea. The kindness all of you showed to me last summer stays with me, and touches me to the heart. I felt I was with you and your parents on that journey we had hoped to make, and that, through these photographs, I could understand more of your beautiful country. One day, perhaps, I shall see it once more in person.

I am more than pleased at your splendid written German. How hard you must have worked! I understood everything, though your word position and your morphology were not always correct: generally, though, I can award you high marks for your written work, if not your oral! I am a teacher always, you see: and to demonstrate it, I enclose a photograph for you. Here I am with my little class of boys and girls, all just nine years old. The two little girls holding hands in front are Hilde and Anna and they are best friends. Are they not very sweet little ones?

Give my best wishes to your parents, dear Edith, and thank you, again, for writing to me.

Your friend,
Paul Herrold

* * *

Note: The following letter was found among my father's papers, apparently returned to sender from an address in Rome, then forwarded to his Berlin address by a Frau Schmidt, from the town of Ulm. This translation for inclusion in the collection in the Benner Archival Repository, Belfast. Rainer Herrold.

25th July 1938

My dear little Irish girl!

You see I've drawn some flowers, gladioli, at the top of the page. The gladiolus, like the gladiators of old, stands for strength of character, fidelity and honour. Someday, if I return to Ireland, I will give you real gladioli, honourable and strong as yourself. For the moment, however, I must face the fact that all good things must indeed come to an end, and that it is time for me to return to serious life, to thinking about my job, and my responsibility. I write these words, and then I hear our little bird sing. Yes: our little Roman Amico is still with me. His broken wing is mended, and he says hello. He reminds me that life is not all responsibility, not all seriousness. I think of you: in Italy, yes, but even more in Ireland, where we first met. '*My Irish child, where dwellest thou?*'

You see I have kept my promise to write again to you. Does it seem strange then to you that I write to advise you not to come to Berlin? It should not seem strange. If ever you are to come to Berlin, I should wish to be able to look after you, and be your companion. I should make proper arrangements, and see to it that you were lodged in a comfortable hotel with respectable people. These are uncertain times, little Edith, and for reasons I cannot at present disclose, I have many new responsibilities. How should I explain it to your parents if I were not able to ensure your comfort and safety? Someday, perhaps, when the world is righted, you may come here. For now, I think it best that, when you complete your visit with your friends in Ulm, you return to your good parents, whom I respect as highly as I do you. Always your friend,

Paul

* * *

9th September 1938

My very dear Edith,

Thank you for your card. Your German improves with every day!

You must excuse me that I have not written before now. Life, you know, does not always go as one plans or wishes and, at the minute, I have very little time. You may have realised that, following the general mobilisation of the 12th of August, my first commitment is to the service of the Reich. Do not think that I am not happy to serve, for I am;

and I hope you will understand that my time is now very much occupied with new duties to my beloved Fatherland. I know 'My Irish child' will understand!

I shall paint you a picture. Art, my greatest love, will always be a line of connection between us; and if I can paint for you a picture with something of my spirit in it, my tenderness for my little Irish girl, you will have it and remember always our time together. I miss you, little Edith. Since that time we spent together I feel a deep longing for the sound of your voice, for the sense of someone who is moved by the thoughts that move me, who understands and accepts me as I am.

Yes, I too think of that evening in Clärchen's. It was indeed a very beautiful dream that we shared together in Berlin. I think of it today as a dream that ended for us too quickly. I think of it, and I believe I always shall; just as I hold you, dearest Edith, and shall always hold you in a special place in my heart.

Yours,
Paul

* * *

Ulm, 29th October 1938

My dear Edith,

It is well after half-past nine, but still I want to respond to you, if only in a few lines, from a place where you have also been. Yes, I am in the beautiful town of Ulm! My post has been forwarded to me, so I have received your dear letter, and the illustrated magazines you sent me. Ireland looks lovelier than ever. How I should like to see it again, one day. How strange that our letters can reach us, when we cannot reach one another.

Nonetheless, the course of history has been changed and, God willing, we may yet meet again. It meant a great deal to me to read that you kept me in your prayers. Only my mother has ever done that for me! You would like her; and I know she could love the girl who came to visit a lonely patient, far from home. Edith, how beautifully you make me remember what your town is like. I could see, as if I flew above it, the road to your school, the sheltering trees in the grounds of the convent, the crucifix and *pietà* outside St Paul's, and all the streets leading up to the twin spires of the lovely monastery where you go to make your prayers. You know, when I was in hospital that is what I saw from the window: a parish church with its *pietà* and the walls of a convent school, from which one day two young girls came to see me. I never saw the lovely monastery you describe, but in this letter yes, I could see its soaring vaulted ceilings, and the secret surprise of that garden in the heart of the city. You described it all so clearly, Edith! I felt I was there. Indeed, my spirit was there.

Were it not for the great and wonderful change in all our fortunes, it might well have been that only my spirit might travel to Ireland. God be thanked for the magnificent and successful efforts of the Four Statesmen! We have survived testing times. Thanks to them, the world has been spared a great disaster. I should gladly have died for my beloved Fatherland, but am gladder still that it has not been necessary. It is hard for me to find words to express the feeling of joy and pride we soldiers felt in witnessing the homecoming to our great German Empire of the poor people of the Sudetenland. It would not be possible, unless you had witnessed it as I did, to believe the utter misery of these people. I had never seen its like. Their wasted faces bore witness to the abuse they had suffered at the hands of the Czech government. You must try to picture the depth of their longing for this homecoming, and, of course, the German people stood ready to act on their behalf. Our Leader ended his speech with these words for the Czech President: "We are determined, Herr Benes may now choose." This crucial speech was broadcast in England and Ireland: did you hear it, Edith? Did you receive the newspaper I sent you? Wherever we went, we were received with such jubilation! Such joy on the faces greeting our arrival! It was clear that twenty years of anxiety and misery were forgotten. The people could scarcely credit that in this very hour they were about to form a link in the chain of our great people's community. The terrible devastation left by the departing Czech army bore clear witness to the days of terror preceding our arrival. Hotels, villas, department stores, railway stations, petrol stations, great forests, bridges and even the houses of farmers and working folk fell victim to Czech vandalism. I can testify from the evidence of my own eyes that the Press reports were by no means exaggerated. In some places, up to eighty per cent of the Sudetengerman population were obliged to leave the homeland as refugees. The wave of those in flight seemed never-ending, and the misery I witnessed was appalling. Only our march into Czechoslovakia saved them.

By the 29th of September, we were in Munich. Watching the enthusiasm of the reception accorded to the great peacemaker Chamberlain by the people of Munich, I felt great pride and joy. Through the declaration made by him and Our Leader that Germany and England would not be at war with one another, his popularity soared among the German people. On that great feast of St Michael the Archangel, surely God was with us!

In all of this excitement, I have neglected to ask how you are, dear Edith. I gather you are busy with your work at the school, little Miss Teacher. Your German is improving, but

I think if I were there I should be your teacher, and save you all the hours of battling with grammar and vocabulary. We could chat, you and I. Wouldn't that be nice? I am a dreamer, I know: yet, I think of our meeting years ago when you were such a little schoolgirl, and then in Rome, so suddenly grown-up, and most of all, of course, the night we danced together in Clärchen's Ballhaus. Only now, thinking back, do I begin to realise how blessed we were to have those brief times. How well we understood one another, Edith! Each time we have gone our separate ways, I think we have both felt the pain of parting. In Rome, we had our little Amico. He, too, was vulnerable, and alone, and in need of my protection. Before I freed him, he liked to watch me as I wrote to you. Do you suppose he knew? We had our time with our Amico: and now, in this changing world, he goes about his own life, as you and I must go about ours.

Winter has begun its slow approach. We have had no snow as yet, but the air is cold and it cannot be far away. I hope to visit my family in Berlin for eight days over Christmas. Sadly, I cannot have longer holidays than that: but I do hope to make progress with my painting for you. Meanwhile, I enclose the photographs I took from my bedroom window of our new Graf Zeppelin; and I do hope you enjoy the little drawing I made for you at the top of this letter. It's my illustration of the story of the Seven Swabians. Do you know this story by the brothers Grimm? It says much about human nature. We must not be afraid to face life's challenges.

With my most heartfelt good wishes,
Paul

* * *

Ulm, 22nd December 1938

Dear Edith,

At last, I have a moment to reply to your last letter. We have had so much work, that time has run away with me; and now, Christmas stands at the very door. It is bitterly cold here, and we have had snow. At New Year, it seems I may be able to have a holiday — perhaps some winter sports in Austria. I should love that, especially now that the magnificence of Austria has been restored to Greater Germany. Thank God for these quieter times. How can we ever make adequate thanks to the statesmen who gave us this gift of peace? Who knows if I should otherwise be alive today to celebrate the glorious feast of love that is Christmas, when joy sweeps once more into our hearts?

I had hoped to send, with this letter, the painting I promised you; but I am afraid it is not dry enough to withstand the necessary journey by freight. I have been working on it with a spatula, which means it needs more time to dry. In time, it will come. Sometimes I dream that I bring it to you in person. I find myself at your door — and I see your dear face when you open to me, rather than your postman. Dreams, dreams: I am a dreamer still.

I leave you with the heartfelt wish that you and your family may have a peaceful and very happy Christmas.

Paul

* * *

Ulm, 29th December 1938

My dear Edith,

Thank you for your Christmas card, which I received with joy. The lovely image of the little bird reminded me, as

I am sure you intended, of our onetime companion, our Amico. Where is he, I wonder, this Christmas? Perhaps he will perch one day upon your windowsill, and you will know he brings you greetings from me. Ah, that brief time we shared together! Only he, free in the world, carries it unburdened through his little life. For us, unable to fly, willingly yet inexorably fettered by responsibility, life means the soldier's march, one foot after another, until we arrive at our appointed destination.

It is the season for wondertales; so let us rejoice in ours while the Christmas bells ring out towards a new year. What will 1939 bring, I wonder, for you, for me, for all of us? Before me, the forest stands elegant and lonely in its winter white: all about it, red-berried bushes and the silver carpet of grass glittering in diamonds against the deepening dusk, prepare for a new life. May this New Year, full of hope, be bright for us!

Your letters are ever dear to this lonely soldier and, with the passage of time, I find they grow dearer still. It is eight o'clock now, and I am thinking quietly of you as I listen to our own local station, the Reichsender München: first the news of our great progress in bringing stability and peace to Greater Germany, then soft music. I shall fall asleep so. Just think, if you tune into this station, our thoughts may meet somewhere in 'the heaven above', as they did the night we danced, and we shall be close once again.

With my heartfelt good wishes,
Paul

* * *

15th January 1939

Dear Edith,
I thank you for your welcome letters from 27th

December, and also 28th December, assuring me that you did receive my Christmas letter. Thank you also, from my heart, for your kind gift of a calendar. I hope you received my later letter, for New Year? My painting is almost ready: soon, I hope, you will receive it.

My holidays are over, now. How sad that makes me!

With my best wishes to you and your family,

Paul

* * *

Ulm, 12th March 1939

Dear Edith,

I am writing only a few words today, so that you do not worry unnecessarily about me. My work has kept me very busy. I have been absent from here for some time. In the next few days, you will, I hope, hear more from me. It may be that I shall soon be stationed in Berlin.

With all good wishes,

Paul

* * *

Berlin, 11th July 1939

Dear Edith,

It is quite a surprise to me to learn that you will be in Munich, and that you intend thereafter to come to Berlin where, indeed, I am now stationed. Naturally, I should wish to see you, but I am afraid that it could prove difficult. Things are not as they were a year ago. All changed, as your wonderful late poet Yeats wrote, changed utterly. I shall write to you again when I can.

With best wishes,

Paul

* * *

18th July 1939

Dear Edith,

I have made what arrangements I can for you to stay in Berlin, and, all being well, I hope to be able to spend some time with you. It would, for many reasons, be important to me to sit face to face with you, and to tell you in person of all that has been happening to me over these past months. It might be best to have your friend Mr Hamilton accompany you: even in our great Reich, it is not always safe for a woman to travel alone. If you will confirm your travel arrangements, I shall meet you, or arrange that you be met when you arrive in Berlin.

Your friend,
Paul

* * *

Note: Letter following found, unsent, among my father's papers: translation for inclusion in the Benner Archival Repository, Belfast. Rainer Herrold.

Berlin, 1st September 1939

Dear Edith,

My letter must of necessity be short. I wish simply to say that I was saddened and shocked to receive your telegram concerning the death of your dear father, whom I remember with the greatest regard and respect, and to express my heartfelt sympathy to you and your mother. Years ago, he wrote to me when I lost my wife and my little boy. With that letter, and with your own dear letters over these last few years, the wound of loss began to heal. There was much more on this subject that I would have wished to say to you, had we been able to meet as planned. It was not to be, and I shall not intrude upon your grief by speaking of my own circumstances, or the sadness of the situation in the world about us.

Now, in every way, our lives and our relations seem irrevocably changed. Who knows when, if ever, we may meet again? If not, may God bless you, my dear Edith, and keep you. Remember me, if you will, in your prayers, as I shall you in mine.

Always your friend,
Paul

* * *

Resident Office,
United States Commission for the German High Command,
Ulm,
June 7, 1950

Miss Edith Barratt,
19 Sandringham Avenue,
Belfast,
Northern Ireland

Dear Miss Barratt,
After receiving your letter of May 14, this office placed a notice in both Ulm newspapers requesting information on the whereabouts of Mr Paul Herrold. Please find enclosed a copy of a letter received today from a Mr Friedrich Hermann.

Very truly yours,
A.N. Wylie
Resident Officer

* * *

Translation

Dear Miss Barratt,

Through my sister, Mrs Unger in Ulm, who saw the search advertisement published in the newspaper, I have learned of your enquiry. I have lived near her since the end of the war, and have resumed my former profession as baker and confectioner. Of my comrade Paul Herrold, I can unfortunately tell you relatively little for, though we were stationed together first in Ulm, and then in Berlin, we were ultimately separated in France in 1940. From another comrade, I know that he was in Russia. If he yet lives, or how his life may have been, I cannot tell you. This unfortunate war has disrupted many ties and foreign connections.

Believe me,
Yours sincerely,
Friedrich Hermann

Ruth

❧

Das Mädchen

Ruth looked up from the letters, and saw that she was not alone. Rainer Herrold, standing by the issue desk, was watching her. Silently, he walked over and sat down. Between them, as earlier, sat two empty cups, now stained and cold.

"I don't know what to make of these letters," Ruth began. "For a start, these are translations. Where are the originals?"

"Here," said Rainer, tapping his inside pocket. "As I said, I believe the copyright resides with me. Don't worry about any work you may want to carry out," he added. "I plan to donate the translations I made to the collection, and I have no objection to scholarly study."

"I'm not worried about that," Ruth said, irritated, because she had forgotten to worry about it. "I am concerned, though," she added, to recover something of her position as scholar, "that I — or any other researcher — would not have access to the originals. Much may be lost in translation, as I am sure you are aware."

"Indeed," he said, eyebrow raised. The beginnings of a smile seemed to play about the corner of his mouth. "I am well aware of that. Do remember, however, that I have not said I would not make the originals available — to the proper scholar."

Ruth, conscious that she had lost the point, began again.

"I can't say K— I mean, your mother, comes out of this well."

"Call her Kitty, if you want to. I sometimes think of her as Kitty. How do you mean she doesn't come out of it well? She's not mentioned in the letters, unless you count a passing reference to the day the two schoolgirls came to visit."

"I'm not thinking of the letters. It's what she did later. I think she behaved very badly to Edith. And so did Paul, if you ask me."

There was a pause.

"Really," said Rainer, and again she saw that play of amusement round his mouth. "So, to be clear: are you seriously telling me you think Edith loved only Paul, Paul only Edith, and that Kitty was ... what, shallow, heartless ... predatory?"

It was Ruth's turn to pause. "I believe Edith may have thought so," she said.

"Ah, but how well did Edith really know Kitty?" he said. "Theirs was little more than a schoolgirl friendship, as far as I am aware. Yes," he added, seeing her expression, "I know something of Edith Barratt too."

Ruth opened her mouth, then closed it.

"As for me," he continued, "I suppose I was too young to remember Kitty beyond the sensual memories of a young child: the warmth of her face, the smell of her hair, the touch of her hand to calm my fears in the night. I remember a presence, a painful absence, and then a confused memory. My grandparents, however, knew what she went through. My mother, I believe, was brave and resourceful. She gave birth to me and looked after my grandparents, in a hard and difficult time, and she stayed with me as long as she could."

"But she left," said Ruth, bluntly. "And she didn't take you with her."

He looked at her, long and hard. His eyes, hazel at first, had turned a dark brown. "It was apparently too dangerous," he said, "and I understand I was not the strongest of children. Asthma."

For no reason, Ruth thought suddenly of another German child left behind: Hilde, lonely, forgotten Hilde.

"Hilde?" he said.

Ruth, unaware that she had spoken the name aloud, felt herself grow hot with embarrassment.

"No-one. I'm sorry. I didn't mean to interrupt you."

He looked curiously at her for a long moment, and her embarrassment grew.

"Please," she said. "You were saying?"

"I was," he said slowly, still looking at her in some puzzlement. "So — where was I? Right. Well, according to my grandmother, Kitty stayed as long as she could, to nurse me and get me strong. When she had to go into hiding, when it became clear that they were coming for her, my grandmother pleaded with my mother to leave me, not to put me in more danger."

"Why didn't she come home, then, here?"

He paused again, his look this time more of patience, or possibly pity.

"What do you think communication and travel were like in the middle of the war? And don't forget, her own position was ambiguous and therefore precarious. She was not

265

German. My father had managed to marry her only by being able to prove — and I think it was a tricky enough business, involving the suggestion, I believe, that she was illegitimate — that whatever Jewish ancestry she may or may not have had was far enough back, enough diluted by good Aryan stock, to enable him to marry her and —"

"She was Jewish, then?" interrupted Ruth. "I know Edith wondered about that, whether her grandparents were, but not very seriously."

"Yes," he said. "Her grandparents certainly were, so yes, on that side of her family. I'm fairly sure Brown wasn't the name they started out with."

Ruth thought of her own relations, the Bauers, who had taken a strategic decision to become Bowers.

"Anyway," he said, "Paul managed to pass Kitty off as Aryan enough to give me a chance, one degree further removed, of escaping whatever lay in wait for me, should I be found to be a Jewish child. I was just about safe; and I gather she was persuaded, in the end, that I was safer at that time without rather than with her."

Breathing hard, as if he had been running, he spread his hands out on the table, as if in explanation, but he did not look up at her.

Ruth could find nothing to say. Kitty. Kitty, the schoolgirl vamp? Kitty the spoiled, self-centred rich kid? Could Edith's Kitty really be this man's brave, selfless mother?

Then he raised his eyes: hazel again, clear, light-filled. Ruth had a sudden recollection of the *Memory Book* and Edith's description of the schoolgirl Kitty, with the hazel-brown eyes that suited her name. Yes, she was his mother.

He turned away, and looked out of the window, to the bare winter trees and the vast, pretentious dome of the City Hall.

"This town was bombed during the war," he said.

"Yes," said Ruth. "Badly. And more than once. By your lot."

"I know. But don't forget, we were bombed, too. By your lot. The air pirates, we called them. We could look out the window and see where our neighbours' houses had been the night before, where their children — my friends — had played, and see nothing but rubble, and bodies. What had we done, my grandmother and I? Or my mother?"

Ruth shook her head. What had they done, any more than people blitzed in London or Coventry or Belfast; any more than William, or Kitty's own parents?

"But she never even came home for her parents' funerals. Or, maybe she was dead by then, herself?"

"She probably never knew they were dead," he said, ignoring her second question. "And not everyone could get out of Berlin, even if they could negotiate the whole rigmarole of papers and permits. You can't imagine. No, she did all right, my mother. And she had hard choices to make."

"Still, I don't like the way she behaved towards Edith. And, you know, because she knew her so much longer, I think I blame her more than I do Paul."

"Think further then. History reminds us, almost as often as cliché, that it takes two to make any relationship. Whatever connection existed between Edith Barratt and Paul, it was with Kitty that he fathered me. Both my parents made whatever choices had to be made. My existence is surely evidence that both held to the bargain. You know, I'm all there is of my father, beyond these letters. I have no memory of him. I'm told he brought my mother to my grandparents' house for her sake and mine, but I don't remember anything about him. He was in France when I was still an infant, and then he was in Russia. Few came

267

back from Russia. He wasn't one of them."

He stopped, and turned again to the window. Dusk creeping onward, lamps began to throw their comforting pools of light across the streets: high up in tall offices and stores, squares of brightness gradually appeared. In front of the City Hall, extravagantly illuminated, a crowd was gathering and growing. Musicians tuned their instruments; snatches of Christmas carols began, then stopped, then began again. People chattered, stamped their feet and flapped their arms like penguins; the lowering sky sat heavy with snow; the very town seemed waiting in breathless expectation. Soon, the American President would arrive, and, behind the relative safety of a perspex screen, turn on the lights of the large, gaudy tree.

Rainer, still looking through the window, seemed lost in thought.

"I'm afraid," he said, then, quietly, "I don't care for your Christmas tree. In Germany, no matter what, even in the darkest times of the war, we had the loveliest Christmas trees, even if they were tiny, hardly more than a branch, even if they were decorated with cotton wool or scraps of wire from the debris of enemy bombs — your bombs. Nothing was wasted. They were simple, our trees, and beside them there was always a Nativity scene, a crib. For all the talk of God and religion, that Christmas tree looks, I don't know, tawdry, somehow. And no crib, that I can see."

"Be that as it may," said Ruth, suddenly and irrationally annoyed, "come back to the question of Kitty, and the hard choices she had to make."

She saw his Adam's apple move as he swallowed.

He said nothing for a moment, then: "All right," he said. "Let me tell you something else about her. I remember this, though I must have been very young. A woman came to the door one day, in a desperate state. My mother knew her;

she was a neighbour, though not a close one. She had a child about my size. She wasn't a beggar, she was simply Jewish, and her only request was to be allowed to hide herself, her child and, if possible, her husband, in our cellar, or our attic, or anywhere. She had been warned that they were about to be arrested. She knew my grandfather had been a kind man, and that he had suffered for his tacit protection of his neighbours. My mother brought her in, and said she would have to see whether she could help. She would have to think. I see that woman's eyes still, and the eyes of the child. My mother asked about among those she could trust: by then, they were not many. 'Do you know the penalty for hiding Jews?' I heard my grandmother's voice, so sharp, so unlike her. 'Do you want us all to be sent to a camp?' My mother let them stay that night in our attic, the woman and the child. In the morning they were gone."

"You knew about the camps?"

His face closed. "We knew there were camps. We knew we did not want to be sent to a camp."

Hilde, she thought again. Herr Herrold, who got her out just in time. If Paul knew, then so did his family.

"What happened to them? What happened to the husband? Where did he spend the night?"

"I don't know. I suppose my mother couldn't risk the husband, but she did what she could for the woman and the child. They got that one night. She gave them that."

"Hardly very much," Ruth said.

"You haven't lived through a war," he said, "or you wouldn't say that. She did what she had to in the circumstances. She did her best. That was my mother's strength. She made a difficult choice, and then she did her best. That is what you have to understand."

"Well, in our own way, we have lived through a war," said Ruth.

"In your own way," he conceded. "But bad though that may have been or be, and in fact I do know more about it than you may imagine, I don't think you are comparing like with like; but perhaps what you who live here need to understand is that compromise is the key to a solution. Haven't you noticed how the causes of war are forgotten once people become embattled: how the war becomes self-perpetuating, as like looks to like, and the other becomes the enemy, and war itself becomes the goal? Isn't that what all these diplomats are trying to help you with? Look out there."

Sure enough, the noise of the crowds was swelling to the frenzy of a cheer, rising with their frosty breath from the pool of light below: the Clintons must be on their way. Ruth's heart sank: getting out of town would be a nightmare.

"Is that not the reason for the presence of the President of the United States? Things are not always black and white, Ruth. I'm sorry — may I call you Ruth?"

"You may," Ruth heard herself say, a little to her own surprise. She looked at him, standing up, stretching to see more of the spectacle outside. He was quite lightly made: indeed, he moved lightly, like a dancer. And as she thought this, something dropped into place: there came back to her Edith's dreamlike memory of dancing with Paul at Clärchen's Ballhaus. Yet, if he were to be believed, it was not Edith who was his mother, but Kitty.

"Come back to Kitty," she said.

"Well, that's what *she* did. Kitty came back. And she organised us, me and my grandmother, to get out of Berlin in those days after the Russians came."

"How?" asked Ruth. "What did she do?"

Once more, his face shut down.

Ah, thought Ruth, just what did Kitty do?

270

"I don't know," he said, and his closed face gave nothing away. "I presume she used whatever contacts she had to get us out."

Contacts: that was new.

"What contacts?"

He did not reply. Ruth thought again of the Kitty Edith described in the *Memory Book*: no schoolgirl, she. She wondered again about the nature of the contacts.

"Where was she taking you to?" she asked. "Somewhere in Germany?"

"Munich, she planned, then Ireland. Neutral Ireland. There was a charity that helped children, specifically Catholic children, mainly orphans. It went from Munich, and she knew Munich, a little."

Again, something came back to Ruth: was it not Munich where Kitty and Edith were to meet in March 1939? Did that mean she and Paul ...? Could Edith really have seen Kitty? This was racing ahead too far: she pulled herself back to the facts.

"You weren't an orphan. How could the charity help you?"

He was silent. Yet, again, Ruth found herself wondering just what Kitty had had to do to get her mother-in-law and child out of Berlin.

"I was an orphan, *de facto*," he said. "The train was bombed when we were just outside Munich: your air pirates, again. A direct hit. I was lucky to survive: one of the few pulled out, unhurt. My grandmother died, and, as for Kitty, like many others she wasn't found or identified in the wreckage and the conclusion was drawn that she was dead. That happened a great deal, you know."

Ruth thought of the letter Edith had received, telling her Paul was presumed dead. He had never been found, either.

"So you see, I did qualify as an orphan, and a Catholic

one, at that."

As before, the bones on his face stood out, very fine, very sharp.

"And in Ireland? Where in Ireland?"

"Dublin," he said. "Kitty's father — my grandfather — was safely there by then; and he took me in."

Ruth took this in. Kitty's father, of course, the wandering musician, always one step ahead of his daughter.

"I wondered where your accent came from. Not quite Irish, not quite not."

"There is something else," he said, without comment, "that you might like to see."

He reached into the inner pocket of his jacket, and removed a smallish card packet, yellowed with age at its creases, but carefully preserved. He pushed it across the table.

"What is this?" asked Ruth.

"Look at it," he said, "and you may find out."

Opening the worn cover she found, beneath carefully folded tissue, a pencil sketch. It showed a young woman, little more than a girl, half-in shadow, hair swept back, fine eyebrows arching over delicate features; and in her tip-tilted eyes, the most slyly watchful expression Ruth had ever encountered.

"Turn it over," he said.

She did so. On the back, she read the faint pencil inscription: "*Das Mädchen*, Belfast, June 1932. P.H."

P.H.: Paul Herrold. *Das Mädchen*. June 1932, when the two schoolgirls first met him in the hospital. *Das Mädchen*: The Young Girl. Remembering the strong, almost mannish features of Edith Barratt, and the direct gaze apparent even in her smiling graduation photograph, Ruth understood what she was seeing. This was the sketch Paul had been making when Edith looked back from the door of the ward:

272

he was already thinking of Kitty; yet, already, seeing the calculation in her eyes.

Neither spoke; outside another rousing cheer went up.

"You know," she said when the noise died down. "There is something I think *you* need to read," and she pushed the *Memory Book* towards him.

He placed his hand on it and looked at her inquiringly.

"I want to know what you make of it," she said, and catching a hint of a smile, that creasing at the corners of the mouth, felt herself redden once more. "I give you permission, but I need it back tomorrow." She looked at her watch: "At about this time."

She got up then: it was a perfect moment to make an exit, and yet, almost at the door, she turned back.

"Tell me something," she said.

He looked up from the book.

"What was the point in the letters about the Seven Swabians? What did Paul mean?"

His face broke into an unexpectedly wide smile. "Ah," he said. "The Brothers Grimm. I grew up with this story. Seven Swabians, clinging together to one great spear, did not think to use it: instead, afraid of every small thing, they died unnecessarily. They had no courage; and lack of it is what killed them. No weapon will protect you if you are afraid to live."

"Was he talking about the German people? That they were afraid of what might be coming?"

"I think it's simpler than that," he said. "He's talking to her like a teacher. It's very much in his tone to her, teacher to pupil."

"Like Monsieur Heger to Charlotte Brontë, you think?"

He leaned back in his chair, and looked at her for a moment.

"If you like," he said slowly. "That hadn't struck me."

"It's only just struck me," she said.

Thanking him, she left, finding herself puzzled and more than a little intrigued by the encounter with Rainer Herrold.

Seven Swabians

Outside in the heaving crowds, Ruth had to acknowledge that Rainer had been right. That tree did look gaudy, especially lit up, and surrounded by all the trumpeting tawdriness of a town attempting, despite its still unresolved hatreds, to appear festive. When was it, about ten years before, that the City Fathers, united against the latest attempt to bring peace to Northern Ireland, had decided that with an inexpensive stroke of genius, they might transform (for the duration of the Christmas season) the bleak intransigence of the banner above the City Hall, by adding two letters. With two, crass, Scrabble-like strokes, "*Belfast Says No*" became "*Belfast says Noël*". Given that Belfast liked to say no to practically everything, from political settlements to children playing in the park on Sunday, it was almost funny, and people almost laughed: still, on the 6th of January, Belfast said *No* once more, and there was little laughter. And yet, perhaps, this year, the winter darkness passing, the ceasefire might hold long enough for peace to take root; perhaps the clever

Comeback Kid who had risen to the office of President of the United States could bring about what no-one, anywhere, had managed until now. Perhaps.

Deep in such thoughts, negotiating, without thinking, the crossing and criss-crossing through crowds and police and barriers, Ruth was startled to feel a hand on her arm. Turning, she saw to her surprise that it was Chris.

"Hi," he said, and she knew something was wrong.

The hand on her arm was trembling, and a hint, just a breath on the wind told her why. It was early, even for him.

"Chris," she said.

He was pale, the cheekbones too prominent. Immediately she thought of Rainer, whose own sharp bones sat easily under lean health. Chris looked simply sickly, and weak.

"What brings you into town?"

He gestured towards the podium, empty now of its distinguished occupants.

"Oh, the circus," he said. "Couldn't help it. You know, old dogs. I just followed my nose."

"Well," said Ruth. "Maybe you can get an article out of it."

He said nothing, and he did not move.

"Chris," Ruth said, wearily. "I need to get on with … all sorts of things. If you've something to say to me, tell me what it is."

"Here?" he said.

She shrugged. "Why not?"

"All right, then," he said, and something in Ruth braced itself. "I think we should try again."

"Try what again?" said Ruth, a cold hand inside her tightly gripping.

"Us," he said. "Being together. Being … married."

Somewhere a loudspeaker burst into merry melody.

276

"My God," said Ruth. "Why do they insist on doing all this so early! It's ... it's so ... tawdry." She stopped, seeing in her mind Rainer's almost handsome face, hearing his phrase.

"I mean it, Ruth," Chris said. "I want to come home for good."

Ruth came home, then, suddenly understanding.

"Latimer's left you again, hasn't she?"

He said nothing. She knew she was right.

The voice of Nat King Cole, drifting towards them, sang of mistletoe and chestnuts.

"Latimer's left you, and you thought you might try your, what, your fall-back, your insurance policy? Is that it?"

"No, I mean, not the way you mean. I want to try again."

Ruth felt her resolve harden. "She's dropped you. Say it."

He nodded, helplessly. "I think she has someone else," he said.

"I'll bet she has someone else," said Ruth, without pity. "She would always have someone else. But you never learn, do you?"

And until now, she thought, the same could have been said of me.

"Some big German," he said. "I saw them together. Over there." He indicated the Benner Centre.

Ruth's heart, for no reason, turned over, and something of the shock she felt must have shown in her face.

"Ah," said Chris, in quite a different tone, "I get it. The Barratt papers. The German soldier. You never at home. She's put her eye on your fancy man, has she?"

He did not look sad or pathetic now. Thin as he was, his eyes held the quick, rheumy anger of the alcoholic.

"Listen, Chris," she said. "I've never asked you this, but I'm going to, now. Who was the woman in Dublin you'd

277

just broken up with the day I first met you? At my father's funeral?"

He said nothing. His eyes told her what she wanted to know.

"You sad bastard," she said. "You didn't just happen to have an affair with Cory Latimer this summer, did you? You just picked up where you'd left off. Or," and another thought struck her, heavily, "did you ever leave off? Is that it?"

There was silence.

"*Now* I get it," said Ruth because, finally, she did. "Well, do you know what? That's it, Chris. We're done."

Thoroughly angry, she began to turn away

"So much," he said, "for good Catholic girls and their marriage vows."

Ruth spun round, almost, in her haste, knocking over with her whirling briefcase a young, lovingly entwined couple.

"Dr Deacon!" said the entwined girl.

Oh, my God, Ruth thought. Not Sky McDougall. Not now.

"Oh Dr Deacon," Sky breathed, "isn't it wonderful? Isn't the President just the most marvellous man you've ever seen? He's just the — the coolest."

The young man beside her affected to look hurt.

"Apart from you, Brad," said Sky, folding herself round him. "Dr Deacon, this is Brad." She detached herself briefly and leaned across to Ruth: "He's a Republican," she whispered, then aloud, "We're engaged!"

"Well, many congratulations to you both," said Ruth, though quite on what she could not have said. "Isn't that marvellous news!"

"And I'm so glad to have met you today, Dr Deacon. You see, now that Brad has come all the way over to bring me home, we've decided I should give up my studies."

For the second time in ten minutes, Ruth's heart paused. "Give up?" she said, then suddenly, hotly, remembered the phone calls and messages she had refused to hear.

Sky looked abashed, the boy beside her suddenly protective, and large.

"Sky's going to have a baby, Professor," he said.

Now that Ruth looked, she saw that the loose, oddly-assorted clothes favoured by Sky McDougall were quite capable of hiding a pregnancy.

"We think it best to concentrate on that."

"Just for a while," said Sky, with the pleading note she normally reserved for deadline extensions, adding, with just a trace of reproach, "I did try to tell you."

She did, Ruth thought: she did. And now, it was clear that she would very soon need to get on with another production, and no extension would be granted.

"Well, Sky," said Ruth, "it's hardly the time or place — and there will be paperwork, you understand, not to mention the question of the funding you received, but ..."

Sky nodded earnestly. The young man beside her looked stern. Ruth suddenly saw him in fifteen years, and felt for Sky.

"We're putting the baby first, Professor," he said, setting his jaw.

In that moment of insight, Ruth was sadly certain that Sky's academic aspirations, whatever she might think, were over: in the same moment, something perverse in her did not want to see this scattered but bright young woman lose herself.

"Sky," she said, "you can still think about your thesis while you prepare for the baby. You can use any piece of time as thinking time. Even putting the nappies in to wash doesn't stop you thinking. And if you like, you can send me anything you want me to read." She thought: what am I doing?

"Nap—? Oh, diapers! Yes, Dr Deacon: you're *so* right." She turned to Brad. "I never even thought about diapers!"

"You won't have time to think about anything else, sweetheart," said her young Republican; and the look he gave Ruth, over Sky's head, was cold as the air all around them.

She's finished, Ruth thought, but she felt no elation. Her eyes following them as they drifted off into their narrowing future, she was surprised to see the dark thin shadow of Chris, still standing where he had been.

"So now I don't even get introduced?" he said, his mouth turned down in resentment.

"How would you like to be introduced?" asked Ruth, still watching the young people. Anger at him, sorrow for Sky met in her. "Alcoholic philanderer?"

"Husband," he said, his voice shaking.

Only for the crowds on every side, Ruth could have slapped him.

"We're divorced, Chris, or soon will be. I'm going ahead with it."

"Unbreakable vows, before God. Till death do us part." Again that low, trembling voice, the red-rimmed eyes narrow with dislike.

"We were married," Ruth said, evenly, "in case you have forgotten, without the benefit of clergy. Over there." She pointed to the City Hall. "You refused a church wedding. Remember? A decree absolute is all I need to be rid of you, Christopher, since God was not allowed to be present at any point in what passed for our marriage."

He stared at her. "I never knew you were such a …"

"Say it," she said. "You've said worse many a 'time, not that you'd have any memory of it."

She turned once more to go.

"Oh Ruth," he said, and for a moment his voice was as she remembered it, when he was himself, when he was merry and funny, and they were young. "Oh Ruth, I can't be alone."

Ruth did not need to turn round then. She straightened her back, and lifted her head.

"There are worse things," she said. "Believe me."

This time, she walked on and she did not look back. For once, she said to herself, I am not one of the Seven Swabians.

Advent

When I was a child, Ruth remembered, clearing away the last of Chris's possessions into the garage, I was not allowed even to mention Christmas until the beginning of Advent. Advent meant joy and anxiety equally mixed. Something wonderful might happen, or nothing would: like now. She closed the door of the garage, walked back to the house, and breathed in. Half the night, until three o'clock, it had taken to tidy, to pack, to sort: but wherever Chris went now, it would not be with her, and it would not be her responsibility. If she had the slightest doubt, and she did not, the morning's post, like a sign, had brought the decree absolute. She and Chris Applewood were no longer legally bound: and since, as she had in her cold fury pointed out to him, that was the only tie which in the end they had, she was finally free.

It was, therefore, with a light step that Ruth set out once more for the Benner Centre. She did not expect Rainer to be there yet, having specified the afternoon for their meeting. Something in her, however, rather thought he might. It had occurred to her even as, fairly unusually, she slicked on some lipstick before leaving the house, that if he were there they might go for lunch; or if he did not arrive until later, a drink, perhaps even dinner. That way they could discuss not only their differing views of the odd and old triangle of Paul, Edith and Kitty, but also the best way for Ruth to work on the papers. It seemed a reasonable plan.

It was a reasonable plan, except that he was not there; and why should he be? It was, therefore, with only the tiniest, most negligible lurch of disappointment that she took her place at the good window seat, and opened her papers.

A shadow above her made her look quickly up: but it was not Rainer Herrold. Cormac, the assistant she had seen the first day she had asked for the papers, stood hovering above her, like a young and very slight Jeeves.

"Dr Deacon?" he said.

Ruth nodded. "Yes," she said. "Is something the matter?"

"Professor Herrold," he said, "sends his apologies. He was called away unexpectedly this morning."

The blow was unexpectedly painful. And Professor. He had not told her that. How foolish she must have seemed, insisting on her rights.

"I suppose Professor Latimer's not here, either?" she heard a flat voice ask, knowing it was hers.

"She isn't available" he said, cautiously. "I'm sorry. If there's anything I can do to help you …?"

He looked so young and so earnest, it saddened Ruth a little not to be able to think of anything he could do to help her. Yet, who could help her? No fool, she thought, like an old fool.

"This is for you," Cormac was saying. He held out an envelope, bulky, sealed.

She knew without looking that it was the *Memory Book*.

"Thank you," she said, dully, taking it from him.

He stood on.

"There's something else," he said nervously, "and it's my fault."

Ruth saw, to her surprise, that his hands were trembling, and that in them he held a file.

"What is it?" she said. "What's the matter?"

"Well," he said, and he held out the file, "it's this. I don't know how it got in the wrong place, but it did. I may have dropped it myself the first day you asked to see them. I'm so sorry."

Ruth remembered that day: how Latimer had almost taunted him in her warnings to be careful.

"Anyway," he continued earnestly, "it's back where it belongs and in case it's important to your work, here it is, if you would like to see it."

Ruth took the file from his shaking hands. There was no need to tell him she already knew its contents.

"And, Dr Deacon, could you ... would you mind not ...?" He paused, biting his lip.

"Don't worry," said Ruth. "I'll tell nobody."

He looked worried still.

"Nobody, Cormac," she said again, and saw a slight smile of relief upon his face.

As he walked back to the desk, a shaft of sunlight suddenly caught the polished wood of the table; and it was as if, in an instant, Ruth's world had righted itself. She looked out at the tree, and the calendar on the wall: December 1st. Of course it was. Advent had begun, and with it the return of optimism. Ruth gathered herself, straightened her back and walked across to the desk. The young assistant looked up.

"Cormac," she said. "There is something you could help me with. Did Professor Herrold say where he was going?"

285

"Well, yes," said Cormac, "he did. He got me to look up the times of the Dublin train." He riffled the papers on his desk for a few moments and, then, with a slight sound of satisfaction, produced a timetable. "He was going for this one," he said, pointing with his finger to a pencil mark upon the open page. "He asked me to get him a taxi."

Ruth looked at the page he held out, glanced up at the clock, and took a decision.

"Could you get me one? A taxi?" she said, and had the satisfaction of seeing his face light up with pleasure, as he lifted the receiver and dialled.

"On its way," he said, a minute later.

Ruth thanked him and turned to go; then a cold thought occurred. Latimer, she thought: maybe he's with Latimer. She turned back.

"Cormac," she said, "where did you say Professor Latimer is today?"

On his desk, his telephone began to buzz.

"She was supposed to have an early meeting with Professor Herrold," he said and before Ruth could speak, picked up the receiver. "Hello?" he said into the telephone. "Thanks. There's your taxi, Dr Deacon and — oh!" He looked over her head. "There's Professor Latimer now, if you want her."

Turning, Ruth was just in time to glimpse the opening of a door, and see a figure, huddled, head down, walk quickly through the reading room, waving aside the attempts of at least one reader to speak to it. Light from the back office illuminated the face; for one moment Ruth glimpsed the man's crumpled handkerchief in Cory Latimer's hand, and a dark streak of tears about her eyes. Well, she thought, I wonder what that's about? She thanked Cormac again, put her papers into her briefcase, unintentionally including the forgotten folder the young assistant had given her and ran, light-hearted once more, down the stairs and out to the waiting car.

The train was still standing when she arrived, still standing by the time she had anxiously queued and rapidly bought her ticket, and just about still standing when she jumped into the nearest carriage. Seconds later, all doors slammed shut, the guard waved his flag, blew his whistle, and the train began to move.

Now, Ruth thought, all I have to do is find this man. She started to make her way down the length of the train as it picked up speed, holding on where possible, lurching here and there when not, holding on to this seat and that, apologising every two seconds, all the while scanning left and right, looking for Rainer Herrold. But there was no sign. Oh God, thought Ruth; what am I doing? What sort of wild goose chase was she on now? He might not even be on the damn train! And she leaned against the rocking, rolling concertina-corridor between the carriages, almost colliding with the ticket collector. She apologised, so did he: then he held out his hand for her ticket.

"Beyond this is First Class, Madam," he said as he punched it, and his voice, though polite, carried the faint suggestion that she had been trying to sidle past him into First. Ruth felt too dispirited to protest. "There should be some seats free in Standard," he added, then, more kindly, "if you care to go back through the train."

"I'm looking for someone," she said. What else could she say?

"Aren't we all?" said the conductor with the first hint of a smile.

"He could be in First Class," she said, not quite able to respond to his smile. "I don't know. He's not back there, anyway."

"No," said the conductor, and she saw his eyes were

kind. "They never are. I'm guessing you want to look in First Class?"

"Could I?" said Ruth, a little spring of something hopeful bubbling up again. "I'll pay the difference."

He smiled properly then, took her ticket and wrote some illegible initials on it.

"Go on," he said, and he winked. "Maybe there aren't any seats in Standard today."

"You're very kind," said Ruth, and she meant it. "Thank you. Really."

"Not at all," said the conductor. "Good luck", and he stood back to let her past.

Well, thought Ruth, that's two lucky encounters so far. What are the chances of a third? And even as she thought it, she saw him, Rainer Herrold; and her heart, once more, turned right over.

End of the Line

She saw him, he saw her, and for a moment neither spoke.

"Ruth," he said quietly, unsurprised, and his face broke into a smile. He half-rose to greet her.

"No, sit, do," she said, but he did not. She moved towards the seat opposite.

"No," he said, moving out of his window seat. "You come in here."

And, waving away her protest he handed her in. Then, to her surprise, he sat down not opposite, but beside her.

"I like to face in the direction of the engine," he said.

"Me too," said Ruth, and a little warm happiness stirred in her.

For a moment, neither said anything. It was suddenly, surprisingly, as though they had planned to make this journey together, as if nothing needed to be discussed. Of course, a great deal needed to be discussed. Yet, where to begin, this man beside her, elegant, relaxed, his aftershave — subtle, expensive — tingling her nerves. Where to begin, little sleep last night, running about half the morning. I am

289

sure, Ruth thought, that I look as if I've been pulled through a hedge backward; and then she pulled herself together. What did it matter what she looked like? She was here to gather information, full stop. And, she told herself sternly, she was not going to be distracted because he was attractive. All she needed to understand was what he had to say about the *Memory Book*. That was all.

She heard an apologetic cough. A waiter stood above them, holding out a menu.

"Ah," said Rainer Herrold. "Tea, yes. Would you like tea, Ruth? Or coffee? Aren't you a coffee person?"

So, he had noted that she took coffee.

"I'd like coffee, yes, please," she said.

"Coffee for two then," he said to the waiter, then turned to Ruth. "And now, maybe you could tell me why I have the pleasure of your company this morning?"

"Yes," Ruth said. "Good question. I'm sorry for barging in on you."

"Not at all," he said. "I'm glad you did. But why?"

Yes, why? Why could she not have written, or found out his email: it was probably in the envelope she had not even opened. Her skin grew hot. Why had she acted on impulse?

"I wanted," she said, with a calm assurance she did not feel, "to know what you thought about the *Memory Book* — assuming you have managed to read it — and, to know more about Kitty, about Paul and — most importantly for me — their relations with Edith Barratt. You see, everything I thought I'd gathered from the *Memory Book* has been turned upside down. And to write whatever I am to write about Edith Barratt, I do need to understand."

He said nothing, and in the momentary silence she heard herself say: "Sometimes these things work best face to face."

Hadn't Paul said that in one of the last letters: that he

wanted to see Edith face to face to tell her — what? That the war made their connection impossible? About Kitty?

"I see," he said. "Ah, here's the coffee."

It came, steaming and fragrant in a silver pot. Pouring some into a small gold-rimmed cup, he slid it towards her on its delicate saucer.

"A little better than a cardboard cup, isn't it?" he said.

"Much," she said. "Thank you. Much better."

They sipped their coffee. The train rattled past misted drumlins and bare, wintry trees.

"All right, then," he began. "Let's start with the *Memory Book*. And, yes, I did read it."

"What did you think?" said Ruth.

"What did I think." He looked past her, through the window, the train speeding into the farmlands and hills of the countryside.

"I think," he said, "it showed an entirely other picture of all I thought I understood from the letters. Clearly, Edith Barratt did love my father, or her memory of him, in her own way; and her account of her life shows a touchingly steadfast fidelity to that memory. But I suppose what interests me most about it is that it is quite different from the picture I had of Edith Barratt."

"But I thought you didn't know who Edith Barratt was?"

"I didn't say that. I said my mother's name was not Barratt. I did know the name when I arrived, and not simply because I had read the letters."

"How then?" asked Ruth.

"You may remember I said my mother wasn't found or identified in the train wreckage and the conclusion was drawn that she was dead?"

"Yes, I remember."

"Well, that was not the whole truth. She didn't die. My

mother was a survivor."

That, thought Ruth, I can believe.

"As I told you yesterday," he continued "it was owing to her that we made it to the end of the war. That's true. Lots of people, people we knew didn't, but I did. She wanted me to survive; and what she wanted, she generally got."

No argument there, said Ruth to herself.

"So when she discovered — don't ask me how — that there was an organisation in Munich dedicated to helping orphaned Catholic children get to Ireland, she decided I should be an orphan. And it was as an orphan that I came to Ireland. Later, quite a bit later, when she got out herself, she found me, and we became reacquainted."

"Did you know she wasn't dead?" asked Ruth.

"No," said Rainer, shortly. She looked across at him, and saw his mouth had set itself in a hard line. "Not for a long time."

There was a silence; no sound but the low hum of conversation from a silver-haired couple a few seats away, and the train's rolling rhythm.

"I suppose," Ruth said, to say something, "it would have been too much to ask a small child to keep that information to himself."

"I suppose," said Rainer, but his mouth stayed set. "I can see the logic of it. She ensured my survival the best way she could. All the same, after my very early childhood which, as I said, I scarcely remember, I can't say we were ever very close. I didn't want to know of any more skeletons in the family closet. As for Kitty, I think she didn't want to talk about it either. Anyway, we avoided the subject for years; until very recently, in fact. These days, she seems to want to talk about her life. I gather it's a feature of old age."

"Oh, it is," said Ruth, with feeling.

"You know about that?" he said. "Well, okay. So much

the better. You'll understand then that I wasn't specially willing to hear it. All the same, I let her tell me the story, including her connection with your Edith Barratt. Edie, she called her: and I can tell you that the person she described and the person I met in the pages of the book you lent me, were two very different people. I don't mind admitting it took me by surprise, and, you know, though I didn't plan your coming today, and wouldn't have been so presumptuous as to ask you to hop on a train with me, I'm glad you did."

He paused. The train whistle blew, lonely against the empty fields.

"I was sitting here thinking about the *Memory Book* when you appeared through that door," he said, and paused again. "Well, actually, I was thinking about you. And suddenly, there you were."

The train swung round a long, slow bend and for a moment his shoulder brushed against hers, then back again. Below them, the landscape fell away; and high in a leaden sky two winter birds made lonely circles.

Ruth, taken aback, sat still. "You were thinking about the *Memory Book*," she said then, as evenly as she could. Out of the side of her eye, she saw his Adam's apple move as he swallowed.

"Yes," he said after a moment. "I was. Before I read my father's letters, I thought I knew what to expect. I had heard of Edie as the pleasant, rather plain friend whom — according to my mother, always vain — every pretty girl liked to have by her, to set off her own good looks. Does that shock you?"

"No," said Ruth, calm again, fit for him again. "It doesn't. I knew Edith, years ago, in her Jean Brodie prime. She was quite strong-featured. Interesting face, but not, you know, pretty-pretty."

"I see. So you know another Edith and, with the letters and now, this *Memory Book*, I begin to as well. But, you see, that's what I'm telling you. My mother's Edith, her Edie, isn't one I think you'd recognise."

"Try me," said Ruth.

"Well, this girl — and she was always a girl — said little, tagged along, and got in the way, notably where my father was concerned. According to Kitty, she and my father were attracted to one another from the time they met in the hospital, though little was said, and Edie did all the talking. It was Edie, apparently, who got in the middle of their romance in Rome."

"Was it a romance, though?" Ruth asked. "Would you call it that? Or was it an affair?"

"Call it what you will," he said. "According to my mother, her own first attraction to Paul was something that lay dormant. Edith's book describes her as saying little at that first meeting in the hospital: but look at what else Edith says, of the way Paul's eyes follow Kitty. My mother told me that she didn't really begin to discover her feelings for him until Rome, while Edith seems to have carried her torch from day one."

"True," said Ruth, because it was. "She was smitten from the outset."

"That's it, you see. For Kitty, according to herself, when she ran into him by chance in Rome, it was flirtation."

Ruth thought back.

"Edith says she was always going off by herself, it's true. And not coming in at night. But isn't there the hint that Kitty had a number of flirtations on that holiday?"

"Maybe. She said herself she wasn't looking for anything beyond a holiday romance. She also said she was trying to make up her mind about him the day he and Edith met in Castel Gandolfo."

"When Edith went with the German family, and ran into Kitty, and then Paul?"

"That day, yes."

"You don't think she and Paul arranged to meet at Castel Gandolfo?"

"I don't, no." That did not seem to have occurred to him. "Do you?"

"I don't know what I think, at the moment," Ruth said, which was also true.

"No. She said she was taking time to think. I suppose she could have been alarmed by the possibility that she might be falling in love. That wouldn't have sat well with her plans."

"To travel, you mean?"

"Exactly. Remember, she wasn't without means, and she was in Europe to travel and have a good time. She was her father's daughter. Whatever Edith or anyone else may have thought, Kitty knew her father's concert schedules; and it's quite possible that she intended all along to dovetail her travels with his. I gathered she had become rather bored with friend Edie, and even more bored with the family who'd adopted her in Rome. But she said she was quite fond of her. She didn't want to dump her without a word; she said she took the trip to Castel Gandolfo on impulse, half to surprise Edie, and also to tell her she was probably going to travel on alone. Even about that, she was still in two minds."

"And then Paul appeared."

"And then Paul appeared. Yes. She wasn't too pleased to see that he had spotted Edith and was about to walk past without seeing her, and that decided her. She confronted him, then and there, and told him the romance, affair, whatever, was over."

"But she didn't want him, or didn't want anything

beyond holiday romance. You said so."

"Oh, come on," he said, swivelling round in his seat to look at her. "Don't tell me you haven't come across this before. She may not have wanted him for herself, but she didn't want anyone else to have him."

"Well, yes," said Ruth, thinking of her last encounter with Chris. "I do know that one. And it's not confined to women either."

He looked across at her, a quick questioning look. "Right," he said slowly. "Well then, you know what I'm saying. Anyway, knowing Kitty, she wouldn't have liked to be upstaged."

I'm with you there, Ruth said to herself. She was a piece of work, the same Kitty.

"And the little bird, Amico?" she said.

"Did she hit it, you mean? I don't know. Perhaps he was injured anyway. Edith gives her own account of what *she* believed happened after that. But don't forget, it was Edith who insisted on coming to Germany after Rome, even when advised against it by my father."

"That's not accurate," said Ruth, immediately. "Or fair. She didn't get the letter he sent her telling her not to come."

"True. But if she had, do you think it would have stopped her?"

Ruth thought. Would it?

"It might," she said slowly. "But, then again, this had been building up in her for a long time, six years; and he had given her the impression he wanted to see her again. What was he doing?"

"I'm not sure," said Rainer. "That puzzles me, too. He seems to have felt a real tenderness for her, but he was clear that she shouldn't come to Berlin."

"Tenderness, yes: I saw that was a word he used. Especially in those early letters. And it can have a range of meanings, I do accept. But then, when she does go to Berlin, he takes her dancing, and look at the effect the evening in Clärchens had upon her."

"Oh yes," said Rainer, "it's dramatic. But Kitty can't have known anything about that."

"Unless she was in Berlin too," said Ruth.

"She never said she was," said Rainer, and the puzzled frown on his face showed this had not occurred to him.

"But she might have been, mightn't she? Weren't they to go together, she and Edith?"

"Yes, but ..."

"And why was he nervous when Edith told him the room was the one Kitty had booked for them? Was he afraid Kitty might turn up there? And then, why did he take her to a restaurant and almost immediately decide to leave? Did he see somebody there he didn't want to? Was Kitty there?"

He was silent. The hedges sped by, cold slanting rain dashing the windows of the carriage.

"Isn't it possible?" persisted Ruth.

"I suppose it might be," said Rainer, "but what if she was?"

"Well, if she was, that was the reason he took Edith on to Clärchens, and we know what happened there."

"But, what is there to know?" Once more, he turned towards her in his seat, "Paul and Edith danced. They had a pleasant, social, memorable evening. They weren't lovers, whatever Edith may have thought."

"That's the thing, you see," Ruth said. "In the *Memory Book* she remembers herself and Paul as lovers, as a couple in love. I did wonder about the entry where she describes that night when they danced. She doesn't tell us what happened, whether the evening ended with him bringing her home – or whether it went on, whether he stayed with her. She says she won't or can't write about it: but she says there was a morning that dawned too soon. What is that? A Romeo and Juliet fantasy? Or something that is too precious to relate?"

Once more, he sat silent.

"I know her, you see," said Ruth. "She's not a liar. Clärchen's changed her whole perception. Rome may have fed a schoolgirl fantasy, but whatever happened the night of Clärchen's changed it forever in her mind. Whatever that was."

"You know her," he said, then. "And I know Kitty. I have to absorb Edith's version to balance what my mother has told me, but you have to take in Kitty's version to address the task you've set yourself. You surely don't need me to tell you that you can't identify too closely with the subject of a biography, or a study, or an edition, or whatever you're planning. Detachment is essential."

Now Ruth sat silent. He was right; she was committing the sin of over-involvement with her subject's point of view, and she had been caught in the act.

And then, he did a curious thing: he reached out his hand and placed it over hers. It was warm, and that little scent of something exotic wafted up at her for a second.

"I'm sorry," he said. "I'm lecturing you, when I have no right."

He lifted his hand away almost as soon as he had placed it there but Ruth, silenced, sat still. Was Paul like that, she heard herself think. Was it that kind of elusive charm that confused Edith, young as she was? For Paul's son had charm. Something in her steeled herself against it, against him; and then she realised he was speaking again.

"So, what do we have?" he was saying. "We have Edith carrying her romantic dream all through the next six months: and yes, my father's letters, warm and friendly, buoying her up. He was her pen pal. And as for my mother — I'm pretty sure she wasn't in Berlin when Edith was there."

I'm not, said Ruth, silently.

"No, I think she was travelling round Europe, part of her father's entourage, and I'd say, loving every minute of it. Maybe she had forgotten all about Paul; maybe not. She said what changed matters was that she and Paul met by chance in Prague, in March 1939."

"When Edith was there with William. Or rather, after Edith was there. They were meant to meet, she and Kitty, and then Edith was called home."

"Exactly. Kitty's father was giving a concert and Paul, as part of the occupying army, was there. That was, she said, the turning point. To Kitty, it was a *coup de foudre*, and she thinks it was to my father as well. A *coup de foudre*: that was the phrase she used, not looked for or even desired, but overwhelming, and not to be denied. Look again at the letters. I mean, you only have to look at the dates. Who wanted to see whom in the spring of 1939? The summer of 1939? It's all Edith. And when you are looking at dates, remind yourself that I was born in December 1939 and, as our American friends like to say, do the math."

"I don't need to," said Ruth. "That one's self-evident. It's just the rest: there are so many things I'm not sure about — including his letters, the way he writes to her, especially in the early letters, right up to New Year 1939. He's far more than a pen pal. There is love there. I think, if only for that one night, he fell in love with Edith."

"Yes," said Rainer, "but there are many kinds of love."

"*I've known a hundred kinds of love*—" Ruth began.

"*All made the loved one rue*," he finished. "I noticed she had a fondness for the Brontës. That one's Emily, isn't it?"

"Yes," said Ruth. "And Emily's a good example of

someone who understands love — even passion – without direct experience of it. But then, there was also Charlotte, and those letters she wrote to her teacher in Brussels."

"Yes," he said slowly. "You mentioned that yesterday. That was largely fantasy; but it gave us *Jane Eyre*. And *Villette*."

"I did mention it," said Ruth, "in the context of wondering what Paul was doing, writing to her like that, unless what he felt for her was a kind of love."

"Well," he said, then, "I'm glad we agree."

"Do we?" asked Ruth.

"Yes. You accept that the love is Edith's fantasy."

Did she? *A hundred kinds of love …*

"I'd be disappointed if it were otherwise," he said, "from the scholar who published so worthy a study of fiction's unreliable narrators. I'd say you're in an ideal position to judge whether you have met at least one in real life."

And you, Professor Herrold, thought Ruth, think everyone should see things exactly as you do.

"Far be it from me," she said, "to disappoint you."

The sea was on their left; then the estuary. They rattled over a narrow causeway, water lapping at either side, white houses stretched along the shoreline, swans paddling in the shallows.

"Soon be in Dublin," Rainer said, as the grime of the city began to close round them. "End of the line."

End of the line, Ruth thought. I wonder if it is.

They whizzed through a junction.

"You know," Rainer said. "I'm surprised you haven't asked me why I had to go away so suddenly."

"I didn't like to," said Ruth. "It's hardly my business. Wasn't it bad enough to land in on top of you?"

"I told you — I'm glad you did. Anyway, there's something I want you to think about. I do have some urgent personal business to attend to; but in any case I would have had to leave today or tomorrow. I've been appointed head of a new research programme, jointly funded by the Irish and German governments. The idea is to investigate Irish-German relations, concentrating on the years before and during the war."

"I see," said Ruth. "Congratulations."

"Well, thank you," he said. "But I'm telling you, because it may be of interest to you."

"To me? How so?"

"Because I've a proposal to make to you."

For one mad split second, Ruth thought of Mr Darcy, loftily condescending to Lizzie Bennet; then she composed herself, and paid attention.

"Because the Barratt papers may be of more than local interest. There's a Fellowship, not perhaps quite in my gift, but largely dependent on my recommendation. And my instinct is that you should apply."

Ruth stared at him. This, she had not expected.

"A Fellowship?"

"Yes. I think it would be of real benefit to you and your career. There's an application process, naturally; but I think your candidacy would be strong. The post begins in February, based between Dublin and Berlin. You'd have a chance to work on an edition of Edith Barratt's papers, if you wanted; or you could use the information you have to consider the spaces between memory and history, and combine what we've just been discussing with the evidence of the papers. That would be up to you. And you know, there are some other letters from my father. I'd be happy to let you see them, if you wanted to."

"To Kitty?" said Ruth. Those would be worth seeing.

"No," he said, and his face closed over again. "There aren't any to Kitty. They are to my grandmother — his mother."

Ah, Ruth thought: none to Kitty, and he's clearly not going to say any more about that. So he didn't write to Kitty, his wife, this man who loved to write letters. But letters to his mother. His mother who, he thought, would love his Irish girl.

"And I have some of my father's paintings," he said, "if you'd like to see those."

"Thank you," said Ruth, mind spinning. "I would."

She hardly knew what to say. What was happening?

"And, just by the by," he said, very casually, "I gathered from Professor Latimer that she thought she might be first in line to receive the Fellowship. I want you to know she didn't have any encouragement from me in that."

Ah, thought Ruth, that *is* interesting: I wonder if that is what caused Latimer's tears this morning?

They were speeding towards Connolly Station. He began to gather his papers.

"Nearly there," he said. "What will you do now?"

"About …?"

"No, I mean today," he said. "I have to pick up my car and go on to my mother."

"Your mother?" said Ruth, genuinely surprised. "Here in Dublin?"

"Wicklow. That's why I was suddenly called away today. She's developed a chest infection. It's not uncommon with her, but she's a good age and you never know."

"I'm sorry," said Ruth. "I've kept you talking, and you probably wanted to speak to her or the hospital or …"

"No, I told you, don't worry about that. I had just spoken to the nursing home before you arrived, and they would have phoned me if anything had changed. She has the beginnings of senile dementia. There are good and bad days."

"I'm sorry," said Ruth, once more. What else could she say?

"It's all right," he said. "Mostly, she's fairly content. With the trees around the nursing home, she thinks she's in Germany."

"Germany has happy memories for her? I'd have thought otherwise."

"They're just memories," he said. "Some good, some bad. Like Edith's. And, I suppose like Edith, she adjusts them to suit."

Ruth let that go.

"Do you think she remembers Edith?"

"Well, I know she does. In fact, for what it is worth, I believe she thinks quite often of her. She told me quite recently that she feels badly about her. When I asked why, she said: 'I suppose I let her down.' I asked if she was sorry. 'Sorry?' she said. 'Maybe. Yes, I suppose, I'm a little sorry about her. She was a good sort, Edie.' She laughed, then. 'But, you know, an innocent abroad. Not unlike your father.'" He laughed then, a little ruefully. "No-one ever accused my mother of sentimentality."

"An innocent abroad," Ruth repeated. "Two innocents abroad. But was he innocent? Paul? Or did he simply live his life in compartments?"

"Lots of us do," said Rainer.

Yes, said Ruth to herself, I'd say you do. And as for Paul, he was after all a Nazi, who knew about the camps; who could save a former pupil from them because he knew about them. Another compartment, but not one she wanted to discuss with the man who was his son. Or, and she could not easily say this either to the man's son, was his love for Edith, whatever kind that was, growing with absence and the tenderness of the letters until Kitty reappeared? Was he holding out against her in Rome, maybe in Berlin — if she was even there — and only really gave in to whatever it was in Prague? Then a pregnancy, and the doing of the right

303

thing as he saw it. Another compartment.

The train came to a grinding halt. Rainer stood up and reached down his grip: soft, well-tooled leather, landing with a soft sigh on the seat where he had been sitting.

"Will you spend the day in Dublin? I'd take you for a late lunch, but, as I said, my mother ..."

"No, that's all right," said Ruth. "I haven't decided. I may take the next train back up. I don't know yet."

She slid across the seat and stood up. He opened the door of the carriage, stepped down and then held out his hand to her. They walked together, companionably, down the platform.

"Well, look," he said, as they approached the barrier, "think about what I've said to you. That Fellowship would mean travel to Germany. There are more archives there, not least in the military repositories — and if you happened to be there when I was, I could take you — in the interests of research — to Clärchen's, and you could at least see where Edith and my father danced their dance, and walk the streets they walked."

And would you, Ruth thought, turn my head in Clärchen's the way your father seems to have turned Edith's?

They arrived at the barrier.

"Will you come into Dublin? We could share a taxi."

Ruth thought for a moment, and wavered. The National Library. Maybe. Or Grafton Street. Bewley's? Sharing a taxi with this man on a winter afternoon before Christmas?

"Do you know," she said, "I might just head on back."

"As you like," he said, and she thought she saw a fleeting, pleasing shadow of disappointment pass over his face. "But, there is one other thing. Please don't think I'm prying, but I gathered from some references in Edith's book that your own family had its share of suffering. And I did hear you say the name 'Hilde' during our conversation yesterday. I don't know if you have opened that envelope I left for you this morning? I'm guessing not."

'No," said Ruth, wrong-footed. "There wasn't enough time."

"No matter," he said, in charge again. "But there's something in there that may be of interest to you — as a scholar. I mean, that's what we are, isn't it? Seekers after truth?"

Then he went through the barrier, with a wave of his well-kept hand; and all Ruth could think of was suave, duplicitous Harry Lime in *The Third Man*, waving goodbye to the innocent who thought Lime was his friend.

Home

There was a wait before the mid-afternoon train to Belfast. None of the coffee shops looked specially inviting, but the bar looked tolerable. She went in there. Settling herself on a high stool with a glass of water, as far as she could from the cheery conviviality of a group who seemed to have made a gleeful escape from the office, and the blare of noisy sport from an elevated screen, she reached into her briefcase and retrieved the envelope Rainer had left her that morning. So long ago it seemed; yet it was only a matter of a few hours. Yes, as she thought, here was the *Memory Book*. And, what had he said — something in there of interest? She reached into the envelope again, and drew out a smaller envelope, unsealed; and in it was a photograph. Holding it up, Ruth realised why she had recognised Rainer's face. It was a print of the photograph she had found in Hilde's trunk. He might have Kitty's brown eyes, but his face was his father's. The two little girls were, of course, Hilde and Anna, in the days when Anna was indeed still in Berlin, and Hilde's bright hero was her teacher, Paul Herrold.

Yes, there was something in what he said: the exploration of memory and its revisions of history might indeed help her understand not just Edith, Paul and Kitty, but possibly Hilde, Mimi and David. Interlocking triangles, she thought, drifting off through the darkening, sleepy afternoon. She was suddenly, the previous night's broken rest catching up, profoundly tired; and the next thing she knew, the train was slipping into Central Station, and she was home.

Edith

꧁ꕤ꧂

Fred Astaire

At first, arriving back at her house, she failed to notice what was or, rather, was not there. Chris's things were gone. Chris was gone. Yet, it hardly impinged. It was, for the moment, enough that he was simply gone. After she glanced quickly about the rest of the house to ensure that this was so, she lit the fire, pulled the curtains and uncorked an early bottle of the Christmas wine. Glass in hand, she sat down once more with the letters, but she did not read them. A Fellowship: could it be real? Dublin and Berlin; more papers; more of the story; Clärchen's; a publication; release from all of this? It was a scholar's dream. In fact, it had to be a dream. It could not be this easy. How could it be? She set the letters down. The fire crackled; the wine was smooth.

All the same, she drafted an email to Rainer, expressing gratitude and interest in his proposal. If I think it is real in the morning, she decided, I'll send it. Then, resuming her seat, glass in hand, she turned again to the letters. She took them one by one out of their envelope, and this time she did read them, carefully, hearing in her head the voice of the man whose father had written them. As she did, it came home to her that she needed to see the originals again. She recalled, despite her inadequate German, some phrases from that first brief perusal, before their interesting disappearance. Austria, she remembered, from Paul's pre-Christmas letter of 1938, had been *züruckgekehrt*. Rainer had translated this as "restored", yet the dictionary told her it could mean "swept back". Was it restored, or was it swept back to Greater Germany? There was a difference. And the painting, never sent? Surely the paint eventually dried enough for him to send it. Was it because of the war, or because Kitty would not permit it, that it never came to Edith? Was it perhaps among those to which Rainer referred? Then, in Paul's letter of March 1939, where the tone began to change, Rainer had translated the words "I have been absent." Ruth clearly remembered the word, "*abwesend*", from the verb "*abweisen*", to turn away, so frequently employed in Hilde's German reproaches. Hilde — who, after all, knew the real Paul Herrold! — might have been able to help with at least some of these questions. Too late for that; but Ruth knew that to be absent was not the same as turning away. What was Paul telling Edith? And what was he, in that last letter, never sent, planning to tell her? That it was Kitty who was his love, or that, because she was expecting his child, he must do what was proper, and once again turn away? So many more questions: so many more possible answers. Was Edith mistaken? Were the letters truly as loving as she remembered them, or merely friendly as in Rainer's translations? Had he, consciously or unconsciously, sanitised or excised them?

And then, seeing with a guilty realisation that she had

inadvertently taken away the folder Cormac had handed
her in the Benner Centre, she picked it up, and almost
immediately dropped it again. It did not, as she had
presumed, contain the originals of the letters. Here, before
her eyes, was the typescript of the story Edith had called
"The White Stormtrooper". Of course: that is what he was
to her, her white stormtrooper, her white knight. Ruth read
it and, by the end, knew why David Marcus had published
it: true and unflinching, it showed the writer she might and
should have been. With it, she counted ten others,
presumably the unsent and unpublished. And they were of
the same calibre. She had done it: at last, Edith had written
from the depths, and it was good.

Ruth went reluctantly to bed that night; indeed, it was
not until the next morning that she realised she had quite
forgotten to eat the previous evening. Too much to do; and
too much to do today.

It was Saturday, so the College, neglected for days, need
not be a concern; yet perversely she almost wished she did
have the constraint of work. There was nothing to stand
between her and speaking to Edith Barratt. Perhaps a call
to Sandra, to talk it over; to tell her about Rainer's offer?
Ruth reached for the phone and picked it up; then set it
down again. Perhaps not. She opened the computer; looked
again at the email to Rainer, paused, and then pressed
"send".

She threw her bag over her shoulder, deadlocked the
door, got in the car and drove to the nursing home before
she could change her mind.

Yet, arriving in the carpark, she quailed. Why did so
many of these places, no matter how good their reputation,
somehow resemble prisons? And there was Natalia to face.
Edith might still be in hospital; perhaps it was a mistake to
have come. Even if she were here, Edith might be too

unwell to see her. It might be best to write up what she had, prepare a summary of all the findings so far?

Ruth locked the car door, and walked herself into the place. Meeting no-one, she pushed her feet towards Edith's room, half-hoping she might not be there, yet knowing, somehow, that she would be. And still, she did not know what she would tell her. The truth? What was that? That Paul had loved her but not enough? That whatever that love, that tenderness, might have become in a world without a coming war, something had overwhelmed him? That a dreamer had rudely wakened? Or, that he had been trapped by one of the oldest ploys in the world, and by her old sparring partner? Which was true? Whose truth should prevail?

What about Hilde, to whom no-one, herself included, wanted to listen: what of her truth? Rainer was right: there might indeed be records in Berlin to tell her something of her own family history, to fill in the gaps in her own understanding of the war and its legacy. And then, passing what had been Hilde's door, she made up her mind.

She was at Edith's room: and Edith was there. She lay on her back in the high, barred bed as if upon a bier, majestic, her features sharp against the spartan white. Some kind of drip was attached to her arm; a machine bleeped and stuttered as she breathed. Ruth sat down by the free arm, and took her hand. There was no response.

"Miss Barratt," she said. "Edith."

Was there a faint movement? Did she imagine it? The breathing continued, steady, the machine quietly clicking its rhythmic assurance.

"Edith," she said, again. "It's Ruth. Ruth Deacon." She felt a faint pressure on her hand. "I've read the *Memory Book*," she said, "and I will edit the papers. I will be your literary executor. I will tell your story. It will be a privilege."

The pressure on her hand increased. Her own breathing was coming fast.

"I ..." she began. "I met someone who would have liked to come and see you, but could not. He is ..." She paused. "He is Kitty's son."

The breathing in the bed grew deeper; the machine thrilled, and shook.

"Kitty is still living. She is very poorly at the moment. Her son has gone to be with her; but he wants you to know she remembers you, with affection. And," Ruth stroked the bony one so lightly holding hers, "she is sorry."

The breathing grew faster; the machine kept anxious time.

"But I will tell *your* story," she said again, and knew as she spoke that she would. "I will tell the story of you and Paul, and the love you shared."

And now, extraordinarily, the hand attached to the needle and the machine raised itself and, hovering for a second in mid-air, as if about to push back a stray lock, stroke away a headache, fell instead suddenly and heavily over Ruth's hand, and the grip was almost firm. Edith was pulling her near. Ruth leaned in, close as she could over the railed sides, close to the eyes, half-open now behind the heavy, bluish lids, and tried to hear what she was attempting to say.

"Can't," she made out.

"Can't what, Edith? Do you need something? Shall I ring?" The hand on her hand gripped harder, and the words at last, in a rasping whisper, came slow and painful.

"Take" she heard, then "that" and, after a long, painful break, "away".

She understood. George Gershwin. Fred Astaire.

"Of course," she said. "The way you danced till three."

For answer, she saw only that one tear rolled down Edith

Barratt's face, and the bruised, purpled hand gripping hers suddenly relaxed its hold. The machine, disturbed and distraught, whirred and bleeped and sent out alarms and red lights; and the room grew full of urgent people.

What, then, was there for Ruth to do? Stepping back from the noise and confusion, unnoticed and, for the moment, unnecessary, she walked out into the corridor, past the room that had been Hilde's, past the enforced gaiety of the Christmas decorations, past the faltering water feature. No matter about the College or Latimer or Chris, no matter about distant Thomas: she needed none of them. Whether Rainer Herrold's Fellowship came to something or not, a fresh beginning was possible. What was there to do, a shaft of winter sun suddenly piercing the skylight, but pass gratefully through the door and step, collar up, gloves on, into the winter morning, and a new day, of which she could as yet know nothing.

And for Edith, what was there to do, but surrender to the music, and step into the heaven of her lifelong dreaming.

ᄋᢍᧈ

Acknowledgements

Over ten years ago, when I was still a full-time academic, I was fortunate to supervise a most unusual Master's dissertation. Written by Ann Heggan, it examined the work and achievement of Margaret Grant Cormack, a Belfast writer and teacher, who donated her papers to the Linen Hall Library. What made this dissertation unusual was Ann Heggan's discovery in the archive of a cache of letters, written in 1938-9, in German. They came from Albert Linder, a serving Nazi soldier, with whom Miss Cormack had a relationship, and to whom she may have been married. Further correspondence indicated that he died in Russia. Most interesting of all was the fact that, though she kept the letters all her life, Margaret Grant Cormack seems never to have told anyone of the relationship, and never touched upon the subject in her writing.

The story stayed with me, and, as I discovered, with my former student. Thinking more and more of a fictional exploration of the dilemma that would face a young woman in pre-war Northern Ireland finding herself in love

315

with an enemy soldier, I wrote to see whether Ann Heggan had published her dissertation or, indeed, explored the intriguing story in any fictional form. She had not, although, as she told me, she often wished she could have given them a happier ending, and hoped that I might. Whether I have or not, I thank Ann for her original discovery of and research into the real-life story, and give full acknowledgement to the work of her MA dissertation, "*Struggling to Write: The Work of Margaret Grant Cormack*" (Institute of Irish Studies, Queen's University Belfast, September 2003).

Just as Aeneas Benner College, the Benner Centre and those associated with them, are figments of my imagination, let me also be clear that my Edith Barratt is not Margaret Grant Cormack, and Paul Herrold is not Albert Linder: yet, my characters would have no fictional life if the very different situation of those two people had not provided the impetus to this story. The letters written by Albert Linder inspired the letters of the fictional Paul Herrold, and the diaries and war articles so ably written by Margaret Grant Cormack allowed me to see the world Edith Barratt might have inhabited, and the style in which she might have written. I cannot thank them or acknowledge my debt to them in person, but as Margaret Grant Cormack left her papers in her will to the Linen Hall Library, I thank instead the former Librarian, John Killen, who kindly gave me all necessary permissions when I was working on the Grant Cormack archive. I also thank the present Director, Julie Andrews, the Librarian, Samantha McCombe and all the staff of the Linen Hall Library for their continued support and assistance in all aspects of my work.

In a time when the pity of both World Wars is properly remembered, I have had the opportunity to learn a great deal about the Belfast Blitz, not only from radio and television documentaries on the subject, but also from Dr Brian Barton's excellent work on the subject, *The Belfast Blitz: the City in the War Years* (Belfast: The Ulster Historical Foundation, 2015).

I had never been to Berlin until my son John undertook a trip there as part of his doctoral research. It was he who, with his girlfriend Anne McAuley, first introduced me to the wonderful Clärchen's Ballhaus in Berlin's Auguststrasse. The story was forming in my head at the time and, as I watched the dancers magically spinning and dipping in candlelit darkness, in that extraordinary building, survivor of two world wars, I knew not only where Paul and Edith would have their pivotal moment, but also what my title would be. For that unforgettable visit, I thank John and Anne. I dedicate the book to John and to his sister, my daughter Judith, for all the help they both gave me in finding my way through the difficult moments.

Finally I owe, once more, a great debt of gratitude to my agent, Paul Feldstein, to my publisher, Paula Campbell of Ward River Press, and to my outstanding editor, Gaye Shortland, all of whom have kept my feet on the path.

Also by Ward River Press

The Friday Tree
by Sophia Hillan

Belfast 1955: our past was still their future . . .

In the summer of 1955, Belfast is a quiet, apparently peaceful backwater. Trolleybuses run in a leisurely way through sparse traffic, and lamplighters go about at night. Still, though Ulster's eruption of 1969 is fourteen years away, all the seeds of that conflict are being sown. There is an uneasy, palpable tension in the air, yet, for the most part life seems ordered and calm.

In this sleepy, pleasant world, Brigid Arthur, five, and her brother Francis, eleven, live right on the edge of town in a close circle of family and friends. But over that long hot summer, everything begins to change and Brigid struggles to understand the complex adult world around her, a hidden world she often misinterprets. Through a series of events and revelations, some magical, others painful, she learns that the world is full of anguish but also full of hope and wonder.

Then Brigid and Francis know what it is they have to do, separately and together, as, like the "Brother and Sister" of Grimms' tale they "go forth together into the wide world".

A poignant and lyrical story of a family, a town and a time at once distant and disturbingly familiar.

ISBN 978-178199-9523